Jerusalem
by
Moonlight

To Nick with
best wishes.

A free copy for
a fellow-author!

Roger

12/10/22

Jerusalem
by
Moonlight

THE GREATEST STORY NEVER TOLD

ROGER BUTTERS

Matador
Unit E2 Airfield Business Park,
Harrison Road, Market Harborough,
Leicestershire. LE16 7UL
Tel: 0116 279 2299
Email: books@troubador.co.uk
Web: www.troubador.co.uk/matador
Twitter: @matadorbooks

ISBN 978 18031 3251 8

British Library Cataloguing in Publication Data.
A catalogue record for this book is available from the British Library.

Printed and bound in the UK by TJ Books Limited, Padstow, Cornwall
Typeset in 11pt Minion Pro by Troubador Publishing Ltd, Leicester, UK

Matador is an imprint of Troubador Publishing Ltd

'Doubt may be an uncomfortable position,
but certainty is a ridiculous one.'
(Voltaire)

Contents

Main Characters

(Historical characters are in bold type)

NARRATORS OF THE BOOKS

Simon bar-Cleophas, called **Zelotes,** disciple of Joshua bar-Josef

Mary of Magdala, a wealthy widow

Quintus Pontius Pilatus, Prefect of Judaea

Tiberius Rotgarius Teutonicus, chief centurion, First Cohort, First Judaean Quingenaria

ROMANS AND THEIR ASSOCIATES

Ursula, Pilate's wife, a freedwoman

Silvius, his chief scribe

Dio Syrianus, centurion and friend of Teutonicus

Publius Vulpino, lieutenant to Teutonicus

Gnaeus, servant to Teutonicus

Darius, a Greek auxiliary

Regulus, physician to the First Judaean Quingenaria

Dmitrios, a Greek physician

Maximinus, centurion, second Cohort, First Judaean Quingenaria

Sergius and Columbus, members of the Second Cohort

JEWS

Joshua bar-Josef, aka Jesus of Nazareth, rabbi and preacher
Levi, called Matthew, tax-collector and disciple of Joshua
Simon, called Peter, Joshua's favoured disciple
Jacob bar-Zebadiah, another favoured disciple
Johan bar-Zebadiah, his brother
Judas Secarius, a disciple, son of Simon Zelotes
Josef bar-Caiaphas, High Priest, Temple of Herod
Jethro, his deputy
Herod Antipas, Tetrarch (King) of Galilee
Herodias, his wife
Simon of Cyrene, a man from the country
Josef of Arimathaea, an honourable counsellor
Salome, slave to Mary of Magdala, and servant at the Roman
    camp in Caesarea
Miriam, landlady and mistress of Simon Zelotes
Nathan, a Pharisee, scribe to Herod
Elias bar-Abel, Zealot leader for South Jerusalem
Izaak bar-Lavan, another leading Zealot
Rayshan, captain of Herod's palace guard
Malachi, an innkeeper of Bethany
Moshe, owner of some Upper Rooms
Aaron bar-Nahum, proprietor of the Fig Tree Inn, Jerusalem

Book I

Caesarea

According to Simon

IT DOES NOT often happen that on the way to an important meeting one comes upon a dead body. Possibly it may occur in Rome on occasion, but never having been there I cannot say. In Caesarea such a thing was all but impossible. Yet it had happened.

The man lay face down on the paving stones at the street corner. He was quite a young man; less, I judged, than thirty years of age, dark of hair and complexion, and in life not ill-favoured. His leathern helmet lay a few feet away, against the foot of the city wall. He had not been wearing it at the time of his death. His right fist was twisted backwards at his hip, as he had tried to draw his sword. For as is well known, Romans wear the *gladius hispaniensis* at the right side. This man was an auxiliary in full uniform. He had died on duty, and been taken unaware.

Not that I felt sorry. It is over a hundred years since the Roman curse fell on this holy land, and every moment of that time has been an offence against Almighty God. Surely the great *Elohim* (I dare not write the holy name, to be read by unbelievers and blasphemers) will not permit such a state of affairs to last much longer. The day of the Messiah draws near.

Whilst I may have rejoiced at the death of one of the oppressors of our country, the manner in which it had been achieved was perhaps open to question. Soldiers would assert that killing an enemy in combat is one thing, stabbing him in the back another. And this man had been stabbed in the back, from a point low in the left rib-cage upwards into the heart. He had died within seconds.

There had not been much blood. What there was had mostly run into the cracks between the paving-slabs, where it had congealed amidst the moss and tufts of grass. I could say with confidence that the body had lain here for at least an hour. Early in the spring month of Nisan, half an hour after sunset there was still some twilight left. It was inconceivable that none had noticed it meanwhile.

But that no-one had made it his business to report the matter was unsurprising. Any witness would have been dragged before the Prefect, accused of *maiestas* and murder, tortured to confession, and as like as not condemned out of hand. So far as Pilate was concerned, the essential thing was to cause fear and consequent obedience throughout the community. Convicting the right man was comparatively unimportant.

It occurred to me that such a risk applied equally to me. And my status as an Essene would tell against me further. I could hear footsteps and voices approaching. After an apprehensive glance around I turned away and, in the words of our Lord in his parable of the Samaritan, passed by on the other side.

*

THE IMPORTANT meeting I had was with my son, young Judas. I must concede from the outset that I have never felt towards Judas as a man should towards his only son. Things might have been different had his mother not died bringing him into the world. At the time I was guilty of wishing that he had died instead. And though I have tried to disguise it, I fear this may have coloured my attitude toward him ever since.

I tell myself that it may not be too late to rectify matters. He is but twenty years of age, and still in some ways immature, preferring words, and pretentious words at that, to action, much in the manner of students everywhere. Even as a student he had disappointed me, giving up his studies with the Pharisees to hover on the fringe of radical groups such as the Zealots. Were he truly committed to the Zealot cause, as I am myself, it would be a different matter, but I fear he lacks the stomach for it.

Sitting in a corner of the Fiveways Tavern, we must have made a curiously contrasting couple. A slim young fellow, in a woollen cloak of the latest fashion, bicoloured in red and orange stripes, facing a plainly-dressed man in early middle age, dark beard flecked with grey, and I fear, somewhat overweight.

I had decided not to inform Judas of what had occurred on the way to the inn. For one thing there were too many customers within earshot, for another, I confess that I did not entirely trust him. Should he subsequently be interrogated by the Prefect's men, the less he knew the better.

The innkeeper placed a flagon of cheap wine before us as I handed over the few shekels required. We waited until he was out of hearing.

'To the success of our mission,' I said.

'Success,' Judas repeated, his thin young face briefly alight with enthusiasm. 'And now,' he continued, replacing his cup on the table, 'to business. In particular, how to convince our Lord of the error of his ways.'

'If he is in error.'

'Well, we shall see. In my view he shows signs of reneging on our original purpose.'

I inclined my head thoughtfully. 'That may be so.'

'Assuming that it is, we have to ask ourselves how much support we would have amongst our colleagues were we to put pressure on him to become, shall we say, more militant.'

'We have to ask ourselves.' 'Shall we say.' How pompous the young can be. The failings in our relationship are not all on my side. He was talking as if addressing a public meeting instead of chatting with his father.

'Methinks most of the Essenes should support us,' I said. 'Depending upon how they are approached. It'll have to be done carefully.'

'Obviously. Which in any case only gives us four, out of a dozen or so. The remainder will probably drift with the tide.'

'I dare say. Apart from Levi.'

'Yes. Levi is a problem. The Lord alone knows why he has attached himself to our cause.'

'Perhaps,' I suggested, with a feeble attempt at humour, 'he's tired of being rich.'

Judas granted me the favour of a thin smile. 'Indeed. I'm still waiting for him to bestow all his goods to feed the poor. Methinks we may have to wait a while yet.'

There I was not disposed to argue with him. Why our Lord had welcomed the greediest man in Caesarea to join his band of disciples was beyond me.

'What think you of the Magdalene woman?' I asked.

Again Judas smiled in superior fashion. 'Well, she certainly knows enough sinners.'

We spoke of a rich and eccentric widow, who ran a hostel for former harlots, to whom she attempted to teach the holy scriptures, besides finding them respectable employment. Not surprisingly she met with indifferent success. Rumour had it that she loved our Lord Joshua bar-Josef not as her spiritual leader, but as a woman loves a man. I returned his smile, albeit faintly. For some reason I found the jest, which in another might have amused me, distasteful coming from my son.

'But all this is neither here nor there,' he continued. 'It's a question of our Lord. I fear – and I speak just between ourselves – I fear I begin to be disappointed in him.'

'It's too late to change horses now,' I pointed out.

'Oh, far too late, I agree. The following he has attracted are his choice alone. A strange choice in many ways, but the Passover is almost upon us. There's no chance of rectifying matters at this late stage.'

I took a further swig of my drink and gazed around. A very average tavern. The score of customers present were a fair cross-section of society in the cosmopolitan city of Caesarea: merchants and artisans, labourers and drunks, mostly conversing in the local tongue, as did we. A couple of studious-looking men nearby preferred what sounded like a form of Peloponnesian Greek, though I caught little of what they said and understood less. There was a Roman auxiliary, helmet on the bench beside him, seated at a table near the door, and chatting with a buxom little tavern wench who had taken his fancy. Judas had noticed them too, and could not resist passing a crude remark. One of my son's less attractive qualities is that of voicing his sexual fantasies in public. So far as action in that direction is concerned he seems to do very little. I often doubt whether I shall ever be a grandfather.

Eventually I broke the lengthy silence. 'So what do we do? Try to persuade our leader of the error of his ways?'

Judas shook his head. 'Hopeless. He is convinced that he is always right, for all that his teachings often conflict with one another. No, whether he is, or is not, the promised Messiah, he is moving in the direction of believing that he is.'

'That may not be a bad thing. If it encourages him to behave as the true Messiah should.'

He inclined his head in qualified assent. 'If. Unfortunately at present he seems incapable of making up his mind whether the freedom of Judaea is to be achieved by military means with the aid of Almighty God, or by divine intervention alone.'

The auxiliary finished his drink, said a few words to the wench he was sitting with, and made his way over to us. I felt more than a touch of apprehension. In all probability he was one of the Romans' soldier-spies. But he was unlikely to have overheard us, or to understand Aramaic. A man in the early thirties, with soldier written all over him, he addressed us in colloquial Greek, which I speak adequately if not fluently.

'Are you Simeon bar-Cleophas, called Simeon Zelotes?'

He used the Greek form of my given name. I prefer the Hebrew, Simon.

'Who wants to know?'

He hesitated. Evidently he was not accustomed to having his words and actions questioned. 'The Roman Prefect,' he said at length. 'More immediately, *I* want to know. Men call me Teutonicus, centurion of the First Cohort, First Quingenaria.'

Quingenaria is the official description of the hated auxiliary troops used to govern Judaea, so called because their cohorts are five hundred strong. 'And if I choose not to answer?'

'Then I shall have to take you to the Prefect. He has methods of interrogation not available to me. In any case, my question was harmless enough.'

'Suppose for the purposes of argument that I am this Simon. What is it to you?'

'I understand you are a follower of the rabbi calling himself Joshua bar-Abbas, or the Son of Man.'

This time he preferred the Hebrew to the Greek form, Jesus. 'What of it?' I asked.

'The Prefect is becoming a little concerned regarding some of his reported teachings. So long as he confines himself to matters of Jewish religious dogma, or well-meaning nonsense about loving one's enemies, it is of no concern to him. Claims to be the Messiah are another matter.'

I said nothing, though mentally I heaved a sigh of relief. Evidently his enquiry had nothing to do with what I had seen on my way to the tavern. Somewhat disconcerted by my failure to reply, the man continued, 'I take your silence to be neither an admission nor denial, and will ask in so many words: have you heard your leader claim to be the promised Messiah?'

'I have not.'

'And you.' He turned to Judas. 'You are also one of his adherents. Is that not so?'

'And if I am?'

'I ask you the same question. Have you heard Joshua bar-Josef, or bar-Abbas, claim to be the Messiah?'

'Do you know what "the Messiah" means?'

'I'm not here to answer questions, but for what it's worth, I do. According to your prophets, he is the promised one, who is to lead Judaea to freedom from Rome. Is that not so?'

'It might be.'

Neither of us volunteered any further comment. 'I shall report this conversation,' said the centurion at length, 'and your reluctance to co-operate will be noted.'

'We're terrified,' I said.

'Scared out of our wits,' Judas agreed.

'You would do well to be apprehensive. From now on you and your colleagues will be kept under observation.'

'I take it that's a threat?'

'Warning or threat: you may take it how you will. Good evening, gentlemen.'

The man returned to his table and raised a hand to the innkeeper, who hastened to supply him and his whore with further drinks.

'What do you make of that?' asked Judas.

'Only to be expected, methinks. Evidently the Romans are becoming nervous.'

'And are as much in the dark regarding our Lord's plans as we are. Or more so.'

'Quite. It seems improbable, for instance, that they know of his intention to visit Jerusalem for the Passover.'

'They must realize it's a possibility. And from their point of view a dangerous one. Oh, God.'

A prosperous-looking man in late middle age had just entered from the neighbouring taproom. He was dressed in

Roman style, in the simple *tunica* worn informally by men from all classes of society, dyed fashionably maroon. Unlike the centurion he appeared amiably inclined, if somewhat pleased with himself. Overweight and sparsely bearded, he stood with thumbs stuck in his ample belt as he surveyed the scene in a proprietory manner. Matthew, called Levi, the local tax-collector, and for all his superficial bonhomie, one of the most hated men in Galilee.

'Simon! And young Judas! My friends. Let me order you more wine.'

I would have preferred to say that we were just leaving, but he was not a man to offend with impunity. 'Too kind,' I said with an effort, while Judas murmured a similar sentiment.

Levi snapped his fingers at an attendant, who hurried over. 'Yes, sir?'

'A flagon of the best wine for myself and my friends. Not the muck you usually serve, but the best.'

'By all means, sir. We've just received delivery from Rome of some of the finest Falernian ...'

'That will have to do, I suppose.' Levi returned his attention to us as the servant hurried away. 'I observed the centurion talking to you just now. What did he want?'

'He was anxious to know what our Lord was teaching. In particular whether he claimed to be the Messiah.'

'And what did you say?'

'Nothing.'

He nodded. 'Probably wise. The Romans are becoming nervous. Perhaps not without cause.' He broke off as the wine put in an appearance. He tasted it briefly, and nodded again. 'Acceptable. Here. And something for yourself.'

'Many thanks, sir.'

'I find myself in rather a difficult position,' he said, after we had toasted the Emperor in half-hearted fashion. 'On the one hand, I accept the teachings of our Lord, yet on the other I count myself a loyal subject of Rome.' Judas and I received this assurance without comment. 'And I feel it would be to everyone's benefit if our Lord were to clarify his teachings in some respects.'

'You are right enough there,' I said.

'What would you say, gentlemen,' said Levi, 'was the single matter causing most friction between Rome and our people?'

'The occupation, of course.'

'Quite, but I meant more specifically. I should have said, what is the matter most likely to trigger what the Romans would call treasonable rebellion and the Zealots a war of liberation?'

I considered carefully. For his part, Judas already appeared to have lost interest in our companion. As is common amongst the youth of today, he did not trouble to disguise the fact, his lack of participation in our discourse falling little short of discourtesy. Eventually I said, 'The question of imperial images?'

'Precisely,' replied Levi, in the manner of one congratulating the least obtuse amongst a class of backward children. 'Imperial images. They have already caused trouble for the Prefect on one notorious occasion, and may do so again.'

He referred to an incident a couple of years earlier, when Pilate had brought regimental standards bearing the image of the Roman Emperor into the Temple, albeit at night when no-one was likely to have seen them. This gross breach of the second commandment had rightly caused serious offence amongst all shades of religious opinion. 'For instance,' Levi continued, 'coins bearing the Emperor's portrait still circulate here, despite the efforts of those in authority to discourage the practice.'

I shrugged. 'What's the adage? That bad money drives out good. Coins with the Emperor's head on them may one day no longer constitute legal tender in Judaea. Those with abstract designs will always be negotiable. So people spend the dubious coinage, and save the more reliable. Result: there are more coins in circulation with Caesar's head on than without.'

I seemed to have taken the wind out of Levi's sails. Doubtless he had intended giving the lecture on fiduciary finance himself. 'Yes, yes,' he replied irritably, 'we all know that. But how do we take advantage of the fact?'

'Go on, then,' said Judas sourly, making his first contribution for some time.

'Quite simply. We show our Lord a coin with Caesar's head on it, and make a note of his response.'

'How will that help?' I asked.

'If he condemns the graven image, he will be in trouble with the Prefect, and incidentally myself, for discouraging people from paying their taxes. If he sees nothing wrong in it, he will lose support amongst his more radical adherents. Either way he will have clarified his position, whereupon we can make a more informed decision as to whether he is, or is not, claiming to be the promised Messiah.'

Judas and I were considering this suggestion without enthusiasm when the centurion's voice rang out, so loudly that it made us all jump.

'Attention, everyone!'

He stood at his table, alongside a young auxiliary who had apparently just conveyed a message to him. Other soldiers were making their way into the room. 'Those of you who have entered this tavern within the last two hours will stand.'

Reluctantly I complied. Despite his bulk, Levi had beaten me to it. Judas remained seated. Of the twenty or so customers present rather more than half had stood, some more readily than others. I formed the impression that the sharp-eyed centurion had made a note of those reluctant to comply. The little whore sitting at his table had attempted to draw attention to herself by giving a choking cry, and fainting. Despite the fact that one of her breasts was on the verge of spilling from her tunic, most eyes remained on him.

'Innkeeper!'

The man hurried in, wiping his hands on his apron. 'Yes, sir?'

'Is there anyone not standing who to your knowledge has entered this tavern within the last couple of hours?'

The fellow scratched his head. 'Well, now.' He looked around, frowning a little with the effort of concentration. 'I'm not sure about them,' he said, nodding at a couple of young fellows and their companion, a fat pompous-looking man, 'and him.' He pointed at Judas, who quailed visibly. 'The others have been here since midday, or even longer.'

'Evidently,' grunted the centurion, observing the stupor of many of those present. 'My men will now take the names and addresses of those of you who are standing. The four who should have stood but failed to do so will accompany me to the praetorium for questioning.'

'What's this all about?' demanded Judas in a shaky voice.

'I hope for your sake that you are unaware.' After a brief pause the centurion continued, 'One of my men has been murdered not two hundred yards from here, just within the city wall. This appears to have happened at least an hour since, probably more, in broad daylight, yet no-one admits even to having seen his body.'

'That's nothing to do with us,' said the pompous-looking man truculently. 'Why should we be detained?'

'Because you should have been quicker getting to your feet.' One or two customers gave nervous giggles. 'And if any here think this a matter for amusement, I should mention that the deceased, Dio Syrianus, was a good friend of mine.' There was respectful silence for a period during which one might have counted slowly to half a dozen. 'That's better.'

A couple of his men removed Judas from our table. He made no verbal protest, but rose unsteadily and was clearly terrified. Fat Levi, being in the Prefect's good books, seemed but little perturbed.

For my part I tried not to show that I was hardly in better case than my son. Fortunately I had not mentioned what I had seen to anyone. But if there were any that had seen me with the corpse, the consequences could be well-nigh fatal. And I knew Judas. For all the bravado of his talk of liberation, he was no hero. If it suited his purposes, he would not hesitate to incriminate me or anyone else.

*

THE PRIESTS have decided that this year the Passover will fall on the Sabbath. They calculate it by the phases of the moon, but precisely how I know not. All I know is that ten days before the Passover the moon was in first quarter, and waxing. It loomed over the western horizon as I made my way home, throwing gaunt grey shadows in the yellow light. It was not entirely the cold that made me shiver. I have never been at ease on moonlit nights, which I find more sinister than complete darkness. Evil-doers are abroad, and some say that the spirits of the dead are often seen.

I arrived home about the fifth hour of the night. I say 'home.' It is a lodging-house in which by now I am more or less permanently resident, and I share the bed of the proprietress, a widow called Miriam. When Joshua bar-Abbas commanded us to follow him, he also ordered that we abandon our families to do so. I saw no reason to take this too literally. The widow scarcely counts as family, we have no children, and I lost touch with my parents and siblings years since, as soon as I became a committed Zealot.

Miriam was waiting up for me at the kitchen table. A plump woman of middle age, still desirable, with hair dyed fair in the current Roman fashion.

'About time. I take it you've been drinking.'

'A little. I've been conducting important business.'

I had no intention of telling her the true reason for my being late. The number of people I trust nowadays is extremely small, and does not include her, or for that matter any woman.

'What does he want now?'

'Who? Joshua bar-Josef?'

'Who did you think I meant? Tiberius Caesar?'

'Very funny. I told you, I haven't seen Joshua for well over a week. He then said it was his intention to enter Jerusalem riding upon an ass. I think the idea is that such a beast, as opposed to a warhorse, will indicate his humility.'

'Humility is not an attribute I associate with him.'

'Well, there we shall have to differ. Come, let's to bed. I must set out for Jerusalem on the morrow, and am not likely to return for some time. So …'

*

A WHILE later she said, 'I thought your leader disapproved of carnal relations. At least between those who are not married.'

'So he does. He never seems to have been tempted. Anyway, he teaches that we are all sinners.'

She gave a lecherous chuckle. 'Well, you certainly are.'

'I don't deny it. So long as we confess our sins, we shall be saved. Or so he says.'

'I don't much care for the thought that you'll be discussing me with him.'

'Oh, that's unnecessary. I shall simply admit that I have strayed from what he calls the strait and narrow.'

She sighed. 'You know, I wish you'd give up this mad idea you have about freeing Judaea from the Romans. Let someone else do it.'

I hesitated. 'I won't say the idea has never occurred to me. I'm still not entirely clear what he wants.'

'I don't think anyone is. Even himself.'

*

FROM Caesarea to Jerusalem by the coastal road is three days' journey, broken at Joffa. The last day, ascending into the hill country around the holy city, is the most strenuous. By the hour of sunset I had reached Bethany, three miles from my journey's end, and taken lodging at the stables of one Malachi, a fellow who makes a decent living from those visiting from the north. For the standard of accommodation he provides, his prices are reasonable. Otherwise it means a choice between a variety of hovels, or paying through the nose for anything better.

'There's a gentleman to see you, Simon bar-Cleophas,' he said as soon as I set foot across his threshold. 'He's been waiting an hour or more.'

A government official, from the sound of things. Malachi knows most of my acquaintances among the disciples, and apart from them none but the Romans could have known of my intention. Their spies are everywhere.

I was right. The man emerging from the inner room was the centurion who had accosted me in the tavern after the killing of his countryman, and subsequently interviewed me at his headquarters.

'I need to speak to you again,' he said without preliminary.

'By all means,' I said, trying to disguise my unease. 'But I gave you all the help I could the other day.' This was not the whole truth, though I had signed a formal statement telling him as much as I had been prepared to reveal.

'Perhaps,' he grunted. 'Why are you staying in Bethany? It's not *en route* to Jerusalem. You've come five miles out of your way.'

'This is the way our Lord should come. He is preaching in the Jordan Valley, east of here. I propose to enter the city with him.'

'What were you doing in Caesarea?'

'You asked me that before.'

'Well, I'm asking you again.'

'I had financial affairs to attend to.'

'I thought Joshua's disciples were expected to live as impoverished holy men, or to put it another way, mendicant vagrants without means.'

'Not all of us. Some do casual work for the benefit of the group. And we have one or two wealthy patrons. My son Judas keeps the group's accounts, and lends the moneys to various usurers at interest. For myself, I previously owned a farm in Galilee, and a prosperous smithy.'

'And still do.'

'You're well informed. For the most part others now run it for me, but I still occasionally have profits to invest.'

Again the centurion made an unenthusiastic sound. One or two other residents were showing an interest in our business. He jerked his head at the door. 'We'll continue this conversation outside.'

We made our way to the lunging ring, where I first leant against one of the posts, then hitched myself to the top rail and sat there. 'Very well. Here.'

'You told me that you were lodging temporarily with one Miriam, widow of Nathan bar-Gideon.'

'That was correct. I also informed you that it was my intention to visit Jerusalem for the Passover.'

'Quite so. But for the moment I am more concerned with your activities in Caesarea on the evening of the murder. Your lodgings lie some quarter-mile from the tavern in which you were drinking.'

'True. What of it?'

'The Street of the Flags is on the direct route from your lodgings to the inn. It's strange that you failed to observe the deceased's body.'

'Perhaps he had not then been killed.'

The centurion shook his head. 'By the time the body was discovered, the deceased having failed to answer to roll-call, he had been dead well over an hour, perhaps two. According to your account of matters, confirmed by the innkeeper, you had been in his premises no more than half an hour.'

I shrugged. 'I must have failed to notice it.'

'Along with half the population of the city, it seems. Another curious thing. When we saw your lady friend Miriam, she was evidently unaware of the murder. It seems odd that you did not see fit to mention it to her. It is after all not every day that one is interrogated regarding a murder, and sees one's only son arrested into the bargain.'

I kicked myself mentally. For I should have told her of the murder, concealing only my finding of the body. Not having done so, it now looked as if I had something to hide, which of course I had. 'I... thought it would worry her unnecessarily.'

'Well, she's worried now, I can assure you. Not so much on your behalf, as her own. She seemed most anxious to distance herself from you and your activities.'

That was no more than I would have expected. Few nowadays are prepared to endanger themselves for others. The arrangement we have suits us both, but I did not imagine myself to have been the love of her life, or worth risking arrest for. I said nothing. The centurion continued, 'Your son Judas, with whom you were drinking, is, as of course you know, another of the disciples of Joshua bar-Josef. And as you are doubtless also aware, suspected of being one of the *Secarii*.' I still remained silent. 'The *Secarii*,' he repeated, 'or knifemen.'

'He denies it.'

'Yes, so he does. So far.' He had no need to say more. I wondered what Judas had told them. Whatever they wanted him to say, probably. The Romans know how to make men talk, but no-one has yet discovered a way to make them tell the truth.

'The killing seems typical of a *Secarius* murder. A knife in the back at dusk in a secluded place. The usual victims are those Jews believed to be well-inclined towards Rome. For a soldier to be thus singled out is unusual. And in Caesarea, so far as I am aware, unique.'

'Perhaps it was not a *Secarius* murder at all. Some private grudge.'

'Conceivably, but I think not. As I said, Dio was a friend of mine. He was well-liked, and so far as I know had no enemies.'

'Has Judas been charged?'

'He is still being detained. At the time I left Caesarea he had not yet been charged.'

'I see. And how do you think I can help?'

'You can tell me what you know of his recent activities, for a start. He has told us quite a bit about you.'

It is of course common practice for interrogators to set accused persons one against the another by telling each of them that the other is seeking lenity by incriminating him. Nevertheless I judged the man to be telling the truth. For all that he was my son, I had no illusions about Judas. If by blaming me he could save himself, he would do so. I tried to console myself with the thought that few men have sons they are unreservedly proud of.

'He is thought to be one of the Zealots,' the centurion continued, 'as I believe they now call themselves.'

I shrugged. 'He is an Essene, as am I. One of those who believe in strict observance of the Torah. Whether he has also joined the Zealots, I know not. If he has, what of it? The lad is all mouth, and quite harmless.' I sighed. 'In a few years' time I hope he will have gained some sense.'

'He alleges that you are one of the leaders of the movement, as evidenced by your *cognomen*.'

'I'm not responsible for what men call me.'

'Most men's *cognomina* have some basis in fact. He said that he pretended to agree with you so as to learn of your plans, and then report them to us.'

I laughed as convincingly as I could. 'That is the purest fantasy. He was always talking about overthrowing the oppressors of the Jewish people by force. Mere juvenile bragging. In my opinion our leader made a serious mistake in accepting him as one of his followers.'

'I thought,' said the man sarcastically, 'that he preferred the company of sinners. If so, Judas would appear to fit the bill admirably.'

I tried a sardonic smile. 'Methinks there are limits.'

He paused. 'Hm. You will report to the Prefect's headquarters in Herod's Fortress upon arrival in Jerusalem, and every day thereafter. On each occasion you will state anything you have learned of your leader, his followers, and their intentions.'

I shrugged. 'I appear to have no option.'

'Exactly. Where are you staying in Jerusalem?'

'I have made no arrangements yet. The place is likely to be so crowded during the Passover that I may have to return here at night. Or even sleep rough.'

'Again, let us know what you are doing.' He mounted his horse, a bay colt tethered to the fence-rails, and turned in the saddle. 'You stand on the brink of arrest as an accomplice to murder. If I had the men, you would be in custody already. As it is, you would do well to co-operate with Rome.' He gave a rather bleak smile, before raising a hand in valediction. 'We shall meet again, methinks.'

'Roman bastard,' said Malachi venomously, appearing at my side as the centurion's bay trotted back to the north.

I scrambled down off the top rail. 'Do you know him?'

'Not well. He was drafted in a year or so since, from one of the Syrian legions I understand, as a centurion of the local auxiliaries.'

'A man on a special mission?'

'Something like that. He doesn't strike me as a Roman born, somehow. But certainly not a local man. Probably one of the Emperor's personal spies. He has them everywhere.'

According to Mary

THE FORCES of evil are all about us, even, I fear, amongst those closest to our Lord. But first I will copy out the brief notes that I have made from time to time during this last few months. I shall not edit them, but leave my comments as they were at the time they were made. That will enable me to recall the capricious fluctuations in my train of thought, inconstant creature that I am.

I first met my Lord in the month of *Elui*, which the Romans call September, when he saved my life. Had it not been for him I should have been permanently tormented by devils, and in all probability have destroyed myself.

From earliest infancy I had not received from my parents the loving care which a child should have, being regularly beaten and ill-used for the smallest misdemeanour. As a result I was determined to marry early. This came to pass, in that at the age of sixteen I was given to a rich fish merchant from Capernaum, thirty years my senior. Within days of my marriage I realized that I had made a terrible mistake.

My husband regularly abused me in ways too vicious to describe. Over the years I grew to hate him with my whole being, and began to pray that he might die in great pain. My prayers were eventually answered, for indeed he did die, after days of exhaustion and screaming in agony, from what the physicians called an obstruction of the bowel. For my part I was consumed by hellish joy. The only thing preventing my joy from being complete was that he had descended into *scheol*, the grave of oblivion, and thus existed no more. I should have preferred him to live for ever, tormented ceaselessly in the lake of fire and brimstone while he begged unavailingly for death.

He died unexpectedly, and thus had no opportunity to ensure that I inherited nothing. As a rich widow, I used much of my wealth to found a home for fallen women, and those who had suffered at the hands of men. It pleased me to think that I was spending my husband's riches on a cause that he would utterly have despised. I succeeded in finding respectable employment for many of the women, some even at the holy Temple of Herod. Others found men prepared to marry them, but I was never happy about that. I hated all men.

Yet this good work failed to satisfy me. From time to time I was confined to my bed with severe attacks of the headache, or obscure digestive complaints, for which my physicians were unable to find any cause. At other times I heard voices, telling me to do dreadful things. One day, I thought, I would poison the wells to the Temple, so that all the priests would be killed. Or go out and stab men by moonlight, in the manner of the *Secarii*. Although I could never bring myself to act upon them, these delusions obsessed me, and sometimes I would spend days in delirium. I failed to recognize that these thoughts and desires emanated from devils and evil spirits. For surely it was the Evil One who had answered my vicious prayers, and was now exacting his reward.

One day a neighbour told me of a young rabbi from

Nazareth called Joshua bar-Josef, who preached love and forgiveness towards all men, and could perform miracles, including curing the sick. He was unmarried, and not apparently interested in women, or not in any physical sense. It occurred to me that if that were so at least he was not an abuser of women, and therefore a most unusual man. He was said to be teaching in the neighbourhood of Mount Eremos, near the northern coast of the lake known as Gennesaret, now called by the Romans Tiberias, after their Emperor. This was but a few miles from Magdala, where I lived. I had no interest in his teachings, but hoped he might cure me of my illnesses. So I made my way there.

I soon found myself surrounded by a crowd of pilgrims, so diverse in nature that I cannot adequately describe them. For there was no typical pilgrim. The majority were family groups, with children of all ages. Some appeared intent merely on enjoying themselves, having brought bread, cheese, fishes and wine to consume as they sat in the open air. There were serious learned men, some of whom I recognized as Pharisees, given to grumbling and discussion amongst themselves. I even noticed three or four girls from my house, not, I am glad to say, plying their former trade, but talking seriously to one another. One even carried what I took to be a copy of the Holy Torah. As at most public gatherings, there were bands of ill-behaved young men who would probably try to interrupt and shout down the preacher, not through any considered disagreement with him, but for pure mischief and desire to cause trouble.

At the foot of the mount the pilgrims began to take their places, unpacking their food and drink, and laying down blankets upon which to sit. Fishermen were standing or squatting in their boats, moored at the lakeside. Gentiles were present too – Syrians from the eastern hills, and a couple of Roman soldiers, one in the uniform of a centurion.

Finally there were men alone, from all nations and classes of society: Some looked like wealthy merchants, amongst whom I was surprised to see Levi, the rapacious and much-hated publican. One or two other lone men seemed to be doing nothing in particular. Very likely they were Roman spies, or observers as Pilate and his henchmen prefer to call them. So far as I could tell, I was the only lone woman.

*

A FEW moments later I had the first sight of my Lord. He came down the mount and stood amidst the scrub and grassland, on a level piece of ground acting as a platform. He was accompanied not only by his disciples, as they are now called, but a multitude of people from all over the north country, from Calchis and Ituraea to the coastal ports of Tyre and Sidon. From the east too they came, from Gaulanitis and Batanaea, and even further afield. All converged at the foot of the mountain to join the pilgrims assembled from the south.

Joshua bar-Josef was a slim man perhaps thirty years of age, slightly above the middle height, with a lean pale face, dark hair and beard, and simply dressed in a white robe and sandals. By the time he began to preach the crowd was immense, and from time to time would punctuate what he said by cheering and shouting slogans.

Despite this it was surprisingly easy to hear him. He knew how to make himself heard better than any priest or rabbi I had ever known. The rowdy youths, heavily outnumbered, were soon silenced by those who had come to hear him preach, or be healed of their diseases.

As for what he taught, miserable sinner that I am, I was at first unimpressed. He began by preaching to those already converted to his message, including his disciples. There were twelve of the latter, though at the time it was not possible to distinguish them from his other followers. He blessed them all, saying that they should inherit the earth by their meekness, bringing peace to the world by suffering for the sake of righteousness.

Then he went on to teach love for one's enemies, and the doing of good towards those who hate. To my troubled mind he appeared to be advocating submission to evil. Someone in the crowd asked if he came to destroy the law as taught by the prophets of old, who had preached eye for eye, and tooth for tooth. He replied that he came not to destroy the law or the prophets, but to fulfil them. His argument was that any man, even the worst of sinners, could love those who loved him. It was more admirable to love one's enemies, and ensure that one's righteousness exceeded that of the temple scribes and Pharisees.

Here one of the Pharisees interrupted, and asked him to give further examples. He replied that the Torah taught that one should do no murder, nor commit adultery. But one should aim higher than that. As anger tempted men to murder, one should avoid anger. And the committing of adultery in one's heart was as sinful as adultery in the flesh. The Torah forbade taking the name of the Lord God in vain. But in fact one should not swear at all, not even the mildest oath.

Then one of his disciples asked how one should pray. I expected a long answer, but he replied simply:

> 'Our father, which art in heaven,
> Hallowed be thy name,
> Thy Kingdom Come,
> Thy will be done,
> In earth as it is in heaven.
> Give us this day our daily bread,
> And forgive us our debts,
> As we forgive our debtors,
> And lead us not into temptation,
> But deliver us from evil.
> For thine is the Kingdom,
> And the Power, and the Glory,
> For ever,
> Amen.'

Strangely I was able to commit this to memory at first hearing. And I began to see the light, albeit dimly: that the young rabbi might indeed be the Messiah, or promised one, whether he came to bring peace, or a sword.

He was then asked whether it was possible to be a good man, and yet rich. To the disappointment of the questioner he replied that where one's treasure was, there was one's heart also. One could not serve God and mammon. As he said this, I glanced at Levi, half-expecting him to stalk away in disgust. In fact he sat there frowning and nodding thoughtfully, as if making a genuine attempt to understand.

A man accompanied by a large family enquired what provision one should make for the future. Our Lord said, curiously I thought, that one should not take thought for the morrow, because God would provide whatever was good for us. Sufficient unto the day was the evil thereof. The way leading to destruction was broad and wide, whereas that leading to salvation was strait and narrow.

He had set the standard of righteousness so high that I was further surprised when he said that one should not judge others. We were all sinners, and those who presumed to judge their fellow-men would themselves be judged.

It crossed my mind that in recent times many men, like him, had claimed to be divinely inspired, but nothing had come of their teachings. And at that very instant, as if he had read my thoughts, he warned everyone to beware of false prophets.

After he had finished preaching there were members of the crowd who departed unsatisfied, including some of those who had previously been his followers. I supposed that they disliked being told to love their enemies, but the main complaint voiced was that of being told to desert their families, follow him and bestow all their goods to feed the poor.

Those more favourably impressed besieged him with questions. Many wanted to know if he was the Messiah who would free them from Roman tyranny, asking him when the day of vengeance would arrive, though even I had understood enough of what he said to realize that this was not what he had been advocating. Never had he suggested physical resistance of any kind, which was the main reason why I had judged him an appeaser of the Romans, in the manner of the Sadducees. Not that I had much sympathy with those who desired rebellion either. The Romans seemed to me neither better nor worse than the Jews. They were men, and therefore abusers of women.

Others wanted him to heal them of their sicknesses, including those like myself, who were troubled by unclean spirits. Many tried to touch him, believing that he exuded magical powers which would cure all illness. With some he succeeded, with others he failed.

Somehow I found myself next to him. I must have pushed myself forward, but have no memory of having done so. He turned to me and said, 'You are Mary of Magdala, are you not?' That meant nothing, for I was fairly well known in the neighbourhood. I replied, 'Yes, Lord.' Why I should have called him Lord I know not. He said, 'You are much troubled by guilt. Your mind is poisoned. Repent, never hate anyone again, and you will be cured.'

My heart stopped. He knew. I asked, 'Is it possible, Lord, to repent, yet keep the fruits of one's evil?'

He replied, 'There is a Roman saying, that the first punishment of the guilty is that in their own heart they can never be acquitted. You have punished yourself. Now let God be your judge. Spend your money wisely, in the good cause upon which you are engaged. And hate no man ever again.'

He placed a hand on me and turned away. And I suddenly knew that from that moment on I should be a different person. And I was right. The devils have never troubled me again.

I followed him to the town of Capernaum, which was on my way home. And there the centurion I had observed during the sermon approached him and said, 'Rabbi, my servant, one Gnaeus, is at my home, extremely sick. Can you cure him?'

Our Lord offered to go and heal him, whereupon the centurion replied that if he said the word, the servant might be healed without his needing to attend. Hearing this, our Lord said that he had not come across such great faith in all Israel. Those with faith would be saved, but those without would be cast into outer darkness, amid weeping and wailing and gnashing of teeth. The centurion said nothing further, but saluted and left for his home. I reflected that I should never know the fate of the man's servant, and my faith was being put to the test.

Within days I knew that I should devote my life to the cause of which the young rabbi had spoken, spreading his word throughout the land of Galilee, and beyond. The work for women upon which I was engaged in Caesarea I turned over to one of my senior helpers, Susannah. I would call in from time to time, guide her as best I could, and continue to provide financial aid. But henceforth my main mission in life would be to help spread our Lord's message.

In this I was helped by some of his disciples. I say, some. Others I was not happy about. Granted that our Lord was calling upon sinners to repent, it seemed to me that several of his followers had sinned more than most. I particularly mistrusted an effete young man called Judas, who took every opportunity to hang around the refuge trying to catch sight of those of my girls who had taken his fancy.

But who was I to judge? After all, I had killed my husband.

*

I HAD been in our Lord's service about four months when I met the centurion again. It was the afternoon of a bitter winter's day, and I had been seated at the fireside of the women's hostelry with some of my girls, explaining my Lord's teaching to those who would listen. I recall that I resented having to go to the door.

At first I did not recognize the man, for he was not of striking appearance, though he bore himself well, as became a soldier. He was about my own age, broad-shouldered, clean-shaven in the Roman style, and slightly above the middle height. I remember his breath steaming into the icy air. He had called the previous day, seeking a couple of laundry maids for the military barracks at Caesarea. I cannot say that he made any strong impression on me, perhaps a sign that I no longer regarded all men as dangerous, or the enemies of womankind. He addressed me in Greek, the *lingua communis* of the eastern empire. His manner was formal and courteous.

'You are the lady Mary, of Magdala?'

'I am.'

'I tried to make arrangements through your assistant yesterday, but she did not feel that she could do so without your authority.'

'She knows that I am cautious regarding our women's future employment, for fear that they fall back into their old forbidden ways.'

'I can understand that. You have no particular reason to trust me. However, I assure you that I shall protect your women to the best of my ability. I cannot guarantee that they will not form liaisons with any of the men, but I shall not allow any pressure to be put on them to do so. And I shall keep you in touch with their progress.'

At that moment I recognized him. 'Did I not see you at

Capernaum some months since, when you asked our Lord to heal your servant?'

He nodded. 'That's right. I'm surprised you've remembered me.'

'It took a little while. May I enquire what happened to your servant?'

'When I arrived home, his condition had improved, and he eventually made full recovery. The physicians claimed the credit, and denied that your lord had anything to do with the matter.'

'What do you think?'

He pulled a wry face. 'Despite what your lord seemed to think, I am not a man who lives by faith.'

'So you gave the credit to your army physicians.'

'Not really. My faith in them is rather limited, too. It may be that your rabbi's blessing did some good. Maybe the doctors played their part. Or it may be that the man would have recovered anyway.'

'If I remember, you mentioned to our Lord that you were a man of some authority. But from your voice, you are not a Roman by birth. Nor Greek.'

He smiled ruefully. 'I thought my Greek was passable.'

'You underestimate yourself, centurion. It is excellent. You are clearly an educated man. Better educated than I should have expected from… but forgive me, I am being impertinent.'

'Not at all. You're right. Neither Greek nor Latin is my first language. By birth I am German.' Again he smiled. 'A barbarian.'

For some reason this admission inclined me to trust him more. Perhaps I found it easier to empathize with one who was neither Greek, nor Roman, nor even a Jew, but an alien, as I so often felt myself. 'Very well,' I said, after some thought. 'I have two girls here, both forced into prostitution from an early age. They speak little Greek and no Latin, and have no skills apart from limited knowledge of the laundry, and the ability to work hard. But I shall expect them to be paid, and not treated as slaves.'

'They will be treated with respect,' he said, which struck me as a strange but not unwelcome way of putting things, 'provided with basic board and lodging, and paid at the minimum rate. Of course as they gain experience and competence they may qualify for more. You are free to visit them whenever you like.'

'That will be difficult at the moment. I am here every *Yom Revi'i*, if you choose to come to see me and report. Most other days I am about my Lord's business.'

'Very well. May I see them now?'

'Of course.' And after brief conversation with them, matters were agreed.

That, as I say, was my first meeting with the man. As I now write, over two months later, the centurion has kept his promise. In particular he has visited me to report every week without fail. Curiously enough that makes me uneasy. Three weeks ago, being satisfied that the girls were being well treated by their fellow-workers and not abused by his men, I intimated that he need not call quite so often. His reply was that he enjoyed his afternoons talking to me.

In other words, though his manner is perfectly unexceptionable, he is interested in me as a woman. I cannot think of any other explanation. Were I a crone of sixty or seventy it would be otherwise, but I am two-and-thirty, and though I say so myself, still not entirely without physical attraction to men. Whilst it is of course unthinkable that things between us should proceed further, I feel curiously unwilling to bring our association to an end. Normally in ethical matters I should seek our Lord's guidance, but for some reason I do not feel inclined to do so. It surely cannot be entirely wrong to continue seeing this man for the time being.

*

OH, by Almighty God, he knows my secret. Blaspheming wretch that I am, I have taken the Lord's name in vain, and ought to strike it out. But striking his name is also forbidden, and what is done, is done. Whether the man be an angel of the Lord, or as I fear, an emissary of the Serpent, I know not. But he knows the secret of my heart.

The matter came about thus. He had invited me to accompany him to the amphitheatre in Caesarea to see a tragedy by the Greek dramatist Sophocles, entitled *Antigone*. I thought carefully about whether it would be right to accept, and concluded that with everything taking place in broad daylight there would be no great harm in it. It is not unusual nowadays for respectable women, especially widows, to attend the theatre. The centurion's Greek was better than mine, so he could explain some of those allusions and turns of phrase that were lost on me.

For all that I cannot say that I greatly cared for the production. The ethic seemed to my way of thinking very questionable, which I dare say is to be expected from anything Hellenistic. For one thing there was no clearcut distinction between good and evil.

On the way back to the women's refuge I mentioned this to the man. His response was that in real life the difference between the two was often obscure, and that one of the functions of serious drama was to encourage members of the audience to query accepted standards and think for themselves. Of course I disagreed with him profoundly, and asked whether he had ever seriously considered the teachings of our Lord. To my surprise he answered yes, saying that although he thought there was much reason in what he had said, in some respects he did not agree with him.

Upon my asking in what respects he disagreed, he instanced his teaching on divorce. Whereas in certain circumstances Mosaic law permits marriage to be brought to an end, the rabbi Joshua had taught that what God had joined together, no man should put asunder. The centurion said that he thought such teaching could lead to much unhappiness and suffering, when two persons who had come to detest one another became imprisoned in their marriage for life.

At this the demons entered my heart, as in view of my own disastrous marriage I was tempted to agree with him. He went on to say, and this is where I realized that he might be the Tempter in person, that in certain circumstances the only alternative to divorce seemed to him to be murder.

What I said in reply to him I know not, save that it was clear he knew my darkest secret, that of my husband's death. He seemed puzzled, and insisted that he had spoken in jest. But it was clear to me that no man with decency, or what the Romans call *gravitas*, could jest about such matters. He is given to misplaced levity. For instance he said that he had derived much pleasure from committing adultery, or at least fornication, in his heart. This was at best a joke in execrable taste, at worst a confession of real evil. After much discussion to little purpose I told him that I should not see him again.

Again his reaction was abnormal. I had expected him to fly into a rage. Instead he remained calm, saying that he did not believe me capable of murder, and asking me to describe the manner of my husband's illness and death, which he assured me he had not known. Since he was obviously aware of the truth anyway, I judged that I had nothing to lose by doing so. This I did, sparing myself nothing.

So far as this man is concerned, my feelings are chaotic. I am still inclined to think he is an agent of the Serpent who tempted Eve, or conceivably an angel of the Lord who is putting me to the test, in which case I fear I have been found wanting.

He is very insistent about seeing me again. I have tried to say no, but I am weak. I have an irrational conviction that for all his misguided views he is not a bad man. And yet evil can visit in many guises. I must ask the Rabbi Joshua for guidance, whilst confessing my sin.

*

FOR some reason I chose first to consult with Levi, the tax-collector. Although he is one of the most hated men in Galilee, I have always found him easy to talk to. He is unscrupulous, certainly. But he does not pretend to be what he is not. Whilst owning a beautiful villa south of Caesarea, he does not flaunt his wealth, dressing and entertaining modestly, like what the Romans style a 'country gentleman.'

Besides which he is faithful to his plain wife of many years. And had not our Lord told us not to judge others?

The taxman sat behind his office desk, as plump, prosperous and pleased with himself as ever. 'You wished to see me, Mary?'

'Yes. I hope I do not disturb you from your business affairs.'

'I have half an hour to spare.'

Another thing: he did not pretend to be busier than he was. 'It concerns a man called Rotgarius Teutonicus.'

'The centurion? Yes, I know the man.'

Levi knew everyone, which was one reason why I had come to see him. 'What can you tell me about him?'

He shrugged and spread his hands. 'His tax affairs are in perfect order. Would that everyone conducted their business as efficiently.'

'Tax affairs? But he is a soldier.'

'He has made some modest but well-chosen investments. The details he provides are invariably accurate, and he pays his dues promptly.'

'So he is an honest man?'

'So far as I am aware. May I enquire your interest in him?'

'He… has employed two of my girls at the barracks, and I'd like to ensure, so far as possible, that they are not in moral danger.'

Again he shrugged, this time with his eyebrows rather than his shoulders. 'I don't know about that. All I can tell you is that he's a man who knows his way around, as one might say. If you ever have business with the army, he's the man to have a word with. He knows all the right people, and how to handle them.'

'So he has distinguished contacts?'

'Oh, certainly. They say he's a legate of the Governor of Syria. Charged with keeping an eye on Pilate, or so rumour would have it.'

'Teutonicus is a powerful man, then?'

'Influential, at least. I would not care to have him for an enemy. But I'm glad to say that we've always been on excellent terms.'

Another thing occurred to me about which Levi might be able to help. 'You are one of our Lord's followers, and therefore know young Judas.'

Resignation was written all over his face. 'What's he been up to now?'

'Perhaps nothing, but he comes round talking to the girls more often than I should like.'

For the first time Levi laughed. 'The damned young fool. He's a lecher in dreamland only. I don't suppose he's ever had a woman in his life.'

I smiled feebly. 'That seems to be everyone's opinion.'

'Can't even keep the group's accounts in order, and they're pretty basic. He's somehow contrived to get them into one hell of a mess. God only knows why our Lord gave him the money-bags job.'

'You think he should have given it to you?'

'I'm glad he didn't. I've enough to do, without taking on unpaid work as well.' Again Levi smiled. 'Yes, I know, I'm supposed to give all my goods to feed the poor, leave my family and other commitments, and live hand-to-mouth following the joiner's son.'

'And you're not prepared to?'

'Hannah has been my wife these thirty years, and has borne me five children. Why should I walk out on her now?'

'She might come with you.'

'Why should she? She's put up with me all this time, and I'd like her to be well provided for. And I'll admit I'd rather live in a villa than a hovel myself. I've worked hard all my life. I don't see why I shouldn't reap some financial benefit.'

'Yet you're one of his chosen.'

Levi shrugged. 'He knows that I have reservations about some of his teaching. It has not yet led to a breach between us.'

'Why do you follow him?'

'I'm honestly not sure. He's an impressive man in some ways, I can't deny it. Perhaps I'm curious. Yes, that's it. Curious. I'd like to see what he does when the Zealots try to persuade him to lead a rebellion against Rome. Which I'm sure they will.'

'And if he does, what will you do?'

'I've no quarrel with Rome. It's thanks to the Empire that I'm a rich man. The Romans have always dealt squarely with me, and I with them. If it weren't for Rome I'd be a tinpot money-lender at the Temple, struggling to make ends meet, and trying to keep on the right side of the Sadducees.'

'So you would choose Rome?'

'The choice has been made for me. As I say, I owe my position to Rome. It seems to me that I'm estopped from arguing that they have no right to rule here.' He grinned. 'Yes, that's the term the Roman lawyers use: estoppel. "When one is forbidden and proscribed to speak against one's own actions – yea, though it be to speak the truth." '

I stood. 'Thank you, Levi. You've been very frank.'

He stood in turn, levering his substantial bulk from his bench. 'Not entirely. If you quote some of what I've said, I'll deny it. But as for Teutonicus, he's one of the most influential men in Judaea, chief centurion in the First Cohort of the Quingenariae, and not badly off either. Due to leave the army in a year or two, I imagine. He's a Roman citizen too, so he should get a grant of land. You could do a lot worse. Despite his being an unbeliever.'

'I've no idea what you mean,' I said stiffly.

Levi's laughter followed me as I left.

After some consideration I decided that I would not consult my Lord just yet.

*

LAST night I sinned, and most grievously. I pray that in his great mercy Almighty God may not damn me forever to outer darkness. I am truly repentant. Or I try to be. However hard I try to be honest with myself, the Serpent keeps insisting that what happened between the centurion and me last night was good. What blasphemous nonsense. And I am not alone a fornicatrix, but what is worse, a hypocrite. I have presumed to lead others through what our Lord calls the paths of righteousness, but utterly failed to practise what I preach. Surely my perfidious arrogance will be judged harshly in the hereafter, and rightly so. And maybe not only in the hereafter. Suppose I discover myself to be with child? Having sinned with the Evil One, to what kind of monstrous creature may I give birth?

It is the first time I have sinned in carnal matters. I was a virgin when I married, and however foully my husband used me, including numerous adulteries, I remained faithful to him. But since his death I have increasingly been troubled by lascivious thoughts. And the centurion aroused them more than any man I have ever met. Until last night his demeanour toward me was entirely proper, such that no woman, certainly no widow, could reasonably have objected. From time to time he would pay me small compliments about my appearance, which pleased me greatly, vain foolish creature that I was, and still am.

He had again escorted me to the theatre. Henceforth I shall know better than to frequent such a place of iniquity. On the way there he told me that he had been instructed by the Prefect to investigate the murder of a Roman soldier called Dio Syrianus, which had taken place in the Street of the Flags the previous day. He mentioned that one of the laundry girls I had provided, little Salome, had been in love with the dead man, and they had planned to marry. I had known nothing of this, indeed I knew nothing of the murder save what I had gleaned from rumour, the affair by now being the talk of the city.

Throughout the evening it cropped up time and again. When we finally reached home, talk of the killing led to discussion of the topic of murder generally. I found myself telling him about my husband again, how much I had hated him and thus brought about his death. He tried to persuade me that I was not guilty, and that my husband had contracted a fatal incurable disease. But I knew better.

I had wanted my husband to die, and bought potions to bring about his death. I hid them away and fantasized about using them. I must have done so indeed, for after his death I was full of diabolical joy, which would not have been the case had I been innocent. Did not our Lord say that anger and hate were as bad as murder? Surely it was my evil desires which had brought about his death.

I poured the noxious substances away for fear of

discovery. But then the righteousness of the Lord God entered my heart, and I confessed, first to the doctor, then to my rabbi, only to find that I was not believed.

The centurion did not believe me either. And in my proud selfishness I felt gratified that he should consider me incapable of such a vicious act.

We continued talking long into the hours of darkness. I tried to convince him of the truth of the teachings of our Lord, whilst for his part he referred to certain pagan philosophers, some of whom I had heard of, others being new to me. At times we agreed, at other times not. And of course we also talked of less serious matters.

Just before midnight he stood and said, 'It's late. Time for me to go.' And, may God forgive me, I said: 'Don't go.'

*

THE MAN was so different from my husband. Throughout the night the Tempter of Eve entered my heart. The joy and fulfilment I felt passed all understanding. I kept thinking, 'This cannot be wrong. I love this man, and he loves me, so surely this cannot be wrong.'

As he kissed me goodbye early next morning, he asked when he might see me again. And I said tonight.

I am capable of terrible error, but as I write this note later in the day, I no longer believe the man to be the Serpent himself. He is flawed and mortal, and has been tempted and fallen too. God forgive me, I was the temptress. He did not suggest what took place between us. It was I who said, 'Don't go.' Truly I am so far gone in evil that it may be that even our Lord cannot help me.

*

THE CENTURION was over half an hour late. I was beginning to think I would not see him again, which should have been a relief, removing further temptation and allowing me to believe that he was indeed an emissary of evil. Instead I found myself filled with bitter feelings, not that he had seduced me, for indeed the reverse was the case, but that he had deserted me. I was a harlot who had been spurned, and feeling angry for the wrong reasons.

I stood at the door waiting for him, aching for him, my eyes searching the dim light. And then he came, just as the twilight was fading into darkness. My heart quickened. As he stood there in the moonlight I could see the three-inch scar on his left cheek. When asked about it, he had simply said, 'Sword-cut,' and seemed to prefer not to discuss it further. Perhaps it was a wound he had sustained when putting down Jewish revolts. Maybe he had killed the man, or woman, or child, who had inflicted it. He was my country's enemy, after all. His slim dark figure throwing a jagged shadow in the moonlight gave him the air of a Demon Prince.

He strode towards me, palms spread. 'I'm sorry. Truly sorry. I've been so busy. And I've just received orders from Pilate to proceed to Jerusalem without delay. But we must talk.'

'We must talk,' I repeated coldly.

'You're offended that I'm late. Especially after last night. You may have thought I'd deserted you. I would never do that.'

'Yes,' I said. 'I thought you had deserted me. But of course I was wrong. After all, you've found a woman of easy virtue who'll answer your physical needs, and free of charge. There's no need to leave her yet.'

'That,' he said slowly, 'is not how I feel.'

'I realize why you're late. You had to deliver your report to Pilate.'

'That's one of the things I had to do, yes.'

'And of course you told him about me. Perhaps it was he suggested you bed me.'

'As a matter of fact, he did. In the interest of obtaining information, you understand.'

'I thought so. Well, you could report to him that the mission was successful. "She lost her husband years ago and hasn't had a man since. A really grubby bitch, frustrated as Hades. A good night's sport, though. She actually said she loved me. So I said I loved her, too. That kept her going, I can tell you." Then you could give details of the more physical aspects of what happened.'

'Don't be ridiculous.'

'Oh, I'm being ridiculous, am I? But of course that's just what one would expect from a stupid old whore.'

He shrugged. 'You blame me for what happened. Hit me if it makes you feel any better.'

So I did. I slapped him as hard as I could. He made no attempt to block or ride the blow but stood there, the marks of my fingers red upon his pale cheek.

By now I was not quite so angry as I pretended. Part of the reason I hit him was to discover his reaction. My husband would have grabbed me by the hair and pulled my face on to a punch. Then he would have beaten me severely about the breasts and belly, and possibly raped me, according to the degree of his drunkenness and arousal. Most of the girls under my care had told me of their men doing the same. If this man did likewise he would confirm my suspicion. I would know where I stood, and that he was just like other men. Instead he smiled faintly, so I hit him again, this time with my left hand. An angry red weal showed on the other side of his face.

'Feel any better?' he asked.

'No,' I said truthfully. 'I feel worse.' And I burst into tears.

He started forward as if to take me in his arms, then stopped. 'You have misjudged me,' he said quietly. 'I am not a very good man, but I am a better one than you suppose. Do you imagine that I deliver my reports to Pilate in the language of a barrack-room lecher? Or that I would speak to anyone about last night?'

'He would have asked you about me.'

'Yes. I told him I was still trying to obtain information from you which might throw light on the murder, or the intentions of the man Joshua and his followers, but that thus far I had failed.'

'Did he ask if we had lain together?'

'No. If he had I would have denied it.'

'So, you are a liar.'

'You seem determined to cast me in the worst possible light. In all other respects my report was accurate. I owe a duty to Rome.'

'And not to me.'

'I hope the two will never conflict.'

'Suppose they did?'

'I can't answer that. It would depend on the circumstances.'

'Perhaps you had better go now,' I said more calmly. 'It

may be that I have misjudged you, as you say. I cannot tell. But it is better that we never see one another again.'

'I will go now,' he replied. 'But I will not promise never to see you again. I am very grieved that you have misinterpreted what I intended as an act of love. And I do love you, Mary of Magdala.' He paused. 'I came to ask you to marry me.'

At first I could not speak. Then I said unsteadily, 'Roman soldiers can't marry.'

'My term of service expires in a year's time. I am not a rich man, but I am better off than many.' He smiled again. 'I would be most honoured if you would consent to be my wife. Do you want me to kneel? I will if you like.'

I shook my head. By now I was sobbing quietly. 'Please leave. I have to think. Alone. Please leave.'

'I leave for Jerusalem,' he said. 'But I shall see you again.'

According to Pilate

'THIS FELLOW Teutonicus,' I said, sitting back in my seat and staring at the ceiling-boss with its design of Mars the Avenger. 'What do we know about him?'

I was being a shade disingenuous. For I already knew plenty about him. I had first encountered him ten months before, when he suddenly appeared from Syria at the behest of my immediate superior, the Governor L. Aelius Lamia, and as new commander of the First Century, thus occupied the most senior rank in the First Judaean Cohors Quingenaria. No doubt part of his duties involved spying on me.

But I had to admit that thus far I had no complaints about the man, indeed he had succeeded in what I had previously considered all but impossible: by ruthless training and punishment, coupled with promotion on merit, he had turned the First Judaean Cohort into a fighting force comparable with a Roman legion. Previously, like most local auxiliaries, they had been little better than a rabble.

My chief scribe, Silvius, unearthed a couple of scrolls from within his desk. 'I have the man's full record here, *domine*. Having anticipated your request.'

'I already know that you are the most efficient secretary in the Empire, thanks. Just get on with it.'

'Er, *domine*?'

'Summarize it, man. I haven't time to plough through the whole thing.'

'Yes, *domine*. It seems he was born in the twenty-fifth year of the reign of the Divine Augustus, which means that he is aged thirty-four or thereabouts. His father was a minor German chieftain named Hrothgar, or as we would term it, Rotgarius, and as the eldest son he was named after his father. Rotgarius the Elder participated in the... ah... imperial setback in the Teutoburg Forest ...'

' "Setback" is something of an understatement, methinks. Three whole legions were lost.'

'Ah, quite so, *domine*. Fortunately Rotgarius Senior reaped the full reward of his villainy, he and his whole family subsequently being wiped out by the military genius of the Divine Germanicus.'

'I knew the Divine Germanicus, as you call him. A prick of the first magnitude. His only genius was for self-publicity. His martial ability was decidedly mediocre, unless you count his skill in slaughtering women and children by way of reprisal. And his son, that youth they call Caligula, sounds like such another. Anyway, what happened to Teutonicus?'

'At the time he was little more than a boy. Precise details are not clear, but it seems that one of the men of the... er... Germanicus, took pity on him and arranged for him to be raised as a Roman. He still uses Rotgarius as a sort of *nomen*, and in view of his background he soon acquired the *cognomen* Teutonicus. His *praenomen* arises from the fact that his adoptive parents had the highest possible opinion of the man who became our present Emperor.'

'Go on.'

'He followed his adoptive father into the army – I say adoptive, the whole arrangement seems to have been decidedly casual, no question of formal *abrogatio* – the boy was a German bastard, after all ...'

'Never mind all that. What sort of a soldier is he?'

'There, *domine*, his record is good. He served in Thrace, in Bythinia-Pontus, and Legion III Parthica in Syria, where he rose to the rank of centurion. Three times he has been wounded in action, and twice formally commended for valour by his superior officer. In view of his antecedents he has not been required to serve in Germany, though there seems no reason to doubt his loyalty to Rome.'

'Does he know of his real parentage?'

'Oh yes. At the time of their death he was of an age to understand such things.'

'Is he literate?'

Silvius inclined his head in reluctant acknowledgment. 'Yes, *domine*. A well-educated man for a barbarian. He appears to be literate in both Latin and Greek. Besides which he has made some attempt to learn Hebrew, and the local Galilean tongue, which they call Aramaic.'

'I knew that, thank you. How comes it that he now serves in Judaea?'

'It seems he came to the favourable attention of the Imperial Legate to Syria, *domine*, that is ...'

'I know all about that. Give me more detail.'

'He arranged for him to be seconded to the Judaean auxiliary force. There he became the senior centurion of the First Cohort, following the death of the previous holder of the office, Gnaeus Sempronius, from wounds received putting down the Jewish riots in, er, let me see …' He fumbled with his papers.

'Don't bother. There are always Jewish riots.'

'Presumably the intention was to strengthen the local auxiliary forces and …'

'And keep an eye on me at the same time, no doubt. All the same, he may have his uses. Anything else I should know?'

'He's believed to be on intimate terms with a woman named Mary of Magdala, a wealthy widow who's among the more fanatical followers of the man Joshua bar-Josef, who …'

'Yes, yes. The Magdalene woman might be a problem. Is Teutonicus screwing her?'

'As to that, *domine*, I have no information.'

I sighed. 'Very well. Send him in.'

*

TEUTONICUS entered and gave the imperial salute, which I returned. A fellow in the early thirties, on the tall side of middle height, albeit shorter than the average male barbarian. Dark for a German, but fairer than most Latins, he was of medium build, and in all physical respects might have passed as an average soldier in the imperial army. He stood in the centre of the great mosaic I had had installed, depicting the miraculous recovery of the Divine Augustus from serious illness and his reception of the *tribunicia potestas*, which glorious events took place in the year when I was born.

'Tiberius Rotgarius Teutonicus, First Centurion of the Cohors Quingenaria. Sir.'

I nodded. 'Stand easy.' I paused, unrolled the papers on my desk and contemplated them awhile before raising my eyes to his. I have found this tends to disconcert those I am interviewing. Eventually I said, 'You know these people, do you not?'

He considered briefly. 'I doubt whether any Gentile ever really knows them, sir. I have made a study of their language and customs.'

'You are friendly with some of them, I think?'

'I am on good terms with a couple of the Pharisees. They've attempted to explain their doctrines to me.'

'And what do you think of them?'

He pulled a face. 'Superstition.'

I paused. 'Could you expound your views in more detail?'

'We seem to have a multiplicity of gods nowadays. It's not impossible that there's one who concerns himself with the Jews. To claim that he's the only god is absurd.'

'You say you are friendly with a couple of the Pharisees. What about the woman Mary of Magdala?'

He betrayed no sign of unease. 'I know her, sir. She is one of the adherents of the man Jesus, or in Hebrew, Joshua bar-Josef.'

'Is she his whore?'

'I think not. He doesn't seem interested in women.'

'Is he then an invert?'

Teutonicus paused, then shook his head slowly. 'I don't think he's interested in men either. Not in any sexual sense.'

I clasped my hands tightly together and placed my chin on them in thought. 'The reason I ask you about him, centurion, is this. I am concerned about the recent increase in the activities of the *Secarii*. There have been three such murders in Judaea in as many weeks.'

I referred to a group of terrorists, whose typical *modus operandi* consisted of stabbing their victims in crowded places before stealing away in the resulting confusion. Recently they had also begun to operate in more secluded places, particularly favouring moonlit nights.

'And you think, sir, that the man Joshua may somehow be involved?'

I shook my head. 'Perhaps not personally. But it's possible that some of the more fanatical of his followers act on their own initiative. Tell me what you know of him.'

'He is thirty years of age or rather more, and native of a village called Nazareth, which is inconvenient for those who believe him to be the Messiah.'

I nodded. 'Their prophesies predict that the Messiah will be born in Bethlehem, near Jerusalem.'

'Exactly, sir. Nazareth is a tiny collection of hovels, hardly even a village. What's more, some Jews believe it's a sort of joke place. I understand they have a saying: "Can any good thing come out of Nazareth?" '

'Hilarious. Anything else?'

'He is the son of a man called Josef bar-Jacob, who was employed in the building trade in some capacity: as to his precise craft, accounts vary. Some say he was a joiner or carpenter. He's been dead for several years. Anyway, this Joshua seems to have led an uneventful life until a couple of years ago, when he was baptized by the man Johan bar-Zechariah.'

I well remembered Johan the Baptizer. A religious crackpot, in a country with more than its fair share. 'At least he won't be troubling us any more.'

Teutonicus nodded. 'Quite so, sir. But before he died, it seems this Johan put into Joshua's head the idea that he had some sort of special mission, acting as a divinely-inspired prophet similar to himself. Thereupon the man left his family – seems to have fallen out with them, in fact – surrounded himself with a bunch of ne'er-do-wells, and has gone around preaching, healing the sick, and so forth. He's rather out of favour with the leaders of Orthodox Judaism, so he seldom preaches in synagogues, but prefers the open air. In fact he hardly ever visits a place of any size. His main message seems to be that we are living in the last days, and this world will come to an end very shortly.'

'The same message that has been preached by a thousand others. It hasn't happened yet.'

'As you say, sir. He also preaches forgiveness of sins, and loving everyone, including those who wrong us, and so on. This doesn't seem to prevent him losing his temper at times, and threatening those who disagree with him with hell and damnation. It seemed to me that he would have done better to teach people less about love, and more about refraining from hatred.' He shrugged. 'That's my opinion, sir, anyway.'

'From what you say I'm inclined to agree. Go on.'

'He's a good public speaker, sir, no doubt about that. Large crowds gather round him, and sometimes approach a state of near frenzy. Some say he is what they call the Messiah: the one who is to lead them to freedom from foreign rule.'

I sighed. 'Not another one. Does he claim as much for himself?'

'That, sir, I know not. There are conflicting accounts of his teaching.'

'But I undertand you've heard him preach yourself.'

'Not recently. I heard part of his notorious sermon on Mount Eremos, teaching the Jews how to pray, and so forth. It continued for several hours, but seemed fairly innocuous. Very likely he has repeated the teaching, or parts of it, on other occasions.'

'Tell me what you remember of it.'

The man took a small slate from his satchel. 'I noted some of it down at the time, sir.'

'Summarize it.'

'Apart from what I've already mentioned, love and forgiveness of enemies, etcetera, they asked him about the Mosaic law regarding divorce. He appeared to disagree with their ancient prophets, saying that what God had joined together no man should put asunder. In other words the marriage bond was indissoluble, at least until death.'

I recalled my first two marriages, one of which had been far from ideal, the other disastrous. 'So, the man's a fool, albeit not necessarily dangerous. Anything else?'

'He played around with some children. And advised that no rich man could enter the Kingdom of Heaven.'

I pulled a face. 'I should be all right, then.'

He smiled. 'Me too, sir. The man went so far as to say that it was easier for a camel to go through the eye of a needle than for a rich man to enter the Kingdom of Heaven.'

The parallel was not as absurd as it might seem. Many Jewish cities have small apertures in their walls known as eyes of needles, whereby pedestrians may enter at night after the main gates have been closed. Beasts of burden are unable to enter unless they are first unloaded of their goods, and even then have to proceed on their knees, in the manner of those at prayer. I had to concede that the allegory was rather neat, and said as much.

'I respectfully agree, sir. In my view it would be a mistake to imagine that the man talks nothing but nonsense. Here and there one can detect nuggets of wisdom.'

'I think it would be well, centurion, if you were to arrange for him to be kept under observation. And keep me informed of progress.'

'Yes, sir. I have a few days leave due, cancelled during the recent disturbances. I could take them, with your permission, and use them to make informal enquiries.'

'Do so. I doubt if we shall ever solve the *Secarius* problem completely, but the situation seems to be deteriorating.' I turned to some papers on my desk and referred to them as I spoke. 'To remind you of what we are dealing with, I have here details of the three most recent murders.

'One, Gideon bar-Reuben, a metal-worker in Galilee. An ordinary member of the public, he was stabbed in the midst of a crowd at a busy market in Joppa, apparently having been selected at random. The other two murders took place at night. One was a slave woman called Dinah, killed in a secluded alley in Jerusalem, and her throat cut. No sign of sexual assault, but she was the mistress of a Roman soldier, and possibly killed for that reason. Most recently, and worst, a man named Caleb bar-Kobe, one of our informants. He was also killed in Jerusalem, and cut open like a pig, while he was still alive. He was found in a pool of blood, clutching at his entrails, as if trying to push them back into his body.'

Teutonicus pulled an expression of distaste. 'It seems, sir, that those who co-operate with Rome are singled out for particularly vicious treatment.'

'Quite.' I paused. 'Of course it doesn't follow that all three were *Secarius* murders, but it seems likely. Conceivably those in Jerusalem were committed by the same man. Unfortunately there seems little chance of apprehending the culprits now.' I paused again before changing the subject. 'This woman of Magdala. Do you know her better than you have told me?'

Again he showed no sign of being disconcerted. 'I have seen her several times, sir. She's an intelligent woman, and I enjoy her company, indeed I find her attractive. But that's as far as things have gone between us. She would not be interested in me, anyway. She's obsessed by the man Joshua.'

'But he's not interested in her?'

'That's right, sir. As far as I know.'

'Cultivate her acquaintance further. If you manage to bed her, so much the better. Find out what she knows about him and his other followers.'

'Yes, sir.'

'You sound hesitant.'

He gave a rueful smile. 'Only that I fear the *dominus* may overestimate my appeal to women.'

'Well, do your best.' Yet again I paused for thought. 'Is there anything else you know about the man Joshua and have not told me?'

'After the Eremos sermon, he told me that my servant Gnaeus, who was ill, would recover. This proved to be the case. Whether Joshua healed him I take leave to doubt. And I think it likely that he and his disciples, as they call themselves, will visit Jerusalem for the Passover, which might be dangerous. It's surprising how many there are who believe in the Messianic prophesies.'

'Nothing surprises me any more. Especially in Judaea. As the Divine Julius said: "Men generally believe what they want to believe." ' I stood. 'All right, centurion. Dismiss.'

According to the Centurion

NO-ONE WHO reads these jottings, set down many years after the events they describe, will have heard of me, so I must introduce myself. My name is Hrothgar, son of Hrothgar of Teutoburg, a chieftain of the Germanic tribe known as the Cherusci. To the Romans I became known as Tiberius Rotgarius Teutonicus, centurion of the First Cohort of the First Judaean Quingenaria.

I am an old man now, but when the events I am about to relate took place I was young. Much has changed since then. Rome herself is barely recognizable, magnificent fora, triumphal arches, statues and places of entertainment having replaced the plain and unassuming city I remember from my youth. The great house of the Caesars has fallen, and the Empire is governed by a former muleteer, who has utterly destroyed the power of the Judaeans and their religion. The followers of Joshua bar-Josef have split from the Jews to become a sect called Christians, following the doctrines of one Saul of Tarsus, who never met the man Joshua and whose interpretation of his teachings was very far from mine. They now revere the Cross, the very instrument of torture and death used to kill the man they believe was God himself. And they persist in the belief that the end of the world will shortly be upon us. How long they continue to subscribe to this fantasy before reality forces itself upon them, I know not.

As for the events taking place in Judaea in the sixteenth year of the reign of Tiberius Caesar, I must rely on my elderly and imperfect memory, aided by a few scribbled notes I made at the time, and the far neater notes and reminiscences of my dear wife. And as I recall those distant times, soon to pass from living memory, I am struck above all by how good the gods have been to me, both then and since. I have lived far longer, and seen more, than most men, and suffered less. And I fancy I may have glimpsed the truth, albeit darkly. Happiness comes not through seeking or cultivating it, but scarcely noticed, as one chooses one's path through life simply and calmly from day to day. As the fashionable young writer Martial now puts it: '... To wish to be none but oneself, no other. Neither to desire death, nor to fear it.'

I was born on the day known to the Romans as the Ides of February, in the Year of the City DCCXLIX. At the age of thirteen I fought alongside my father in the great victory of the Teutoburg Forest, wherein three Roman legions were destroyed. My father was killed beside me. The following year my mother, brother and sisters were murdered in reprisal by the Roman general known as Germanicus. I continued the fight until wounded and taken prisoner by the man who subsequently became Emperor: Tiberius Claudius Nero, who spared my life upon a whim. Inspecting some of those about to be executed, he asked me why I fought against Rome. Others were grovelling and begging for mercy. Certain of death, I felt I had nothing to lose, so I remained standing, and replied frankly that my entire family had been wiped out by his cousin Germanicus, whom I hated beyond all men, and called upon the gods to punish him and his brood for all eternity. I remember the words of Tiberius clearly: 'No-one who hates Germanicus that much can be all bad.'

I repaid his generosity, if such it was, by fighting for Rome, first as an auxiliary on the Danube, then on the coast of the Black Sea, and finally in Syria as a member of the Legion III Parthica. As a legionary, as opposed to an auxiliary, I became entitled to Roman citizenship. And if I were to become a Roman, I needed a *praenomen.* With little more than a dozen to choose from, I decided to adopt that of the man whom I considered my patron. By this time he had become Emperor, and it seemed advisable to enquire whether I had his permission to do so. Not surprisingly I received no reply. If he had received my request, he obviously could not have cared less, for which I could hardly blame him, so I took his silence as consent. As *nomen*, I used a Romanized version of my father's name.

After serving several years in Syria, I was transferred to Judaea, a posting as thankless as the former one had been rewarding. I had taken advantage of my time in Syria to learn something of the native languages, and this proved to be to my disadvantage. It was thought I might use such knowledge to learn of any Jewish plans for rebellion; they were always threatening something of the sort. My resulting transfer was a sideways promotion at best, as employment in a mere auxiliary force instead of a Roman legion. However in appreciation of my assistance the Governor of Syria, Aelius Lamia, promised to use his best endeavours to obtain advancement for me. Rather to my surprise this promise was kept, albeit partly as a result of chance. The senior centurion for the Judaean Quingenariae had just died from wounds received in putting down a minor revolt, as a result of which I was promoted to fill his place.

As for the Jews, I never knew a people so obsessed by their religion. Everything was referred to their one god for his decision. Unsurprisingly, his adherents constantly disagreed amongst themselves about what he wanted, but the general consensus was that he wanted them to get rid of the Romans. That this desire corresponded with their own wishes likewise did not occasion me surprise. According to one of their minor prophets, the man to do this would be the Messiah, a military leader to be born in Bethlehem, near Jerusalem. What follows deals largely with the story of a man whose adherents claimed that he was this Messiah. His name was Joshua bar-Josef, sometimes known as Joshua bar-Abbas, which in their language means 'son of the father.' In Greek his name was hellenized as Jesus bar-Abbas.

I first heard of the man within a few weeks of my arrival in Judaea. He had been travelling around Galilee, preaching that all men should love one another, and allegedly performing miracles. The prestige he thus acquired led to his becoming known as a rabbi, or teacher. He increasingly fancied himself as a prophet, threatening his adherents and others with dreadful consequences if they did not follow his teachings, often expressed as fables, or as they preferred to call them, parables. I heard two or three of them, and can only say that they appeared to me at best trite and at worst positively unjust in the lessons they taught, never approaching the subtlety found in some of the stories of Aesop.

For all that, he at first appeared comparatively harmless,

achieving nothing worse than falling out with other Jews about matters of religious doctrine. As time went by however he seemed increasingly to be regarded by his followers, and possibly by himself, as the Messiah, who would free Judaea from what they called the Roman yoke. Needless to say, that was a different matter.

*

MY personal involvement in the affair began on that most ominous date in the Roman calendar, the Ides of March, when I was summoned before the Prefect of Judaea, Q. Pontius Pilatus. Conceivably he had learnt something of my business in his province, which included, but was not confined to, preparing periodical reports on his own activities. Since I was in a sense a representative of Tiberius Caesar, I should in theory be in no peril of anything beyond incurring prefectorial disfavour. On the other hand, since the Emperor's henchman, the capricious tyrant Sejanus, now held Rome under his sway, one could no longer be certain of anything. I write these notes many years after his well-merited fall from favour and ignominious death. But having no means of knowing that at the time, it was not without a certain apprehension that I presented myself at the Prefect's headquarters.

I heard myself announced, entered and gave the imperial salute. Pilate did me the courtesy of standing to return it, which was a good sign. A man of medium height, plainly dressed in a tunic, with military *caligae* on his feet, he bore a marked resemblance – which I suspect he cultivated – to pictures I have seen of the late great Gaius Julius Caesar, even down to the partial baldness. In formal fashion, I reminded him of my name, rank and cohort. For his part he fiddled with the scrolls on his desk before coming directly to the business in question.

'You know the Jews well, or so I've heard.'

'I've investigated their culture, sir. But I doubt if any Gentile really knows them.'

'What do you know of this man Joshua bar-Josef?'

I paused for thought. 'There are conflicting accounts of his teaching.'

'You have never heard him yourself?'

'Not recently, sir, but I heard him deliver a sermon on Mount Eremos some months since. It seemed harmless. But there was one curious feature. He told me that my servant, Gnaeus, who was sick of the palsy, would recover.'

'Did he?'

'Yes, *domine*. It took several weeks, and I doubt whether there was anything miraculous about it. But he eventually recovered most of the use in his affected arm.'

Pilate made a grunting noise, and in a gesture I later came to recognize as characteristic, clasped his hands together and lodged his chin on them almost as if in prayer. 'It may be that his teachings have since taken a more radical turn. In particular I'm beginning to suspect that his followers, or some of them at least, may be connected with the recent increase in *Secarius* activity, of which no doubt you have heard. I therefore think it would be well if you were to hear him again, and report to me immediately thereafter.'

'Very good, sir. I have a few days leave due, cancelled during the recent disturbances. I could take it with your permission, and use it to make discreet enquiries.'

'Do so.' He riffled through some papers on his desk. 'Just to remind you what we are dealing with, I have here details of three recent murders, probably committed by one or more of the *Secarii*. The first, in Galilee, was an ordinary member of the public, stabbed apparently at random in a crowded market-place. The second was a slave woman involved with a Roman soldier. Killed in a back alley, and her throat cut. Finally there was one of our informants, likewise in Jerusalem. His case was worst of all. He was stabbed, then disembowelled while still alive, guts spilt all over the place.'

'Most unpleasant,' I said inadequately.

'Quite.' He then touched upon a subject of some sensitivity to me. 'This woman of Magdala. How well do you know her?'

He referred to a wealthy widow with whom I was known to be on friendly terms. I replied truthfully, yet without revealing the full extent of my feelings.

'I first met her when visiting the refuge which she runs for fallen women. I was seeking a cleaner and laundrymaid for the camp. I have seen her several times since, sir, a cultured and intelligent woman, and I admit that I find her attractive. That's as far as things have gone between us. She wouldn't be interested in me, anyway. She's obsessed by the man Joshua.'

'But he's not interested in her?'

'That's right, sir. As far as I know.'

'Cultivate her acquaintance further, and see if you can bed her. Find out what she knows about the man.'

'Yes, sir.'

'You sound hesitant.'

I smiled. 'Just that I fear the *dominus* may overestimate my appeal to women.'

'Well, do your best.' He paused. 'Is there anything else you know about this Joshua and have not told me?'

'Only what is common knowledge, sir. He's about thirty years of age, and a native of Nazareth, which is inconvenient for those who believe him the Messiah.'

'Because their prophesies allege that the Messiah will be born in Bethlehem, near Jerusalem?'

'Partly for that reason, sir. Furthermore, some Jews believe Nazareth is a sort of joke place. I have heard them say: "Can any good thing come out of Nazareth?" '

'Hilarious. What else?'

'He is the son of a man called Josef bar-Jacob, who was employed in the building trade. He's been dead some years. Anyway, this Joshua seems to have led an uneventful life until a couple of years ago, when he was baptized by the crackpot known as Johan the Baptizer.'

'At least he won't be troubling us any more.'

I nodded. 'True, sir. But before he died, it seems this Johan persuaded Joshua that he had some sort of special mission, preaching, prophesying, healing, and so forth. Thereupon he seems to have fallen out with his family, left his home, surrounded himself with a bunch of riff-raff, and has gone around preaching, healing the sick, etcetera. His main message seems to be that we are living in the last days, and this world will come to an end very shortly.'

'The same message that has been preached by a thousand others. It hasn't happened yet.'

'Quite so, sir. He also preaches forgiveness of sins, and loving everyone, including those who wrong us. That doesn't stop him losing his temper at times, and threatening those who disagree with him with hell and damnation.'

'When you heard him speak at Mount Eremos, what did he say?'

'Quite a lot.' I summarized what I had heard as briefly as I could, including some teachings about the impossibility of the rich being able to enter the Kingdom of Heaven. Pilate commented drily that in that case he should be all right. Which is true; he seems to be one of the few Roman officials who do not unduly enrich themselves at public expense. I then went on to instance the man's teachings about marriage, and that those not accepting such a bond as indissoluble would be punished in the hereafter.

Pilate pulled a face. 'By all the gods, I hope not.' For he had himself twice been divorced. 'The man must be a complete fool.'

'A crank at least, sir. Which is not to say that he isn't dangerous. It's surprising how many there are who believe in such people.'

'Nothing surprises me any more. Especially here in Judaea. As the Divine Julius said: "Men generally believe what they want to believe." All right, centurion. Dismiss.'

*

CAESAREA is the least Jewish city in Judaea, as Jerusalem is the most. Persons of all nations mingle there freely, and are but little concerned with what religion one professes. Places of entertainment are plentiful.

I had asked the lady of Magdala if I might escort her to the amphitheatre, where they were presenting Sophocles's tragedy *Antigone*. It is far from being my favourite drama, but little else in Caesarea at the time seemed likely to appeal to a respectable woman. After some hesitation she agreed.

From the theatre to her rescue centre for fallen women was a distance of some three-quarters of a mile, and I walked her back. During discussion of the play, which had not been much to her taste, I turned the conversation in the direction of the rabbi who had made such an impression on her, the man Joshua bar-Josef. She asked if I had considered his preaching. I said yes, and although it seemed to me that he spoke some truth, there were aspects of his teaching with which I disagreed. She asked me to instance one of them, and I mentioned divorce.

'In Rome,' I said, 'as you probably know, divorce is easy. Unhappy or inconvenient marriages can be brought to an end by simple legal process. Thereafter both parties are free to marry again.'

'But that would be adultery, which is expressly forbidden by the Torah. Have you read the Torah?'

'I have. But I must say that I find its moral teachings defective in some respects.'

'Such as?'

I shrugged. 'You mentioned that it forbids adultery. It seems to me that there are far worse sexual activities than that – rape, for instance – about which your Ten Commandments have nothing to say.'

'The Torah is divinely inspired, the living word of God.'

'It was written by men. How do you know they were divinely inspired?'

'The rabbis tell us so.'

'The priests in Rome tell us that the city was founded

by a son of the god Mars, who as a child was suckled by a she-wolf.'

'And you believe such blasphemous nonsense?'

'Of course not. I'm just pointing out that folk legends, whether Roman or Hebrew, are not reliable guides to reality.'

'I cannot argue with you,' she said coldly. 'We obviously will never agree about such matters.'

We walked in silence for a hundred paces. Thereafter, by way of re-opening the conversation on a lighter note, I said, 'It seems your rabbi Joshua is in some respects even stricter than the Torah. For besides the act of adultery, he also disapproves of committing adultery in one's heart. I can only say that such a pastime has accorded me much pleasure.'

'If that is intended as a joke,' she replied, 'it seems to me to be in the most appalling taste.'

'It was a joke,' I confirmed. 'But they say that there is many a true word spoken in jest.'

'It may be so. I should have warned you that I have no sense of humour.'

Again we were silent for a while. At length I attempted to bridge the gap between us by returning to serious matters. 'What of divorce? Do you prefer your rabbi's teaching, or that of the Torah?'

She seemed most uneasy at this, and took some time to reply. Eventually she said, 'The question is not a simple one.'

'Surely there must be at least some provision for divorce,' I insisted. 'Otherwise there would be no way to bring an unhappy marriage to an end but to resort to murder.' An even feebler joke than my previous effort, but this time I indicated my humorous intention by a smile.

She stopped in her tracks. Never before had I seen

anyone with dark complexion actually turn pale upon the instant, but I swear she did. Then she said harshly, 'You know, don't you?'

'Know what?'

'There's no need to pretend. You know perfectly well what I mean.'

'I can assure you I don't.'

'How you have found out, I know not. Perhaps the Evil One himself has told you.'

I sighed and shook my head. 'He never seems to tell me anything.'

'There you are again. You turn everything into a tasteless jest.'

'Just assume for the purpose of argument,' I said wearily, 'that I tell the truth.'

'I will spell it out, then. You know very well that you are talking to a murderess.'

I thought for a moment. 'Your husband?'

'There. You knew all the time.'

'Oh, nonsense, woman. It's just been my experience that on the rare occasions that women commit murder, the usual victim is their husband. And you mentioned that your marriage was far from happy.'

'I don't believe you,' she said.

'And I do not believe you. You are no murderess. You are not capable of it. Describe the manner of your husband's death.'

I had expected her to refuse to discuss the matter further, but to my surprise she went into considerable detail. In short, she had fervently prayed for him to die, whether to god or devil, she knew not. Upon his suffering an apparently trifling indisposition, under the pretence of administering a medicine she had given him a potion she had prepared containing hemlock and other noxious substances. He was soon screaming and writhing in agony, with severe abdominal pain, especially low on the right side. After a day or two's intense suffering, death had ensued.

'What did the physician diagnose?' I asked.

'Malignant stoppage of the bowels. I then told him of my guilt.'

'And he didn't believe you any more than I do.'

'The old fool wouldn't have it that he could have been mistaken. He told me that having fervently desired my husband's death, I suffered from severe feelings of guilt when it actually came to pass.'

'He doesn't sound like a fool to me. The symptoms you've described are characteristic of malignant bowel stoppage, and bear no resemblance to those of hemlock poisoning.'

'You invite me to deny my guilt. You are an emissary of the Serpent of Eden.'

'Drivel. I am an emissary of Caesar.'

'Whatever you are, I shall not see you again.'

'That's a great pity.'

Shortly afterward we reached the women's centre, and stood on the paving-stones outside. 'I'm hoping you may reconsider,' I said.

'I'm not sure,' she said, to my relief. For I really did want to see her again, not alone to pursue my enquiry, but for my own sake. 'You have not reacted as I would have expected from a minion of the Evil One. I am now inclined to believe that you are but a flawed and mortal man.'

'I can't argue with that,' I said.

*

NEXT day I visited the elderly physician she had named, a certain Dmitrios, a Greek, and one of the best respected men in Caesarea. Not unreasonably, he was at first reluctant to speak of the case.

'I understand,' I said, 'that you do not wish to discuss your patients' affairs. But the man in question is dead.'

'Some things last beyond the grave.'

'At the time, you diagnosed his death as being due to a bowel disorder.'

'If you know that, why ask me?'

'Did a more sinister explanation occur to you?'

'I suppose his widow has been telling you she killed him. Well, she did not.'

'Are you quite certain?'

'I never claim to be certain of anything. All I can say is that the man displayed all the classic signs of a sudden obstruction of the bowels.'

'Which are?'

'He first complained of a pain low down on the right side of the abdomen. Upon my touching the place in question, even quite lightly, he cried out in pain. During the next twenty-four hours, despite the application of warm poultices, his condition deteriorated rapidly. At one stage the pain suddenly became even more intense, and he screamed in agony. It was as if, as he put it himself, his bowels had burst, and thereafter the pain spread to the whole abdomen. *In extremis,* I tried the traditional remedy of a strong laxative, whereupon he convulsed, again screamed in pain, soon mercifully passed from consciousness, and was dead within a couple of hours. I've often wondered about the laxative remedy; I've never known it work, but there seemed nothing to lose.'

'Is there any poison that would result in similar symptoms?'

'None that I'm aware of. There are plenty that give you bellyache, of course, and interfere with normal bowel movement, but the concentration of severe pain low down on the right side is a sure sign of malignant intestinal blockage.'

'Could such blockage be induced by poison?'

Dmitrios shrugged. 'Again, not that I know of.'

'What is the usual cause of such illness?'

'Unknown. It seems to be commoner in young adults than any other age group. Maybe the changes in the body due to adolescence are an aggravating factor. But any physician who tells you he knows more than that is a charlatan.'

'Why should his wife confess to killing him if she didn't?'

He shrugged again. 'Who knows what goes on in other folks' heads? Perhaps he used to treat her badly, and she wanted him dead. So when he actually died she felt guilty.'

'Have you any reason to believe that he *did* treat her badly?'

He hesitated. 'She never complained to me.'

'But?'

'Well, I had observed injuries which she'd explained away as resulting from domestic accidents. It struck me that such things seemed to occur with unusual frequency.' Again he hesitated. 'All right, I was not deceived. I'll admit I felt sorry for her, and I thought her husband a complete shit. It's never pleasant to lose a patient, expecially in such intensely painful circumstances, but if it had to happen to someone, I was content for it to be him. There now, I've been completely unprofessional, and beg you not to say anything about this to anyone.'

I nodded. 'It won't go any further.'

Later I spoke to Regulus, our regimental physician.

'Have you ever treated men for stoppage of the bowels?'

'Plenty. A good dose of senna usually puts things right. But if you mean the virulent form, with intense pain concentrated on the right side ...'

I nodded. 'That's what I mean.'

He counted silently to himself. 'I make it six.'

'May I ask how many survived?'

'One. And frankly, I was astonished. I'd never heard of anyone recovering before.'

'What treatment did you apply?'

'I admit that I experimented. The death rate normally being a hundred per cent, I thought I was justified. As it seems I was by events.'

'Go on.'

'Since the usual treatment of warm poultices and senna invariably resulted in death, I tried an ice-pack instead. And omitted the laxative.'

'And he lived?'

'Yes. But don't get it into your head that I've discovered a cure for obstruction of the bowels. I've tried it three times, and the other two died. But a success rate of thirty-three per cent is better than nothing.'

*

WITH Pilate's agreement I had deemed it advisable to recruit one of my men to help me with the enquiry. I chose a certain

Dio Syrianus, because he was the commander of the Second Century, transferred with me from Syria, besides which I had found him to be a friend whom I knew I could trust in the matter of secrecy. He also seemed a good choice in that he had formed a relationship with one of the cleaning girls Mary of Magdala had provided for me, a cheerful young wench named Salome. How far matters had proceeded between them I did not think it my business to enquire. I had promised to see that the girls were treated with respect, not to act as chaperon. If she chose of her own volition to go with a Roman soldier, that was a matter for her.

About a week after my conversation with the Magdalene woman, Salome came to see me at my lodging. My servant Gnaeus conducted her to me.

'Excuse me, *domine*.'

'Yes, Salome, what is it?'

'The *dominus* may be aware that I am… friendly with his lieutenant, Dio Syrianus.'

I smiled. 'I had heard something of the matter, yes.'

'Tonight I had an arrangement to meet him at the Five Ways Tavern, in the Street of the Flags. He did not appear.'

The last thing I wanted was to become involved in sorting out the love affairs of servant girls at the *castra*. If Dio had decided that things between them were at an end, that was a matter for him. On the other hand I had promised the Magdalene woman that I would keep an eye on the girl. And I was a little surprised. Dio was a serious young fellow, not given to treating women and girls as playthings. If he had intended to terminate the relationship, I would have expected him to tell her so rather than simply avoid an arranged meeting. Furthermore he had recently informed me of his intention to marry the girl. Clearly it had become far more serious than a casual affair.

'I know what you are thinking, *domine*. But I do not think it is like that. Despite my former occupation, he had not yet invited me to... In fact,' she added defiantly, 'He said he wanted to marry me. Me, a former whore, to marry a Roman soldier. But perhaps the *dominus* does not believe me.'

In view of what Dio had said, I did believe her. Marriage between them would have been unusual, but not impossible. Dio was not a Roman legionary, with a long term of fixed service ahead of him during which he was forbidden to marry, but an auxiliary, a Syrian Greek, whose parents lived in Sidon. Maybe they would have accepted the girl, maybe not. But it was not impossible.

'I hate to trouble you, *domine*, with the problems of a mere camp servant, but ...'

'That's all right. It will certainly be easier for me to make enquiry than you. Have you a couple of hours to spare?'

'Just an hour now, *domine*, before resuming my duties.'

'In that case, I think the place to begin our enquiries is the tavern, don't you? I'll escort you there, buy you a drink, and ask a few questions. And if it takes a bit more than an hour, no matter.'

*

UPON entering the tavern I immediately espied a couple of men I had been wanting to see: Simon, called the Zealot, and his son Judas, two of bar-Josef's followers, or disciples, as they preferred to be called. Enquiries thus far had suggested that such men could conveniently be divided into two categories: honest tradesmen or journeymen, and miscellaneous *polloi*. Simon and his son fell into the latter category. I deemed it best not to rush things, first ordering drinks for myself and my companion. After a few words of explanation to her I made my way over to their table.

'Are you Simon bar-Cleophas, called Simon of Canaan?'

Judas shrivelled into his seat. It was his father who replied, with an attempt at swagger, 'Who wants to know?'

'The Roman Prefect,' I replied 'Q. Pontius Pilatus. And more immediately, *I* want to know. Men call me Teutonicus, chief centurion of the First Cohort of the First Judaean Quingenaria. Now will you answer my question?'

'And if I choose not to?'

'The question was harmless. Should you refuse to reply I shall have to take you to the Prefect to see if he can persuade you.'

'Suppose,' he said in surly fashion, 'that I am this Simon. What is it to you?'

'I understand you are a follower of the rabbi calling himself Joshua bar-Abbas, or the Son of Man.'

'What of it?'

'The Prefect is a little concerned regarding some of his reported teachings. So long as he confines himself to matters of Jewish religious dogma, or well-meaning comments about loving one's enemies, it is of no concern to him. Claims to be the Messiah are a different matter.'

Still the fellow did not reply. 'I will ask again. Have you heard your leader claim to be the promised Messiah?'

'I have not.'

I turned to the youth Judas, who was still looking as if he

profoundly wished he was elsewhere. 'You are also one of his adherents. Is that not so?'

He gulped. 'And if I am?'

'I ask you the same question. Have you heard Joshua bar-Josef claim to be the Messiah?'

'Do you know what "the Messiah" means?'

'I'm not here to answer questions, but for what it's worth, I do. According to your prophets, he is the promised one, who is to lead Judaea to freedom from Rome. Is that not so?'

'It might be.'

Neither seemed inclined to say anything further. 'I shall report this conversation,' I said, 'and your reluctance to co-operate will be noted.'

'We're terrified,' sneered Zelotes.

'Scared out of our minds,' croaked Judas.

'You would do well to be apprehensive, I think. From now on you and your colleagues will be kept under observation.'

'I take it that's a threat?'

'Warning or threat: you may take it how you will. Good evening, gentlemen.'

I returned to my table and raised a hand to the innkeeper, who was attending to customers nearby.

'Yes, *domine*?'

'You know my colleague, the centurion Dio Syrianus?'

'Yes, *domine*.'

'Has he been in here tonight?'

'No, *domine*. I have not seen him since yesterday.'

'Did he then say anything about his intentions?'

'Yes, *domine*. He said he would be entertaining a young lady here tonight, and they would be celebrating. He asked me to make a special effort. I'm surprised he is not here.'

I indicated my companion. 'Is this the young lady?'

'I assume so, *domine*. I've seen her with him on several occasions. And she looked in here briefly an hour or so ago.'

'Did he say what time he would be here?'

'The eleventh hour.'

'And it is now the first hour of the night. Thank you, landlord.'

'You can see why I was worried, *domine*,' Salome ventured.

'I can. He's well over an hour late, maybe two.' I made a decision. 'We'll give him another half-hour, then go back to camp to see if he's answered roll-call. If not, I can justify making formal enquiry.'

I was still not seriously concerned. Syrianus was making enquiries for me, and presumably had been delayed as a result. I expected him to show up at any moment, full of apologies.

During the ensuing half hour little happened of note, save that the publican Levi entered, made his way over to Zelotes' table and engaged him and his son in conversation. They did not seem overjoyed to see him. I managed to overhear parts of what they said, Judas having rather a loud voice. They spoke in the local dialect of Aramaic, probably unaware of the fact that I had some knowledge of the tongue. It seemed they intended to submit bar-Josef to some sort of test to ascertain his attitude towards Rome, a plan which suited me admirably. But as for what happened next, I could not have dreamt of anything worse.

A few men from my century entered and looked around. Upon catching sight of me, one of them hurried over.

'Excuse me, sir. I have bad news. Very bad.'

My heart sank. 'Go on.'

'The centurion Dio Syrianus, sir. He is dead. Stabbed to death in the Street of the Flags.'

As he started to give further details, Salome choked back a cry, half-stood and slumped backward. I caught her just before she hit the ground. 'Look after her,' I said to the young soldier who had given me the news. 'He was her man.'

Then I stood. 'Attention, everyone!'

The habitués, who knew me, mostly looked alarmed. The rest seemed simply bewildered, or in some cases too drink-sodden to react. 'Those of you who have entered this tavern within the last two hours will stand.'

There were three-and-twenty customers, of whom all but nine stood immediately. Zelotes eventually hauled himself to his feet. His son remained seated.

'Innkeeper!'

The man hurried out of a back room, still wiping one of his pots. 'Yes, master?'

'Is there anyone not standing who to your knowledge has entered this tavern within the last couple of hours?'

He looked around. 'I'm not sure about them,' he said, nodding at a couple of young fellows and their companion, a fat, half-drunken man in late middle age, 'and him.' He pointed to Judas. 'The others have been here since the ninth hour, or even longer.'

'I'm sure.' By now several more auxiliaries had entered, and stood awaiting orders. 'My men will take the names and addresses of those of you who are standing. The four who should have stood but failed to do so will accompany me to headquarters.'

'What's all this about?' demanded Judas, half-getting to his feet, his voice shaking.

'I hope for your sake that you don't know.' I paused to ensure that I had the full attention of all present. 'One of my men has been murdered not a couple of hundred yards hence. This appears to have occurred at least an hour since, in broad daylight, yet no-one admits even to having seen his body.'

'That's got nothing to do with us,' said the fat oaf who had failed to stand. 'Why should we be detained?'

'Because you should have been quicker getting to your feet.' Some customers gave uneasy giggles. 'And if any here think this a matter for amusement, I should mention that the deceased, Dio Syrianus, was a good friend of mine.' There was silence during which I counted to ten to control myself. 'That's better. Those who have relevant information about this affair should accompany me to the *castra*. Anyone withholding such information will be regarded as an accessory to murder and *maiestas* and treated accordingly. Get your wife and women to take care of this young lady will you, innkeeper? She's had a severe shock. All right, let's go.'

The fat man and his stupid young friends probably had nothing to do with the business, but a couple of hours interrogation might teach them a lesson, and encourage others not to dissemble when dealing with Rome. Zelotes and his son were of more interest. The latter was so terrified we virtually had to prize him away from his table.

*

EVEN the most perfunctory enquiries would have revealed that the man Joshua and his closest followers intended to visit Jerusalem for the Passover. It was common knowledge, indeed as devout Jews they could hardly have done otherwise. This meant that I was virtually bound to do the same, particularly as Pilate, wary of trouble at that time, had just moved to his headquarters there, which formed part of the Fortress of Herod the Great in the Upper City. And indeed on the afternoon of the *dies Jovis* I received a message from the Prefect by express courier ordering my immediate attendance.

The previous evening I had again invited the Lady Mary to accompany me to the theatre, and after some hesitation she had accepted. This time the work was *The Frogs* by Aristophanes, though I had judged such a lightweight offering unlikely to be to her taste. She had after all recently denied having any sense of humour. It seemed particularly inappropriate after I had apprised her that the scope of my enquiries had been extended to include the murder of Dio, who had been as good as betrothed to her former slave girl, Salome. Apart from the personal tragedy, it meant that the *Secarius* threat, previously largely confined to Jerusalem, had now apparently extended to Caesarea. I gave her the advice, albeit hardly necessary for such a respectable woman, not to venture out at night alone.

Nevertheless my lady seemed to sense that such an outrageous comedy made it appropriate to dress in less subdued fashion than was her custom. Instead of her usual dark-grey costume she wore a striking robe in scarlet, black, and gold which, though I did not dare say as much, set off the lines of her figure to perfection. And after some initial misgivings about the propriety of the piece, she could not help but laugh with me at some of the droller moments, even the saucier jests. It did my heart good to see her thus. Joy knocked a good ten years off her age. By the time the performance finished we were both in relaxed mood.

For the first time she invited me into her home, a small and simple annex to the hostel for her women, albeit decorated in perfect taste, rather after the Roman fashion, though scrupulously avoiding images other than those of leaf-patterns and geometric shapes.

Our conversation ranged over a variety of topics, both trivial and serious. Despite my enquiries of the physicians clearly having indicated the contrary, she persisted in taking responsibility for her husband's death, on the grounds that her evil desires had somehow brought it about.

We talked long into the night, despite the fact that I had such a busy day in prospect for the morrow. At last I stood, and said it was time I was leaving.

She simply smiled and said: 'Don't go.'

*

I WILL not speak of that night, save to say that I knew beyond any doubt that I wanted to spend the rest of my life with that beautiful, complex, troubled woman. I left early in the morning, promising to return before the day was out.

When I did, in early evening, it was as I had feared. Her manner was cold and distant. Through force of circumstance I was half an hour late, but that was not it.

I apologized. 'I've been very busy. For one thing I've been making preparations for my trip to Jerusalem. You may have thought I'd deserted you. I would never do that.'

'Of course you wouldn't,' she said. 'You've found yourself

a whore who will answer your needs free of charge. No need to leave her yet.'

'That's not how I feel,' I said, 'and you must know it.'

'I know another reason why you're late. You had to deliver your report to Pilate on last night. I daresay it was he suggested you bed me.'

'He did, but …'

'As I thought. Well, you could report to him that his orders were obeyed. Implicitly.' She went on to accuse me of reporting to him in the foulest terms.

I shrugged. 'Hit me if it makes you feel better.'

She slapped me twice across the cheeks.

'Feel any better?' I asked.

'No,' she said, 'I feel worse,' and burst into tears.

I ached to take her in my arms and kiss her beautiful, troubled face, but feared to make matters worse. 'You have misjudged me,' I said. 'Do you imagine that I deliver my reports to Pilate in the language of the gutter? Or that I would speak to anyone about last night?'

'He must have asked you about me.'

'Yes. I told him I was still trying to obtain information from you which might throw light on the murder, or on the intentions of the man Joshua and his followers, but that thus far I had failed.'

'Did he ask if we had lain together?'

'Fortunately not. If he had, I should have lied.'

'So, you are a liar.'

'You seem intent on casting me in the worst possible light. My report was accurate so far as it went. I owe a duty to Rome.'

'And not to me.'

'I hope the two will never conflict.'

'Suppose they did?'

'I can't answer that. It would depend on the circumstances.'

'Perhaps you had better go now,' she said more calmly. 'It may be that I have misjudged you, as you say. But it is better that we never see one another again.'

I shook my head. 'I will go now, but I will not promise never to see you again. I am very grieved that you have misinterpreted what I intended as an act of love. And I do love you, Mary of Magdala.' I paused. 'I came to ask you to marry me.'

She seemed to be in the grip of strong emotion, and it was several moments ere she could speak. At length she said, 'Roman soldiers can't marry.'

'My term of service expires in a year's time. I am not a rich man, but I'm better off than most. And as a Roman citizen I'm entitled to a grant of land. I know you are too good for me, Mary of Magdala, but I should be most honoured if you would consent to be my wife. Do you want me to kneel? I will if you like.'

She was crying again, but more quietly. 'Please leave. I have to think. Alone. Please leave.'

She was no longer cold and hard, and I was not quite so discouraged as I had been on my arrival. Before leaving, I kissed her hand.

BOOK II

Jerusalem

According to Simon

I ARRIVED in Jerusalem on the eve of the Sabbath. Unnecessary travelling for the next twenty-four hours would be discouraged. But a week before the Passover it was still possible to obtain accommodation, albeit at extortionate rates. I duly made arrangements at a tavern I had frequented before and found to be satisfactory. Shortly before sunset, and much against my will, I stood at the gateway to the Prefect's palace and announced my business, before being admitted to an anteroom and referred to one of his scribes.

'Your details have been noted,' he confirmed after I had given him my business and temporary addresses. 'Henceforth you need report only on alternate days, unless you change your address, or have dealings with other followers of the rabbi calling himself Joshua bar-Abbas, in which case you should let us know immediately.'

'I understand. I assume you already know of his intention to enter the city on the aftertomorrow.'

'So we have heard.'

'My understanding is that he intends riding upon an ass.'

'An ass? A beast of burden?'

'So it would seem.'

The scribe shook his head and sighed in the manner of one who had given up trying to understand the Jews. I turned to take my leave, then decided to risk a question. 'Have you any news of my son, Judas bar-Simon?'

The man regarded me suspiciously for a few moments before deciding that the question was not unreasonable. After consulting a couple of scrolls, he said, 'There is nothing I can tell you, save that he continues to assist in enquiry into the murder of Dio Syrianus.'

Asking to see him would have been both futile and dangerous, suggesting that I had been involved in his activities. I simply said, 'Thank you. Shall I be notified of progress?'

I knew what he would say, and he did. 'Should he be released, he will no doubt come to see you. If condemned, you will be informed as next of kin at your last known address.'

There was nothing to be inferred from his manner, which was studiedly neutral. I thanked him again and left.

*

THE FOLLOWING morning I was leaving the Temple by way of the Beautiful Gate through Solomon's Porch. The sacrificial beasts had been butchered before the service, so I was no longer disturbed by their screams and bellowing, though the stink of the abattoir was still in my nostrils. As I took a few deep breaths of fresh air to clear my nose, from the Court of the Women behind me there came scurrying a plump, well-favoured little wench, with dyed reddish-blonde hair showing under her headscarf. I fancied I had seen her before, and quite recently, but could not think where. All I knew was that the recollection had disturbing associations.

'Simon bar-Cleophas?'

'That's me.'

'A message for you to collect an animal, an ass, as I am informed, from the premises of Benjamin bar-Jacob at the fourth hour tomorrow, and convey it to the rabbi Joshua in Bethany. Johan says he will meet you there.'

Johan bar-Zebadiah was one of our Lord's most favoured disciples. 'I was expecting to hear from him,' I confirmed. 'Thank you, my dear.'

She left, and was soon lost to sight amongst the crowd of other women leaving the Temple. But where had I seen her before? The question still troubled me.

I knew the man she spoke of slightly. He kept an inn called the Four Winds, not far from the Temple grounds. A well-run establishment; I had patronized it on several occasions.

An inn. Of course. That was where I had seen her. And no wonder the memory had aroused in me feelings of unease. For she had been the young tavern whore I had seen in Caesarea in company with the centurion Teutonicus.

*

MY misgivings were groundless, at least so far as the ass was concerned. The creature was indeed tethered to a stake of the fence surrounding the Four Winds Inn. Johan bar-Zebadiah was just leaving by the front door. As he saw me he raised a hand in greeting.

'God be with you, brother.'

'And with you, brother.'

'I've spoken to the innkeeper and confirmed things. The hire of the ass has been paid for; we may take it away.'

'Fine.' I began to undo the animal's tether.

'I don't know about you, brother,' said Johan, 'but I don't feel it would be right for either of us to ride it into Bethany. Methinks our Lord should be the first.'

'I agree,' I said.

It was no great sacrifice, for asses are uncomfortable mounts, not designed to bear men. And so we walked the creature the two or three miles to the village of Bethany, where Johan said he would take it to our Lord.

'I will accompany you.'

'No, he has another task for you. Do you know one Moshe, a merchant and dealer in wool?'

'Of course. One of the richest men in Jerusalem.'

'He lets out some upper rooms in one of his warehouses on a weekly basis. Our Lord's instructions are that you reserve a room for the period of seven days, commencing on the afternoon of Nisan 13.'

'Including sleeping accommodation?'

'For those who desire it, if they can obtain nothing better.'

'So that means all thirteen of us?'

'More than that, if one includes the women and servants. And others who simply want to be with our Lord. There could be a couple of score.'

'Suppose the room is not available?'

'It will be.'

I hesitated. 'I should like to see our Lord before I leave.'

Johan smiled and shook his head. 'He prefers to be alone for the present. He has to prepare himself.'

'But …'

'Your concern is for Judas.'

'Quite.'

'Our Lord says you need not worry about that. He will soon be released.'

It would have been pointless to ask how he knew. Our Lord seems to know most things.

*

UPON return to Jerusalem, I made at once for the premises of Moshe, and succeeded in obtaining an interview with the man himself. I explained our needs.

'Of course, of course. I have been keeping it. For the Rabbi Joshua, is it not?'

'That's right.'

'For not more than fifty persons, in the afternoon of Nisan 13, for a period of seven days?'

'I'm not sure of the exact number who will be attending, but it sounds about right. As are the other details.'

'Good, good. It's a big room, of course. Would you care to see it?'

'Well, as I'm here …'

'Quite. Follow me.'

We mounted a wooden step-ladder leading through a gap in the ceiling, and thus to the upper storey. As he had said, it was a large room, perhaps fifty cubits by twenty, and rather bleak, albeit soundly built in good timber; cedarwood if I mistook not. Construction materials were strewn about in the untidy fashion of builders everywhere.

'I am in the course of having the upper rooms refurbished as living accommodation instead of being used for storage as hitherto. That's why things look rather basic at present. But I was told that didn't matter.'

'And your fee?'

He waved his hands. 'That has already been settled.'

Not for the first time I began to feel myself superfluous. As if I were taking part in something pre-ordained, a dramatic work in which I had no option but to play my part and speak the lines prepared for me. And it was not only our Lord who knew my role in advance. The Romans were also aware of it, in the persons of Teutonicus and his little whore. Which of course meant that the Prefect must also know.

This feeling was accentuated as I stepped outside into the street.

'Greetings, father.'

I turned in surprise. It was of course Judas.

*

THAT my son had survived the ordeal of interrogation by the Romans unscathed should not have surprised me. What he had told them, or promised them, to avoid torture and possible crucifixion, of course I knew not. He volunteered nothing, and I declined to give him the satisfaction of asking. All he said, with an adolescent swagger, was that it helped to have friends in high places. Presumably he meant the Prefect, or more likely one of his representatives, for I doubted whether Pilate would have considered him important enough to attract his personal attention.

Judas had always been a survivor, if a rather ignoble one. In my judgment there was little he could have told them that they did not already know. It followed that he had promised them something. Whilst he would not necessarily deliver on that promise, our Lord should be warned of his intentions.

Meanwhile there were other things for me to worry about. For our Lord was to enter the city this day. As a devout Jew, he had frequently visited Jerusalem, and it was far from being the first time that he had done so at the time of the Passover. Yet for some reason I felt convinced that this year would be the last.

According to Pilate

I HAVE never liked Josef bar-Caiaphas, but to be fair I cannot call to mind any Jew whom I do like. And at least one can do business with him. Unlike most of their countrymen, the Sadducees have an empirical attitude which I can understand. They can unfailingly be relied upon to act in what they conceive to be their own best interests, unhampered by religious belief or personal integrity. Shortly after my arrival in Jerusalem the rogue was sitting opposite me in my headquarters in the palace of the former tetrarch Herod the Great, where I had deemed it advisable to take up residence during the time of their Passover festival. There is invariably trouble at such time. His robes of office were a riot of colour: red, rich blue, purple and gold. Presumably this was intended to impress me. His manner of speech was obsequious, yet at the same time contrived to suggest a thinly veiled insolence.

'Yes?' I said wearily.

'I am sure Your Excellency will have noted with concern the activities of the man calling himself Joshua bar-Abbas.'

I did not reply. After an awkward pause he continued, 'Whether that be so or not, I have to say that he is causing us some… ah… inconvenience.'

'And what am I being asked to do about it?'

'Your Excellency has resources not available to the Sanhedrin or your humble servant.'

'And why should Rome involve herself in the religious squabbles of a faith she does not share?'

'With respect, Excellency, I feel that she should do so if it involves her security and that of her esteemed Emperor.'

Of course the canting knave knew that once he mentioned that I had to listen to him. 'Go on,' I said.

'His real name is Joshua bar-Josef, son of a prosperous artisan from Galilee, now deceased. A couple of years ago he was baptized by the lunatic calling himself Johan the Baptizer, since of course executed by King Herod Antipas. Soon after that he fell out with the rest of his family for reasons which may readily be surmised, namely that he has abandoned his former work in the building trade, and at the age of over thirty still shows no inclination to get married and start a family of his own. Instead he has become a self-styled prophet on the lines of the late Baptizer.'

I trust that my face remained impassive, even bored. Rather desperately the priest continued, 'Yet despite that – and this is the important thing – he now calls himself bar-Abbas, that is "the son of the father," sometimes rendered into Greek as "the Son of Man." '

I drew a sigh, allowing my eyes to stray to the pile of business papers needing attention on my desk. 'This is riveting indeed. Can you come to the point?'

'The point is, Excellency, that by "the son of the Father," he may be claiming to be the son of Almighty God, heavenly father of the Jewish nation.'

I thought to annoy the fellow by arguing theology with him. 'Are not all men sons of God?'

'That is true in a sense, Excellency, but I fear that Your Excellency misses the point.'

'Which is?'

'That he is on the verge of claiming to be divine. Which needless to say constitutes the most heinous crime of all: that of blasphemy.'

'It sounds more like lunacy. There are places where such people may be detained.'

'Hardly feasible in view of the man's following, I fear. But I repeat, Excellency, should he be claiming to be divine, he is guilty of blasphemy against Almighty God.'

'So, for any man to be called divine constitutes blasphemy?'

I referred of course to the Divine Julius and the Divine Augustus of recent memory, to deny whose divinity comes close to constituting *maiestas,* or high treason. It amused me to see the fat sycophant squirm. 'Ah, well, Excellency, I am aware that Rome views these matters in a somewhat different light.'

'Well, I will tell you the light in which I view the matter. So far as I am concerned this man may travel around Galilee preaching whatever religious nonsense he pleases, so long as he does not demonstrate hostility to Rome.'

'Quite so, Excellency. I am coming to that. Many of his followers appear to belong to the fanatical sect called Essenes, and one or two of them are believed to be Zealots, that is, extremists who believe that the Jewish Messiah will soon return and drive Rome from this land.'

'Names.'

'Of those close to him, a man called Simon of Canaan, surnamed Zelotes, and his son Judas, nicknamed *Secarius,* or knifeman.'

I saw no reason to disclose that I knew them both, and that one of them was in our pay. Evidently sensing that he was not getting very far, Caiaphas continued, 'Worst of all, Excellency, one of Rome's tax-collectors is amongst his followers. A man named Levi, whom some call Matthew.'

'I know him by repute, of course. And as a tax-collector,' I pointed out, 'he is unlikely to be a religious maniac. My experience has been that they mostly concern themselves with the affairs of this world rather than the next.'

Uncertain whether I was jesting, the villain essayed what might have passed for a smile. 'Indeed, Excellency, very true. But this man may be an exception. There seems some evidence that in recent months he has moderated his tax demands substantially.'

'So, the rogue now confines himself to claiming the taxes due to Rome plus his lawful commission, rather than adding multiple extortions of his own. An unusual state of affairs, I concede, especially in Judaea, but scarcely sinister.'

'Ah, well, there I beg leave to differ from Your Excellency.' Caiaphas shifted in his seat. 'Do I take it, then, that your Excellency has no intention of acting upon my information?'

'Most of what you have told me I already knew. You should not imagine that Rome and her humble local representative are ignorant of matters of common knowledge. And if I were to crucify every crackpot who claims to be the Messiah there would scarcely be a tree left standing for miles around.'

'I apprehend that Your Excellency exaggerates somewhat. Does Your Excellency know that the man intends to visit Jerusalem for the Feast of the Passover?'

'So I have been informed.'

'Your Excellency may be of the opinion that preaching

religious nonsense in Galilean villages is one thing, in Jerusalem quite another. Our holiest city is …'

'A hotbed of troublemakers, both religious and civil. The former being the more dangerous. You are right to that extent, at least.'

'I am glad to find Your Excellency in agreement with me.'

'That overstates the matter. As I understand it, this fellow Joshua preaches sweetness and light, and loving one's enemies. Laughable though such a doctrine is, he could nevertheless be a force for moderation.'

Caiaphas seemed somewhat taken aback to discover that I knew more than he had suspected. 'That is true, Excellency. But this harmless, and as Your Excellency has pointed out, naïve teaching, is scarcely consistent with certain other remarks which he has made, such as eternal punishment in outer darkness for those who fail to repent of their sins: "There shall be weeping and wailing and gnashing of teeth …" '

'Few things interest me less than the fate of sinners after they are dead. There's enough trouble to cope with in this world. And I strongly suspect that the Emperor feels the same.' I stood. 'I wish you good day, High Priest. And thank you for your attendance.'

*

SOON afterwards I learned by express messenger from Teutonicus that his second-in-command, one Dio Syrianus, had been killed, in all probability by one of the *Secarii*. Killing a member of the army, even if he was but an auxiliary, was a new departure for them, and very disturbing. It was doubly vexatious that I had moved to Jerusalem to deal with anticipated trouble there, when against all expectation a case of *maiestas* had reared its head in Caesarea, which I had just left.

After some thought I sent orders to Teutonicus to join me in Jerusalem at once, together with the bulk of his quingenaria. The extra troops would be very useful; meanwhile he could leave the murder enquiry in the hands of his lieutenants.

If an unforeseen murder and almost inevitable trouble at the Passover were not enough, Herod Antipas, King of Judaea, had requested an audience with me. Requested, or demanded. I dislike dealing with people in circumstances where seniority of rank is not clear. Does a tetrarch, or client king, outrank a Roman sub-governor? I could not say. Partly for that reason I heartily wished that rather than pestering me, he had gone to see my immediate superior, Aelius Lamia, Governor of Syria.

What made matters worse still, the King would be accompanied by his wife, a stupid and vindictive woman who insisted upon being addressed by the self-style or title of Herodias. Whilst as scribe he employed one Nathan, a learned Pharisee, who could doubtless be relied upon to raise religious difficulties to virtually everything proposed.

Caiaphas also wanted to see me again. I almost welcomed the prospect by comparison. At least I was used to dealing with the greasy rogue. And he does not always see eye to eye with Herod any more than I do; maybe I could play one off against the other.

Nevertheless, faced with four devious Jews, every one

of whom would claim the authority of their Almighty God for his actions and opinions, I felt I needed the support of another Roman. One of my own guardsmen or stewards would have been useless, as was that old fool Silvius. Then it occurred to me to make use of Teutonicus, who should arrive within a couple of days. Meanwhile it would do Herod no harm to keep him waiting.

*

TEUTONICUS appeared promptly on the aftermorrow, together with a welcome reinforcement of some four hundred men, the pick of the Judaean Quingenariae. They moved into the praetorium, next to my palace. I could justify his presence at the meeting by calling him a senior liaison officer, or some such empty title. It would be good to have an ally present. He might be screwing the Magdalene woman, but he had no illusions about her countrymen, or anything else. I know a fellow-sceptic when I meet one.

I saw him alone immediately on his arrival. 'What progress have you made, centurion?'

He shook his head. 'Not as much as I should have liked, sir. One or two of my men have reported to me on the man Joshua. Despite having plenty to say for himself, it would seem that he has still not uttered anything treasonable. He constantly annoys the Pharisees, but of course they're always upsetting one another with their eternal religious disputes. I'm still inclined to think he's a harmless crank. It seems he intends to enter Jerusalem a week before the Passover mounted on an ass rather than a warhorse. What his followers will make of such a spectacle, I know not.'

I sighed. 'The main thing, naturally, is to avoid more trouble. But what about the murder of Syrianus? I gather he was not alone second-in-command of the cohort, but your friend.'

'That is so, sir. It seems that on the afternoon of his death he had been making enquiry of a widow called Eunice, related to a couple of Joshua's disciples, Philip and Barthol. His body was found within yards of her house.'

'Have you arrested her?'

'No, sir, not yet. But it suggests that Syrianus was killed because of his enquiries into the rabbi Joshua's followers. Although I said that the man himself seemed harmless, that doesn't necessarily apply to all his adherents.'

'Are there particular suspects amongst them?'

'Four seem potentially dangerous, sir. Simon, reputed to be a Zealot, and his son Judas Secarius of course, who is already in your hands. Two others are Essenes, and therefore possible extremists: Tomasso and Thaddeus.'

'Not Philip and Barthol?'

Teutonicus shook his head. 'They're Greek scholars, who used to make a modest living from teaching philosophy, which they've given up to follow the man Joshua. In my view they're not dangerous compared with the Jews. The disciples are always in and out of one another's houses, so all of them would have known of their relationship to the woman Eunice.' He paused. 'Might I enquire whether Your Excellency has had any success with the man Judas?'

After preliminary interrogation, Teutonicus had handed the man over to us. 'We could hardly stop him talking,' I said. 'Albeit to little effect. A pretentious pseudo-intellectual, without any backbone.'

Teutonicus nodded. 'My experience of him was similar, sir. He claimed to be acting for Your Excellency already, promising to continue to observe Joshua closely and report upon his activities on a regular basis.'

'He was right up to a point. He's one of those in our pay. How many of such knaves just take the money and do nothing much for it, is hard to say. The mere threat of torture reduced him to a whimpering wreck. According to him he's a loyal subject of Caesar, but the same is not true of many of the other disciples, about whom he promises to report to us, and so forth and so on. In short, exactly what he offered you.'

A slave entered. 'The High Priest Josef bar-Caiaphas has arrived, sir.'

I sighed. 'Let him enter. As for you, centurion, I should be glad of the presence of another Roman. Stand behind me at all times. Both physically and metaphorically.'

*

HALF an hour later we sat in the tablinum of the palace I use as my own residence, after being conducted to our places with all the customary meaningless ceremony. Over the previous four years it had amused me to ensure that the walls were adorned with a variety of pantheistic themes illustrated in graphic detail, which no doubt were anathema to my Jewish guests. Pagan idolatry, I suppose they would have called it.

I got rid of the slaves and servants, apart from a fat eunoch unnecessarily fanning Herod's wife, originally attractive but by now almost equally obese, with a spray of ostrich feathers. Unnecessarily, because on an evening in late March the climate of Jerusalem is cool enough already. Her husband was a thin man of medium height, some fifty years of age, dressed in a simple robe of deepest blue, and bearded in the fashion of all men in the eastern lands. Much as I detested the fellow, I had to concede that he possessed a certain dignity of mien lacking in the High Priest.

As host, I had responsibility for initiating the meeting.

'You wished to see me, sire?'

The last word stuck in my throat, but I had little choice. To have omitted it would have amounted to studied discourtesy, and I had no wish to provide Herod with an excuse to complain about me, as he had on previous occasions, albeit with limited success.

The small courtesy seemed to relax him a little, for he gave what passed as a smile. 'That is correct, Excellency.'

As the old military joke had it when the centurion was speaking to the young tribune, 'I have to call you *domine*, and you have to call me *domine*. But only one of us means it.' Which of us meant it? Neither, probably.

Herod was continuing, 'It would appear essential to do something about this fellow Joshua bar-Josef. He continues to spread alarm and dissention wherever he goes.'

'My information is that he preaches peace and goodwill, and the brotherhood of all mankind.'

'On the contrary, he is a dangerous agitator. As bad as his former colleague, whom they called Johan the Baptizer.'

Whether dangerous or not, the man Johan had been condemned and executed by Herod without reference to me, which was a clear breach of protocol and convention, if not of law. At the time I had let it pass without comment, but now decided to mention it.

Herod scowled. 'A mere formality.'

'I would call it a courtesy, which you did not extend to me. Sire.'

I could have sworn I saw the hint of a smile flicker across Caiaphas's greasy countenance, and then it was gone. Herod's face was as black as thunder. His wife said, 'The man called my dearest daughter, Salome, a lascivious trollop, and the whore of Babylon. She was severely distressed.'

Substitute Judaea for Babylon, and the Baptizer had not been far wrong. The antics of Salome were notorious throughout the province, and Herodias herself when younger had been little better. Her real reason for having the man executed was thought to be that he had called her marriage to Herod incestuous, she having previously been married to his brother.

'That is neither here nor there,' said Herod irritably, '*Excellency*. The fact is, the man claims to be the King of the Jews. Both blasphemous, and politically extremely dangerous.'

Disagreement came from the quarter I had least expected, the Pharisee, Nathan. He cleared his throat apologetically. 'Strictly speaking, sire, I doubt whether calling oneself King of the Jews can be considered blasphemous. The title is after all not divine …'

'Yes, well, I dare say you know more about that religious mumbo-jumbo than I do. The fact remains that the man constitutes a serious danger, both to Judaea and Rome.'

'Teutonicus,' I said, turning to him. 'You have made detailed enquiry, and met this man Joshua. Has he claimed to be King of the Jews?'

'Not to the best of my knowledge, sir. Certainly not in

my presence, and I was at his meeting on the Mount for several hours. There are those amongst his followers who claim the title for him. Or rather, that of Messiah.'

Caiaphas shook his head. 'Messiah. That's bad.'

'Explain,' I said. I knew what the rogue was going to say, but pretended stupidity can be an effective ploy. It has been known to cause others to underestimate me.

'The Messiah, Excellency, is the anointed one, who will one day free captive Judaea from her enemies' yoke. In the circumstances, that means ...'

'Rome. I have worked that out. Very well, King Herod, what do you suggest I do?'

'Arrest the man immediately,' snarled his wife, 'and have him crucified. After prolonged and skilful torture.'

I might have imagined it, but fancied I glimpsed a shade of revulsion flicker across Antipas's face. 'That,' I said, 'might well lead to an immediate insurrection. The very thing it is my duty to prevent.'

'On the contrary,' said Herod, 'if it forces troublemakers out into the open, you can make an example of them, thus permanently deterring others.'

'No-one has yet succeeded in permanently deterring your countrymen from making trouble. Sire.'

'They are not my countrymen,' he corrected me with asperity. 'I am their ruler, not their compatriot.'

That was debatable, to say the least. He had been born in Idumaea, in the south of the province. Admittedly it had been incorporated into Judaea proper only within the last hundred years, and it was certainly true that the majority of Jews detested him.

Not that any Jew distrusted him more than I did. As

a tetrarch of Judaea, and client king of Rome, he owed allegiance to the Emperor, and I was not alone in believing such allegiance extremely suspect. Should it suit his purpose he would have no qualms about betraying us. No enemy is more dangerous than a false friend.

I decided to try another tack. 'Do you know how many men I have to defend the whole of Judaea?' He shrugged. 'I will tell you. Less than three thousand. Is that not so, Teutonicus?'

'It is, sir.'

As soon as I had spoken, I could have bitten my tongue off. I should never have admitted my weakness to Herod. But he had probably been aware of the position anyway.

'You can send to Syria for more,' said the Tetrarch. 'They have close on twenty thousand men. Four whole legions.'

'By the time they arrived, Judaea would be knee-deep in blood, both Jewish and Roman. Rome would win in the end of course, but at great cost, and Judaea would remain a trouble-spot, even worse than it now is.'

'Then you are not prepared to do anything?' he enquired.

'I did not say that. Caiaphas, what think you?'

I knew that the High Priest loathed Herod and his wife every bit as much as I did. It would be amusing to see the fat rogue squirm, as he tried to placate both me and the king.

He hesitated, rubbing his hands together like a miserly moneylender. 'I think the man and his disciples need watching carefully, Excellency.'

Herod made a disgusted noise. I nodded. 'You speak wisdom, High Priest.' The sanctimonious rascal preened himself. 'As it happens I have already put detailed enquiries in hand. Is that not so, Teutonicus?'

'Indeed, sir. And given orders for the men in question to be kept under surveillance. I can provide details, if Your Excellency thinks that would not compromise security.'

'You also speak wisely, centurion. Hostile ears are everywhere.' I tried not to look at anyone as I said this. If any chose to take offence, what of it?

'He will enter Jerusalem on the aftermorrow,' said Herodias. 'Did you know that?'

I smiled and again indicated to Teutonicus that he should speak. 'His Excellency is well aware of that, *domina*. Also of the fact that for reasons best known to himself the man has chosen to ride an ass, and have his followers strew the road ahead of him with their garments and the branches of trees.'

'What on earth does he mean by that?'

'I know not, *domina*. I simply report the facts.'

Herod made an impatient noise, though rather less offensively than before. The Pharisee Nathan again surprised me by demonstrating a mind of his own, albeit a second-rate one. He said, 'Methinks it were best to allow matters to proceed untrammelled for the time being. I have spoken with this Joshua, and find him a good man, if misguided in some ways.'

'I thought he disliked the Pharisees,' I said.

'He dislikes those who do not practise what they preach, whether Pharisees or no. Most of his teachings are strictly orthodox. Here and there I disagree with his interpretation of the Holy Torah.'

Herod and his wife glowered at him. Caiaphas simply looked bored, Teutonicus unmoved. Eventually the High Priest remarked, 'Conceivably the man means well, but I have grave doubts. Would that I knew what he intends. But God's will be done.'

Not to be outdone in the spouting of pious platitudes, I said, 'The gods themselves know not what men think.'

From then on the meeting lost any point it might have had, becoming repetitive, as all present kept repeating their position and arguing in circles. As the sun went down and the Sabbath began, the Pharisee Nathan voiced his fear that they might be offending their deity by transacting business on the holy day. There ensued an indescribably tedious religious dispute in which I took no part, as the eventual result of which all the Jews decamped unsatisfied.

Despite the lack of result I was not displeased at the way matters had turned out. It was apparent that the Jews had been almost as much at odds with one another as with me: Herod and Caiaphas, Sadducee and Pharisee. I had even detected signs of strain in Herod's relations with his wife. Was it not the first Caesar who had said: 'Divide and Rule'?

Teutonicus stayed behind to deliver and discuss his formal report. The man had conducted himself throughout in exemplary fashion, saying and doing exactly what I had wanted, without any prompting from me. Despite our difference in rank, I felt amiably inclined towards him, almost as if he were a personal friend.

'I think we handled that quite well, centurion, don't you?'

I preferred not to mention my gaffe in disclosing the inadequacy of our defensive forces. His reply was appropriately diplomatic.

'Very well, sir. If I may say so without appearing presumptuous, I considered Your Excellency's conduct of the meeting could not have been bettered. The Jewish leaders are in complete disarray.'

'Precisely my thoughts on the matter. Every one of the rogues has his separate agenda, as one might put it, and his own unresolved problems. Not least King Herod.'

Teutonicus raised his eyebrows and smiled. 'His wife, for one thing.'

'By all the gods, yes. Appalling woman. I wouldn't wish her on my worst enemy.' I paused. 'Though come to think of it, Herod is my worst enemy.'

According to the Centurion

I REACHED Jerusalem in what must have been record time, riding through the night, and changing horses whenever possible. Fortunately the weather was perfect, with a cool breeze by day, cloudy and mild at night. Meanwhile the First Cohort, under the temporary command of my deputy, young Vulpino, followed apace.

I even managed to find time to call in at Bethany, three miles to the south-east, where as I had surmised, Simon Zelotes called whilst awaiting his leader. A somewhat strained interview confirmed my suspicion that the man was not being entirely frank, so I ordered him to report daily to the Prefect's headquarters.

On reaching Jerusalem I intended seeking an early meeting with Pilate, but within an hour of my arrival he sent for me anyway.

'What progress have you made, centurion?'

'A certain amount, sir, if not as much as I would have liked. One or two of my men have reported to me on the man Joshua. Despite having plenty to say for himself, it would seem that he has still not said or done anything which could be considered treasonable. He's always annoying the Pharisees, but of course they're constantly upsetting one another anyway, with their eternal religious disputes. I'm inclined to think he's a harmless crank.'

'Does he still intend visiting Jerusalem for the Passover?'

'My Lord, yes. There are arrangements made for him to ride into Jerusalem in triumphal fashion.'

Pilate shook his head, more in bewilderment, it seemed to me, than disapproval. 'A triumph? Such things are now reserved to the Emperor. Whom has he conquered?'

'It does not appear to be a triumph in the Roman sense, sir. According to his followers, or some of them anyway, it is rather a demonstration of his victory over sin and death.'

'Well, if he's been victorious over either of them, he is a conqueror indeed.'

'Quite so, sir. He appears to have limitless confidence in himself and his teachings. But it seems he intends to enter mounted on an ass, to symbolize peace, rather than a warhorse.'

'I thought the ass symbolized stupidity.'

This time I felt safe in smiling. 'I think he means to do it, none the less. What his followers will make of the spectacle, of course I know not.'

Again Pilate shook his head. 'The main thing, naturally, is to avoid more trouble.' He paused before changing the subject. 'What about the murder of Syrianus? I gather he was not alone second-in-command of the cohort, but your friend.'

'That is so, sir.' I went on to report my recent discovery that on the afternoon of his death Dio had been making enquiry of a widow called Eunice, related to a couple of Joshua's disciples called Philip and Barthol.

'Have you arrested her?'

'No, sir, not yet. But it suggests that Syrianus was killed because of his enquiries into the rabbi Joshua's followers.

Although I said that the man himself seemed harmless, that doesn't necessarily apply to all his adherents.'

'So you believe the victim was killed because he was making enquiries, not because he was Dio Syrianus?'

'That's so, sir. He had otherwise been engaged only in routine operations. A few days ago he was on patrol during some minor trouble, helped break a few heads, but no more than the average auxiliary. It seems unlikely that he was singled out on that account.'

'Are there particular suspects amongst Joshua's followers?'

'Four seem potentially dangerous, sir. Simon, reputed to be a Zealot, and his son Judas Secarius of course, who is already in your hands. The latter was particularly reluctant to co-operate, which is why I had him arrested. His nickname appears to be partly self-adopted, and partly derisive. All seem to agree that although he talks big about being a knifeman, he wouldn't have the guts to do anything much. Whether he realizes that he's a bit of a laughing-stock amongst the rest of them, I wouldn't know. Two others are Essenes, and therefore probable religious extremists, Tomasso and Thaddeus.'

'Not Philip and Barthol, then?'

'They are Greek scholars, with interests in philosophy. Hitherto they've made a modest living from teaching, which they've given up to follow the man Joshua. In my view they're not dangerous compared with the Jews. Joshua's followers are always in and out of one another's houses, so they'd all have known about the woman Eunice; for instance Barthol visits her from time to time to sponge on her. It seems he's her favourite nephew.' I hesitated. 'Might I enquire whether Your Excellency has had any success with the man Judas?'

'We could hardly stop him talking, albeit to little effect. A pretentious pseudo-intellectual, without any backbone.'

'I had the same experience of him, sir. He had promised to observe Joshua closely and report his activities on a regular basis. I thought it better to pass him on to Your Excellency none the less, in case he could provide any further information.'

The Prefect's lip curled. 'The mere threat of torture reduced him to a whimpering wreck. According to him he is a loyal subject of Caesar, but the same is not true of many of the other disciples, about whom he promises to report to us regularly. In short, exactly what he had already offered you.' The Prefect added thoughtfully, 'Of course, inadequate men have committed murder before now. Sometimes to convince themselves and others that they are adequate.'

Not for the first time I reflected that Pilate was no fool. I nodded. 'His father, sir, described him as "all mouth." When I interviewed him I was inclined to agree.'

'It would of course be easy to have him convicted of the crime, which fact has been made abundantly clear to him. As a result, for all his heroic rhetoric about being a patriot, he prefers co-operation with us to crucifixion.'

Again I nodded. 'Have you continued to cultivate the company of the Magdalene woman?' he continued.

'I have, sir. I am satisfied she knows naught of the murder.'

'Have you any suggestions?'

For a Prefect to ask advice from a centurion was unusual, to say the least. The surprise must have shown in my face, for he continued, 'Don't worry, centurion, I shan't necessarily follow your advice. But you seem an intelligent man, and I'm interested in your views. What would you do in my position?'

I considered briefly. 'I should detain the man Joshua, arresting him unobtrusively, when crowds are not present. Then I should interrogate him to find out his true intentions. There seems a great deal of doubt and misunderstanding about what he is teaching.'

'What do *you* think he's teaching?'

'I've given some thought to this, sir. He seems to see himself as what he calls the "Son of Man." Whether that's the same thing as the Messiah, I know not. And according to him, the Kingdom of God will come upon earth very soon, by divine intervention.'

'Which presumably means an end to the Roman Empire.'

'Indeed, sir. But I think he believes it will happen, not as a result of armed rebellion, but supernaturally, by their god intervening in person, as he has several times in their legends. The Feast of the Passover celebrates one such event.'

'So, he's a crackpot. As you thought.'

'My lord, yes. And to be fair, a well-meaning crackpot. But some of those he leads could be dangerous.'

A slave entered. 'The High Priest Josef bar-Caiaphas is here, *domine*.'

Pilate sighed. 'Let him enter. As for you, centurion, I should be glad of the presence of another Roman. Stand behind me at all times. Both physically and metaphorically.'

*

I THEREFORE attended the subsequent meeting between him and the Jewish authorities, namely King Herod Antipas and his wife, and the High Priest, Josef Caiaphas. The Prefect seemed to trust me implicitly, which was gratifying, for he was known to trust very few. There was as yet no conflict between my loyalty to Rome on the one hand, and my feelings for the Magdalene woman on the other.

The meeting was tedious in the extreme, but from the Roman point of view not unsatisfactory, in that it revealed significant divisions between the Jews themselves. Assuming that is, that Herod Antipas counted as a Jew: by birth he was Idumaean, and by allegiance a Roman, if indeed he had allegiance to any. His wife defied description.

His scribe Nathan was one of the Pharisees, interested in the teachings of the man Joshua, and not prepared to condemn him out of hand. Bar-Caiaphas the Sadducee, like most of his kind, believed neither in the afterlife nor anything much else except retaining his temporal power and riches.

After the meeting was over, Pilate congratulated me on my performance, though in truth I had done little enough. He seemed to have taken a liking to me. And to be fair, I'd known a good many officials worse than him.

The problem was not only that he had now entrusted me with the thankless task of arranging security for the visit of the man Joshua to Jerusalem the next *Dies Solis*, but that I had to rely simply on men from the First Cohort. The reason Pilate gave was that he did not want to attract too much attention by having a mass of soldiers on the streets. He had a low opinion of the other local auxiliaries, and may have thought they would do more harm than good. But whatever his reasons, I feared the worst.

Book III

Palm Sunday

According to Mary

AS I write these notes, it is shortly after midnight. The day is come. The day when my dear Lord will enter the Holy City, and proclaim the end of the old order of things. Then will dawn a new age of righteousness and goodwill toward all men (and women), and the existing states will be overthrown. Not merely that of the Romans, but of their tools the Sadducees, and the scribes and Pharisees who preach one thing and perform another.

Of course I must be with him on his journey. I shall rise early, to ensure arrival in Bethany before he sets out. Then I shall accompany him every step of the way. Meanwhile I must spend the night in prayer and fasting.

*

I ARRIVED in Bethany in early morning, but our Lord would not see me, nor anyone else but his closest disciples, until he set out about two hours after noon.

O what a truly joyous and holy pilgrimage it was! Our dear Lord sitting upon his donkey-mount, his face shining in the light of the Lord God, surrounded by his disciples and followers, all crying out, 'Hosannah! Hosannah to the Highest! Here comes the Messiah! Captive Israel shall be captive no more!' My dearest, dearest Lord. Not for the first time thoughts of unbelievable arrogance crossed my mind: that by some miracle I could perhaps become closer to him than any, his well-beloved if unworthy consort, sharing his glorious mission and helping him spread it to the world.

At first his following was modest in number, some thirty or forty persons, but by the time we descended the Mount of Olives into the Kidron Valley, numbers had swollen to a thousand at least. We passed the Temple on our right, high upon its mount, awaiting the arrival of our Lord. As we did so, more and more pilgrims descended from all sides of the Mount of Olives, and from Gethsemane, from the Pinnacle of the Temple, and the Mount of Offence. All joining together, and singing in praise of God, ten thousand or more, in a single, happy band, of which I was but one humble member. Salome had preceded me to Jerusalem with the First Cohort, so I looked about for her, but without success.

We passed the King's Pool on our right, alongside the city wall. Thence to the Water Gate, where we entered the City of David. I was among the leading group, barely twenty yards behind our Lord as we passed through the gate. There were Roman auxiliaries on guard, but none attempted to stop us, indeed they were so heavily outnumbered that they would have been hard pressed to do so. Amongst them I noticed my centurion, though whether he saw me I know not. As usual he appeared neither supportive of our cause nor hostile, but thoughtfully observant. How I wish he were a true believer. For despite his failings, I cannot believe that he is a bad man. I now see that my attempt to blame him for what took place between us was inspired by demons. For truly it was my fault more than his.

Many citizens of Jerusalem now lined the route, waving palm leaves, strewing branches and even their garments before us to ease our Lord's passage over the rough and rocky surface. Well over half the crowd were women. The little donkey picked his way most carefully, as if conscious of the glorious load he bore.

We passed the Hippodrome. There was no racing, but some of the grooms and ostlers leant over the fence, curious to see what was happening. Like us, they were swamped by the giant crowd, by now surely twenty or thirty thousand strong. Ahead of us rose the mighty Temple of Herod, six hundred cubits by two hundred, surrounded by its courts. Gleaming pillars and shining rooftops proclaimed it the holiest two acres in Jerusalem, indeed in the whole world. Behind it rose the sinister Antonia Fortress, separate from the Temple and manned by the Prefect's troops, surely soon to fall, along with all temporal powers of this world of darkness.

All were somewhat out of breath, not only from our exertions in climbing the mount, but from excitement to know that we were participating in the greatest revelation of all time: the coming of the Messiah, or anointed one. Could it be, I asked myself again, could it be that our Lord had some special role in mind for me? He was no abuser of women. Indeed …

I pulled myself up sharply. My Lord was not interested in matters of the flesh. Surely it was his mission to stand alone. My thoughts to the contrary, sometimes bordering on the lascivious, came from the Serpent. He was subtle, and knew my weaknesses.

Next came the steps, set in three series of staircases at

right angles to one another: seventy, eighty, a hundred or more, I know not, leading up to the gates in the great temple wall. Here the poor donkey flagged, and our Lord slipped from his back to ascend the stairs himself, accompanied by two of his disciples. Simon Peter was on his right hand, Johan to his left.

The temple guards made no attempt to stop our Lord and his followers as he continued through the Royal Porch into the Court of the Gentiles. Thus far any could proceed, even unbelievers. And here, amongst the tables of dealers in meat and foodstuffs fresh from the abbatoir, and the tables of the money-changers, our Lord paused, spoke briefly to his friends Peter and Johan, and walked around, occasionally chatting to those approaching him, as is his wont.

Perhaps a couple of hundred of us had accompanied him thus far, the remainder of the vast throng having stopped or been halted by the temple guards, who would not have succeeded had our Lord not intervened to assist them.

The tables of the money-lenders extended for many cubits across the forecourt of the Gentiles. Here Roman or Greek currency could be exchanged into that of the Holy Temple. One could also borrow money from the temple funds, as did many of those too poor to afford sacrifice otherwise. Even then they usually had to settle for a dove or other bird rather than a beast.

Our Lord entered into converse with one of the exchangers, though I could not hear what was said. And for the first time he appeared to encounter opposition to his wishes, for I heard his voice raised in argument, which was unusual. One or two of the soldiers who had been wandering about nearby looked uneasy, as did the priests' temple guards. I looked for my centurion, but could not see him. For some reason I had the feeling that he could have settled things amicably. Did I have more faith in him than in my Lord? Did such thoughts come from the Serpent? If only I knew.

*

THEN it happened, all of a sudden. Our Lord moved swiftly along the tables of the money-changers, overturning them one after another, so that their contents tumbled into the dust. So did some of their owners, as they struggled to save them. One or two others tried to lay hands on my Lord. Their language was profane. I heard them even above the moans, bleats and screams of the brutes being sacrificed at the altar of burnt offerings within the Temple Court.

There was a whip in his hand. He struck out blindly, in full fury. 'This is the house of God!' he yelled, kicking the moneys about the floor. 'And ye have made it a den of thieves!'

A den of thieves it soon became, as some of those present grabbed coins from the floor under pretence of restoring them to their owners. As a result a good half of the moneys disappeared. Those robbed were calling for the Temple Guard, who seemed in no hurry to intervene. Meanwhile my Lord marched up and down, striking out at the money-changers with his whip, reviling them in the most dreadful terms, and threatening them with eternal damnation, when there should be weeping and wailing and gnashing of teeth.

I was appalled. Was this the man I had so deeply loved? Furious anger terrifies me. I fear for my safety, cowardly wretch that I am, whenever I see a man in such a state. What had angered him so? Everyone knows of the money-changers and their activities. They perform a necessary task. Not all of them are honest, but the same applies to all professions.

Our Lord turned and stalked out of the Gentile Court, swearing that one stone of the Temple should not stand upon another. His disciples looked embarrassed. I noticed the Greeks, Philip and Barthol, helping the money-changers re-erect their stalls. After some delay our Lord's remaining disciples followed him outside.

I did not. I needed to think. Had the Serpent, cunning beyond belief, somehow managed to enter into our Lord's heart? Surely that was impossible. I reminded myself that my Lord Joshua had cast the minions of the Evil One out of me. But had he altogether succeeded? My thoughts were still inclined to stray along forbidden paths.

Order was soon restored, and a couple of the guards asked me for my account of what had happened. Like many of the others, I told them falsely that I had not seen anything. So I have sinned again. Yet surely there must be some good reason for our Lord's behaving as he did.

There were no Roman soldiers present. Presumably they had deemed it diplomatic to leave maintenance of order in the temple to the Judaeans and their priests. Rightly or wrongly, I could not avoid thinking how much I should have liked my centurion to be there.

*

I SOUGHT him out, I confess it. He was still standing at the Water Gate, this time alone, looking out into the evening mist gathering over the valley. As he turned at my approach, his face lit up. My heart beat more quickly. Was it so very wrong to be gratified that he might feel something for me?

'Ah, there you are, Mary. I had been hoping to see you.'

'I was with the procession, in attendance on my Lord.'

'Yes, I saw you. You looked happy.' He noticed my tear-stained face. 'What has happened since then?'

'In the temple. You may have heard about it.'

'A few vague rumours. The temple lies outside my sphere of responsibility. I was more concerned with seeing your lord safely out of Jerusalem. Which I am glad to say he is, and well on the way to Bethany by now. Will you be joining him?'

'I… I don't know. I'm very confused.'

'As a result of what happened in the temple?'

'Yes. He was like – I dare not say it – but yes, I will. He had been involved in trenchant debate with the money-changers, I assume about the ethics of their trade, though I was out of earshot. Suddenly everything changed. He had been leaning over their tables, but now he stood back, grabbed the table-tops and overturned then. He strode along the row, and every single table was overturned, together with the piles of coins and papers, and the calculating machines. As the changers grovelled trying to pick things up, he took a whip, whence I know not, and laid into them, screaming that they had turned the house of God into a den of thieves.'

'Strange that he was not arrested. Or at least, I assume he wasn't. When he came out there was no sign of anything having happened amiss.'

'No. No-one seemed to know what to do. The priests and guards were taken aback. As was everyone.'

'Hardly surprising.'

'I was terrified. When men become angry, it frightens me. Because of my husband, and others. I'm a coward, you see.'

'One should not confuse fear with cowardice.'

'I'm sure you are never afraid.'

'I am constantly afraid. One hears of men who are fearless, but they're few and far between. Even then I have my doubts. I remember an old soldier advising me soon after I joined the army: "There's nothing wrong with being afraid, son. But make sure you never *show* that you're afraid." '

'It's not only that I'm afraid. I'm ...'

'Disappointed?'

'Yes. When he entered the City I was so full of hope, yet now ...'

'I understand.'

'It was so different from a Roman triumph, you know. Not that I have ever seen one, of course. But – a little donkey instead of a chariot ...'

'I'm not keen on Roman triumphs myself,' he said surprisingly. 'Although I've never seen one, either. But methinks they could teach your lord one thing. The only person allowed in the chariot with the triumphant general is a simple slave, whose task it is to keep murmuring, "Remember, thou art mortal." '

'You mean that Joshua bar-Abbas is flawed and mortal like the rest of us.'

'I mean that he would do well not to forget it.'

'Speaking to you has helped me,' I said truthfully. 'But now I must go to join our Lord in Bethany.'

'Naturally.' He looked into the gathering mist. 'But

you need an escort. I refuse to let you undertake the risk of travelling alone at night. For all I know there could be *Secarii* about. I'll get a couple of my men to take you.'

'No,' I said hurriedly. 'Don't do that. One man will be enough. And I want it to be you.'

*

BY the time we set out it was nearly two hours later. My centurion had had to write out and deliver his report to Pilate on the day's activities. From Jerusalem to Bethany is barely three miles. Had I set out alone I should have been home and in bed already. And yet I did not regret waiting for him.

With the possible exception of our Lord, I would not have entrusted my safety to any other man, indeed I should have felt safer on my own. But I somehow knew that, whether he was a good man, or foully misled by the Serpent, I could trust my ccnturion.

The gibbous moon was high in the south, casting deep dark shadows across the misty valley. At first we were silent, but then began to speak of a variety of things, both serious and trivial, occasionally smiling and joking, then discussing our hopes, beliefs and fears, matters I have never before discussed with any man. As we climbed the Mount of Olives I twice needed to pause for breath, my centurion never. The second time he stopped with me he offered me his arm. I took it.

As we neared the summit I turned to look at the Holy City, silent in the moonlight, at once more beautiful and more dangerous than by day. Deep in the shadow and mists to our right lay the Gardens of Gethsemane. Neither of us spoke for a long time.

'Surely,' I said at length, 'this is a holy place.'

'Are not all places holy?' he replied.

At one time I would have disagreed with him instantly. Now I took my time to reply. 'I think I perceive your meaning.'

'The Stoics believe the stars are divine. I would not go so far as that. But is not the whole world, the whole of creation, a manifestation of Jupiter?'

'Elohim,' I corrected.

He smiled. ' "In him we live and move, and have our being." '

'That sounds the sort of thing our Lord might have said.'

'I can't claim credit for it. It's from the Greek poet Aratus. Invocation to Zeus.'

'Paganism,' I said uncertainly. My centurion simply smiled and said nothing.

After that we spoke but little. The remainder of the journey was without incident, the descent of the mount comparatively easy. Or it would have been, had I not become convinced that we were being followed. I glanced at my centurion, but he gave no sign of concern. Should I warn him? Or would he think it but the vapourings of an hysterical woman? I said nothing. Soon the small town of Bethany lay before us.

'Where do you live?' he enquired.

I indicated my lodgings, near the stables, alongside those of most of the other women. For more women follow our Lord than men.

Then I warned him. But he already knew, and had not

wanted to worry me by mentioning it. How very like him. But I reproved him gently. He must never fear to worry or offend me.

'I will say goodnight, then,' he said as we neared the stables. 'And may your god go with you.'

'And yours with you.' Whence this piece of paganism came I know not.

Then we kissed.

*

THAT night I slept little. Surely, I thought, the way I feel about this man cannot be entirely wrong. Is it sinful to desire that after the act of love I should lie all night with his arms around me, as we talked of our love for one another, and made plans for the future? Foolish, impractical plans no doubt, for our lives were so different. How could I adjust to his ways, or expect him to conform to mine?

Nor were my thoughts entirely for myself, and the distant future. He might be waylaid on the journey back. When I had mentioned the possibility, he had observed that in that case he would probably know who was the knifeman who had killed his friend. Typical of him to think of his duty before himself. And my centurion had fought his way all across Europe and the eastern provinces, against enemies far more formidable than a lone cowardly bandit. Surely, *surely*, he could take care of himself.

In my fantasies I imagined him being wounded, but not too seriously. He would manage to make his way back to Bethany, where I would care for him, tending his wounds, while he would again tell me how he felt about me, and what a comfort I was to him. What joy that would give me, knowing that he was grateful to me, redeeming myself in his eyes, for surely by now he must think me a dangerously unstable creature.

It was some time before I could bring my mind back to my Lord, Joshua bar-Abbas. Passover week had barely begun. He must be planning to return to Jerusalem very shortly. And there his great purpose would be accomplished, and all would be well.

My last thought as I finally drifted off to sleep was that I should then have the opportunity to see my centurion again.

According to Simon

FROM BETHANY, our Lord would be approaching from the direction of the Mount of Olives, and thence along the Kidron Valley, east of the city. In theory he could have scaled the Temple Mount, and entered directly into the temple by its south-eastern gate. This however would have allowed little scope for the triumphal process he had planned. I therefore assumed that he would continue along the city wall until he reached the Water Gate to the City of David, oldest quarter of Jerusalem. Upon entering the city he would back-track, taking the modern road to the temple, alongside a ragged row of stones marking the remains of the original city wall. I positioned myself just inside the Water Gate, opposite the Siloam Pool, the waters of which gave the gate its name. This would enable me to join our Lord and his followers as soon as they entered Jerusalem, and follow them all the way to the temple.

Nisan 9 was a clear spring day, the brisk breeze rendering it a little on the cool side for perfection. There was a gathering of prospective onlookers, mostly small family groups, but as yet no dense crowd. One or two Roman auxiliaries were hanging about trying to look inconspicuous. Amongst them I noticed the ubiquitous centurion Teutonicus. I had expected him to avoid my eye, but he smiled blandly and raised a hand in what I took to be ironic greeting.

Travelling at the modest speed allowed by his mode of transport, I judged that setting out soon after breaking fast our Lord should arrive some time during the ninth hour, in which calculation I proved correct. Meanwhile I attempted without much success to engage in conversation with a couple of family groups nearby. Both seemed intent upon seeing the notorious Joshua bar-Abbas for no particular reason but to tell their friends that they had seen him. There were a couple of middle-aged men talking earnestly together whom I provisionally identified as scribes or Pharisees. Getting involved in discussion with them would occupy time and energy I felt disinclined to spend.

The first indication of our Lord's approach was a distant cheering from the direction of the Kidron Valley. By now the crowd in the vicinity of the Water Gate had increased, to number perhaps two or three thousand, mostly lining the road on the same side as myself. They constituted the usual mixture of the devout and the merely curious, and were for the most part well-behaved. Some carried palm leaves which they waved to discourage insects, comparatively few in number at this time of year.

The noise grew in volume, bursting out in full force as the procession entered the city. It was led by our Lord's disciples, headed by two of his favourites, Peter and Johan, simply dressed in their work-a-day fishermen's clothes, raising their hands in salutation, and trying not to distract attention from our Lord.

He sat on the haunches of a donkey of modest size, dressed in a simple white robe as was his wont, and turning his head from side to side as he acknowledged the tribute of the crowd. For some reason I was expecting him to look different from normal, possibly transfigured in a divine light. In fact he looked much as he had last time I had seen him, his pale, inscrutable face watchful and observant as he surveyed the crowd. All his disciples were with him save the three who had preceded him to Jerusalem, namely myself, Judas and Levi.

A stentorian voice cried out: 'Messiah! Messiah!' which call was taken up by many in the multitude. Our Lord's demeanour did not change, either to accept the tribute or reject it, but remained serene. The same could not be said for some of his followers, who cast off their clothing and strewed it in his path, together with the branches of olive trees. Meanwhile others continued to wave their palm leaves.

Well over half his following were women. Amongst them I glimpsed Mary of Magdala, running alongside the main body of the procession and waving a shawl, her dark, slightly mad face alight with joy and exultation. Upon seeing her, for some reason I looked for the centurion Teutonicus, but without success.

As our Lord's figure disappeared into the crowd ahead I joined those in his wake, but I had delayed too long, and was soon surrounded by miscellaneous *polloi*, some of whom seemed to be present for no other reason than to cause minor disorder, shouting, gesticulating and generally playing the fool. Somehow I found myself next to the man Teutonicus. I say 'somehow': I have little doubt that he had been keeping an eye on me. I ventured to pass a comment to that effect.

'On you, among others,' he agreed calmly.

It struck me that with the possible exception of our Lord, he was less disturbed by events than any. The adjective which

sprang to mind, and seemed appropriate, was 'unmoved.'
I began to revise my first opinion of the man. He was no
mindless tool of Pilate.

'I dare say this is different from the triumphs you are
used to?' I enquired.

'I've never seen a triumph,' he admitted. 'They don't seem
as common now as in the olden days. But very different in
some ways, as you say. A donkey for a warhorse and chariot.
No captives in golden chains, or soldiers singing bawdy
songs. But crowds are much the same everywhere.'

'In what way?'

He pulled a wry face. 'The Roman mob that cheered
Pompey cheered his conqueror Caesar shortly afterward.
Methinks many of those now present would shout just as
loud if your Lord were on his way to be crucified.'

I said nothing, but confess that something of the sort
had occurred to me. We passed the Hippodrome on our left.
It crossed my mind that horse and chariot racing destroyed
men's judgment *en masse*, by substituting emotion for
reason. Might religious fervour do the same? Or were such
thoughts an offence against Almighty God and his prophets?

By the time I managed to reach the Temple our Lord
and his followers had long since entered it. I turned to bid
farewell to Teutonicus, but he had already disappeared,
which meant that I had to mount the massive staircase alone.
Feeling decidedly self-conscious, I forced myself to do so.

'Hey, you!'

As I had expected, one of the guards had raised a hand.
'Yes, you,' he confirmed, as I pointed to myself in silent
query. 'Where do you think you're going?'

As I began a somewhat incoherent reply, he interrupted

me. 'No more of his followers are to be admitted. We have our orders.'

'That's all right, guardsman, you can let this one through.'

The centurion Teutonicus was descending the steps behind him. The guard grumbled and gave way. 'You can join the rest,' Teutonicus told me. 'But don't go off on any jaunt of your own.'

I thanked him and agreed before climbing the remaining steps to the temple building. There I decided it would constitute no very serious breach of my promise were I to purchase some meat and a cup of wine. This I proceeded to do, before making my way through the Court of the Gentiles into the chamber of the money-changers. Our Lord was engaged in heated argument with one of them, though I was unable to catch the words.

Then it happened. Our Lord seized the top of one of the tables and overturned it. Coins, scrolls and abacuses rolled away at his feet. He proceeded to the next, and the next. In all I made it eighteen. Some of the owners stood and shouted at him. Others grovelled on the floor, seeking to salvage their money. Yet others seemed incapable of any action at all, but simply sat open-mouthed. It was scarce possible for them to have been more surprised than me. Was this swearing, raving fanatic the man who had taught us to to love our enemies, and turn the other cheek? Even as the thought crossed my mind he seized a whip and began to belabour those grovelling on the ground. Most of the disciples hovered around in helpless dismay. Amongst them I noticed my son Judas. He stood to one side, attempting a supercilious smile.

And then it was over. Our Lord recovered his senses,

and it was as if the incident had never occurred. The money-changers retrieved such of their moneys as had not been appropriated by opportunistic thieves, while the guards patrolled the room saying fatuous things like, 'Now then!' or 'Are you all right?' The faces of most of the disciples were blank. Judas's supercilious smile had turned glassy. The Magdalene woman was in tears, her expression that of horrified disbelief.

Some names were taken, including mine, though the guards seemed to accept that I bore no responsibility for what had happened. Nor, to be fair, did anyone apart from our Lord, unless the money-changers had said something to provoke him. Even then, did it justify such furious anger? Particularly since our Lord had expressly warned us against such a thing.

I returned to my lodging deeply troubled. Could the Messiah, whether a man of peace or war, have conducted himself in such undisciplined fashion? As for Judas, he remained talking to the guards, no doubt attempting to ingratiate himself both with them and their Roman counterparts.

Revisiting the temple later in the day, I was informed that our Lord had departed from Jerusalem shortly after the disturbance. Yet again I was puzzled. He had intended to spend the Passover here. Had his plans altered, and if so, why?

By now I was seriously considering the possibility that Joshua was not the promised Messiah, but on the contrary might be a dangerously deluded man. Or did these thoughts emanate from the Evil One?

According to Pilate

LATE MARCH or early April is the time when I have to prepare my annual accounts for audit. I therefore had neither time nor inclination to observe the tomfoolery likely to result on the Sunday before the Passover as a result of the man Joshua riding into the city on an ass. I gave orders to Teutonicus to keep him and his followers under close scrutiny, and left it at that.

It was the hour before sunset when he arrived to make his report. As ever his demeanour and salute were impeccable.

'What have you to tell me?'

'The man Joshua duly arrived in mid-afternoon, sir, riding upon an ass, as he had promised. He arrived at the Water Gate during the ninth hour, together with some five or six hundred followers. They were singing and shouting slogans, waving palm leaves, some even strewing the route with their clothes or vegetation.'

'The damned fools.'

Teutonicus nodded wryly. 'As you say, sir. Fortunately those involved were otherwise well-behaved. Some of the women were blowing kisses, calling out that they loved the man, some even in tears …'

'I can imagine. Go on.'

'Joshua entered the City of David, and made for the

Temple of Herod. By this time there might have been a couple of thousand lining the road *en route*, of whom a few hundred had attached themselves to his procession. Again there was no disorder, except for the usual minor trouble liable to be caused by loutish youths everywhere. As the procession reached the temple its numbers had swollen to a thousand or so, perhaps twelve hundred. The rumours circulating of ten thousand or more are absurd exaggerations.'

I nodded. 'There was some trouble at the temple, or so I have heard.'

'Yes, sir, though I did not witness it myself. As Joshua and his followers reached the steps, my men and the temple guards dissuaded most of them from entering with him. Eventually we permitted about fifty to accompany him, the rest remaining outside. Some dispersed, while others awaited his return, which occurred about an hour later. As you say, sir, there had been trouble in the temple, of which I was not aware at the time. Any noise would have been drowned by the hubbub of the crowd outside, and the cries of the beasts being sacrificed within.'

Teutonicus's responsibility for maintaining order had come to an end at the temple gates. Thereafter security was the affair of the priests, assisted by my men from the Fort of Antonia. I began to regret that I had not entrusted him with the temple as well. From what I had heard, he could hardly have done worse than the useless knaves in the fortress.

'According to the High Priests,' I said, 'whose version of matters I would trust about as much as I would that of the average leprous beggar with a hangover, the man Joshua suddenly assaulted the money-changers and lenders with a whip, overturned their tables and lashed them furiously, crying that they were a gang of thieves, and he would not let one stone of the Temple stand upon another.'

'That is the version I heard too, sir. From one of his followers.'

'Which one?'

'Mary of Magdala. Her description corresponded in every particular with that given to you by the priests.'

'I suppose even they must tell the truth from time to time. Go on.'

'After emerging from the temple – when I confess I noticed nothing amiss – he and his entourage retraced their steps back to the Water Gate, and left by the route to Bethany. I have just received reports that they duly arrived there a little over an hour later. There were no further incidents.'

'Things could have been worse, I suppose. Have you had any further indication of his intentions?'

'I understand that he means to return to Jerusalem some time during the week. He may even make his way back and forth to Bethany several times.'

'Without the same circus accompanying him every time, I trust.'

'I think any attempt to repeat the performance would be unlikely to succeed, sir. It was but a qualified success first time. As I say, his followers are exaggerating the numbers and enthusiasm involved. May I enquire, sir, what action is proposed as a result of the disturbance at the temple?'

'I haven't yet heard from the High Priests. Very likely they'll want to see the man crucified. To judge from what you say, it sounds as if he well overstepped the mark. A sound whipping might not be out of the question, plus whatever ecclesiastical penalty they choose to impose.'

*

BEFORE the day was out I duly received the anticipated deputation from the high priests, accompanied by a thinly-veiled complaint that I should have done something to prevent the trouble. As ever, Caiaphas was their spokesman. And as with most of their grumbles, they were vague when called upon to suggest an alternative course of action.

'The fact is, Prefect, that whereas until recently this man confined his nefarious activities to the Jordan Valley and seldom visited a place of any size, he is now intent on invading the holy city itself. Needless to say, this is a matter of far greater concern.'

It concerned me too, but I was damned if I was going to let the rogues see that I was worried, or even acknowledge that I agreed with them. Maybe I was guilty of obstinacy, but I find these canting Jewish knaves and their superstitions very difficult to stomach. 'My information is that the only disorder occurred inside the Temple of Herod, where keeping the peace is the responsibility of your temple guards. Indeed you have always been reluctant to allow my men to play any role there. Did the guards arrest him?'

'No, prefect. They deemed any such attempt inadvisable in view of the large number of his followers present.'

'Then why are you complaining to me?'

The greasy rogue shifted uncomfortably. '"Complaining" puts it too strongly, Your Excellency. What we have said is in the nature of a friendly warning. The man has returned to Bethany for the time being, but there can be little doubt that he will visit Jerusalem again before the Day of the Passover, when the city will be ripe for further trouble. He may, for instance, try to persuade Judaeans to discontinue paying their taxes.'

'Has he done so hitherto?'

'Well, no, prefect, not so far as I am aware. There is of course no means of knowing what he has been up to when my men have not been present.'

I shrugged. 'Speculation as to what persons might have done, without a vestige of evidence, seems to me unprofitable.'

He tried again. 'One thing he did say, Excellency, is: "Think not that I am come to send peace on earth; I came not to bring peace, but a sword." '

I decided it was time to show that I knew more than they gave me credit for. 'The context suggests that he was talking about domestic disharmony. He went on to say that he was sent to set son against father, and daughter against mother, and that no-one was worthy of him unless he abandoned his family to follow him.' I shrugged. 'Families are always falling out. I know I've had enough trouble with mine.'

As usual when uncertain as to whether I was attempting a pleasantry, the High Priest essayed an idiotic sort of half-smile. 'Very... ah... yes. So Your Excellency intends to take no further action?'

'My men will keep a close eye on him, as they did last time. I repeat, they witnessed no trouble. It was your men who apparently failed to keep him in order.'

The priests conferred briefly amongst themselves. One of them said sulkily, 'King Herod Antipas agrees with us.'

'And apparently feels so strongly that he is not prepared to travel the quarter-mile from his palace to add his voice to yours.'

'Well, after all,' said Caiaphas feebly, 'he is a king. And as such, more used to receiving visitors than honouring the habitations of others with his presence.'

I sighed. 'I thought I had made my position clear. But in case I have not, I will do so again. My reponsibility here is to protect Rome and her citizens. It follows that I do not want trouble. Ever since I came here, four years since, your countrymen have complained about matters of the utmost triviality, but I have refused to be provoked. I repeat therefore: I Do Not Want Trouble. I am not looking for conflict with Joshua bar-Josef or anyone else. Should he seek trouble with Rome, I assure you he will find it. Beyond that, I am not prepared to go.' I stood. 'Good evening, gentlemen.'

According to the Centurion

THE DAY came and went, and the outcome was better than I might have expected. I had four hundred three-and-twenty men under my command who were fit for action. I left a handful at headquarters, and employed the others on the route which it was expected the man Joshua and his followers would take. Approaching from the direction of Bethany, he would descend the Mount of Olives to the Kidron Valley, before turning south alongside the city wall and entering the Old City via the Water Gate. I posted fifty men there, and a further fifty at the steps to Herod's Temple, to liaise with the guardsmen employed there by the high priests. The remainder were to mingle with the crowds *en route*, not necessarily to remain *in situ*, but use their own judgment according to how matters developed. I initially took up position amongst those at the gate.

One of the things a soldier has to learn is how to cope with tedium. During the next few hours little happened save that small scattered crowds assembled both in the Kidron Valley and in the City of David along the route to the temple. If there were any religious fanatics amongst them the fact was not apparent. Some formed small family groups, others were couples, and not a few seemed to be alone. Women considerably outnumbered men. Many were doubtless merely curious, indeed I heard some enquire of others what it was they were awaiting.

It was well after noon, about the ninth hour, before we first espied the man and his followers descending the Mount of Olives. There was scattered clapping and cheering, mostly from those already with him, although at their approach some of the onlookers joined in in hesitant fashion. A small number bore and waved palm leaves.

A few more joined them from the direction of the Mount of Offence. One or two started singing Jewish religious songs and psalms, but without musical accompaniment. As they drew near I recognized some of his followers: those named Peter and Johan, and a dozen others, not however including Zelotes or his son, or for that matter Levi the publican.

Then I saw her. Some twenty yards or so behind the leaders, dressed in bright colours, smiling happily and waving her shawl. I caught my breath as I saw her, my throat tightened, and my heart beat louder. Few women had had that effect on me before, none to the same extent. And curiously my thoughts turned not so much to carnal matters, as to how I should like to cradle her in my arms, protect her from harm, and try to help heal her poor wounded mind.

Reluctantly I dragged my eyes from her, for duty called. I glanced from side to side before ordering my men to move from the gates to allow the visitors entrance. As they did I concentrated my attention upon their leader: a man of thirty or so, something above the average height, dark-bearded and gaunt of feature, seated upon the haunches of a small ass, neither astride nor in the fashion called side-saddle, but somewhere in between. Strangely enough my first thought was for the welfare of the animal, and how it could bear so great a weight.

Joshua was dressed as ever in a plain white robe. The sandals on his feet were of the most basic kind, and unusually for a Jew, he went bare-headed, the cape of his robe being pulled down to his shoulders. He appeared satisfied with the reception he obtained, from time to time raising a hand in benediction, smiling and speaking, though I could not catch the words.

Once he and his leading followers had entered the city, I left a score of men on the gate and moved swiftly along the roughly paved area alongside the temple road, indicating to my men that they should scatter and keep their eyes open for possible troublemakers. A small gang of youths were shouting obscenities. A couple of my men soon persuaded them to stop.

By now the crowd along the temple route was appreciable, though still not large or particularly enthusiastic. I noted occasional exceptions: those with fixed stares and open mouths of adoration, or worse, the glazed look and gleaming eyes of the true fanatic. One or two cried: 'Messiah! Messiah!' which was taken up by others in ragged fashion.

A few of the faithful, mostly those already accompanying their leader, ran ahead and strewed his route with their garments. The Magdalene cast her scarf down before him. How I wished she had never met the man, not only for my sake, but for hers. It was tragic that a highly intelligent woman, capable of achieving so much that was good, allowed herself to be deluded by such superstition.

There were further onlookers at the upper windows of the two- and three-storied apartment dwellings east of the road. One or two cried out or applauded, but the majority were content to observe either thoughtfully or with mere casual interest. Nothing more different from a Roman triumph could be imagined.

I suppose the simplicity of it should have impressed me, but the best I can say is that it appeared well-meaning and harmless. For his part Joshua continued administering his blessings, smiling and nodding. As they neared the Temple the crowds were a little denser, but I judged the total involved, including those *en route,* to number no more than a couple of thousand. The normal population of Jerusalem is over twenty times as many, swelling to half a million during the Passover week. A mere two thousand seemed a disappointing turnout, and the attempts by the participants to pretend that their progress was a riotous success struck me as rather pathetic.

At the temple steps the convoy drew to a halt as those in the lead were stopped by the guards, and a lengthy debate ensued. I was about to intervene when the problem was resolved. The guards waved Joshua and his disciples through, but prevented more than a couple of score of others following him into the temple grounds. Amongst them was the man Simon Zelotes, with whom I had already exchanged a few words to little effect.

Once the motley band set foot on the temple steps they were no longer my responsibility. I returned my attention to those left outside, none of whom seemed likely to create any kind of disorder. And so it proved. I had my men walk amongst them, chatting goodhumouredly both amongst themselves and with the crowds, even talking to the children, and giving them a few coppers or a trifling gift here and there. It seems to me that such strategy is often more effective than the traditional Roman policy of intimidation.

An hour later Joshua and a score of his followers descended the steps, and he remounted the long-suffering ass, whom I had had a couple of my men tend and water. Then he set off back the way he had come. By now most of his following were women, but I was surprised to note that the Magdalene was not amongst them.

It was not until later that I learned what had happened in the Court of the Gentiles.

*

I HAD dismissed my men, and was about to return to the *castra* to write my report. But first I dawdled a quarter of an hour by the Water Gate, marvelling at the beauty of the view of the Mounts of Olives and Offence as they faded into the evening mists, and the pale blue sky turned pink and orange. Why do men seek the gods in temples and holy places? Surely everything on earth is a manifestation of Jupiter. We have only to recognize him.

Some such vague musings occupied my mind as I turned to see the Lady Mary of Magdala making her way toward me. I realized that this was partly why I had stayed at my post overlong. I had hoped that not having departed with the man Joshua, she would nevertheless return to Bethany sooner or later, and so pass this way.

'It's good to see you,' I said with a smile.

'I was in the procession with my Lord.'

'I saw you. You looked happy.' I observed that her dark, gauntly beautiful face was now stained with tears. 'What has happened since?'

'My Lord's behaviour in the temple. I am very confused.'

'I've heard something of it, but not in any detail. I was more concerned with getting him safely out of Jerusalem, when he ceased to be my responsibility. He should be in Bethany within the hour. Will you join him?'

'Perhaps not yet. I need to think.'

'Would it help to tell me about it?'

She hesitated. 'Very well. My Lord became heated during debate with the money-changers.' She gave a short, bitter laugh. 'I say "heated," but that understates it. He seemed to lose control completely. Shouting and swearing, he overturned their tables, obtained a whip from I know not where, and lashed them with it. He was like a... it was as if he were possessed of a devil. He screamed that they had turned his father's house into a den of thieves. In fact, some thieves benefited from his action. Of the coins spilt on the floor, many were stolen.'

'I see. There was nothing to suggest anything amiss when he emerged from the temple grounds. Strange that he was not arrested.'

'The priests and guards seemed as taken aback as everyone else.'

'I'm sure they were.' I hesitated, uncertain what to say next. 'It must have been very difficult for you.'

'I was frightened of him. For the first time, I was frightened of him. I'm always terrified when men become angry. Because of my husband, of course. And other men, too. I am a coward.'

'Fear and cowardice are different things. I doubt if anyone is actually fearless. I'm certainly not.'

'I was desperately disappointed. When he entered the city I was so full of hope, but now... It was all very different from a Roman triumph. That's why I loved it. But you would not understand.'

'I understand very well. And I'm not as keen on Roman triumphs as you seem to think. Though I admit I've never seen one. But methinks they could teach your Joshua one thing. "Remember, thou art mortal." '

'Yes. I now believe he is mortal, as other men.' She paused. 'Having this talk has helped me,' she said quietly. 'And now I should return to Bethany.'

'I'll arrange for a couple of my men to escort you. With the *Secarii* about, It's not safe for a woman on her own.' I dared to add: 'Especially one who's known to be friendly with a Roman soldier.'

'I would rather you escort me yourself.'

'Very well,' I said, trying not to let her see how much I was overjoyed. 'But first I must write and deliver my report to Pilate.'

*

ON the way to Bethany in the moonlight we talked. I was determined not to say the usual sort of thing that women like to hear. As I remember we talked of serious matters, she attempting to explain her faith to me, I making reference to the classic philosophers, insofar as I had read and understood them, and throwing in some humble ideas of my own.

Atop the Mount of Olives we paused and looked back at Jerusalem, that savage, bigoted and dangerous city. Never before had it looked beautiful to me, but that night I swear it was, the roofs and columns of the temple gleaming in the moonlight, against the background of the velvet sky studded by a thousand stars. To the north the Great Bear and the Guards: south, the Lion; to the east the golden Bear-star, while to the west the Hunter and his ever-faithful Dogs were disappearing into the mists of the horizon. As usual in those desert lands, the night was cold. Many would have invited their woman to shelter under their cloak, or considered the surroundings romantic. Yet I judged it not the time nor place to tell her of my feelings again. She knew, anyway.

On the way down the mount I could have sworn I heard something. Or sensed something, at least. We were being followed, though the scattered trees and bushes provided but little cover. The man – I assumed it was a man – was taking a risk. But I said nothing, simply reflecting how fortunate it was that I had accompanied her.

We reached Bethany, and she indicated her address. I left her a few yards from its stable block. 'Did you have the feeling that we were being followed?' she asked.

I was surprised. 'Yes. But I didn't want to worry you. Didn't think you'd noticed.'

She nodded. 'So I thought. Take great care when returning.'

I tapped my sword. 'I reckon to be a match for any lone brigand. And there was but one.'

'I repeat, take great care. I shall pray for you. And from now on, my centurion, you never keep things from me, certainly not to try to protect me. Between us, it must always be the truth.'

Then we kissed.

*

THE JOURNEY back was something of an anticlimax, in that I neither saw nor sensed anyone. It occurred to me that were I to be attacked by a *Secarius*, my enquiry might be solved, for what more likely than that the assailant would be the killer of my friend Dio? But I saw nothing, save for a few moments as I began the descent from the Mount of Olives. Here the Temple came into view, and I thought I might have glimpsed a shadowy figure making its way into the South-East Gate. From a distance of half a mile I could not be certain, and there was not the slightest chance of making an identification.

But it merited enquiry. A quarter of an hour later I had crossed the Kidron Valley and scaled the escarpment to the South-East Gate, where I was duly stopped by a member of the Temple Guard. I knew the man slightly.

'State your business... Oh, it's you, centurion.'

'A man entered this gate less than half an hour since. Do you know him?'

'Yes, centurion. His name was Judas. An effete youth, always dressed in the latest fashion, who has attached himself to the man Joshua bar-Josef.'

'Why was he entering the Temple at this hour of the night?'

'He lodges here occasionally, in the Court of the Gentiles. He had accompanied Joshua to Bethany, but turned back upon discovering that no suitable lodgings were available there. His explanation seemed plausible, so we let him in.'

'Yes,' I agreed. 'Plausible. That's the word.'

Book IV

The Final Week

According to Mary

THE DAY after our Lord's triumphal entry into Jerusalem he announced that he would return to the holy city on the aftermorrow, Nisan 12. I am puzzled. From what he says it seems he intends to act in fulfilment of some ancient prophesies, but I am not well enough educated in Judaic law to understand him fully. I was in two minds whether to enter Jerusalem with him again, or to return before then, with the intention, I admit it, of trying to see my centurion again.

In the event the decision was made for me in unexpected fashion. It was the hour of sunset, and I was sitting sewing in the parlour of my lodging, together with other women, when a shadow fell across the doorway. It was the laundry-maid, Salome. She looked around, then seeing me, she hurried over.

'I should like a word with you, *domina*. Outside.'

'Of course.'

In the cloudless sky the low sun made us squint. Once in the stable yard we turned our backs on it. 'What is it, Salome?'

Her question surrised me. 'You know the governor, the Dominus Pontius Pilatus, is that not so, *domina*?'

'I have met him a couple of times. He visited the centre once, and seemed to appreciate the work I was doing there.'

'Dio said …' her little face crumpled, and then recovered.

'Dio said, that Roman officials everywhere are very suspicious of clubs and organizations. The governor may have visited just to satisfy himself that it was not a disguise for a group intent upon what they call *maiestas*.'

I smiled. 'I'm sure that was part of the reason why he visited, yes. Upon my assuring him that men played no part in the organization, he seemed satisfied. He even congratulated me on my good work. A few days later I was surprised to receive a donation from him.'

'So he is a good man?'

'To the best of my knowledge, he is a conscientious Roman governor. And he has a reputation for financial honesty, which is by no means the case with all of them.'

'But he is not popular.'

'No Roman official is popular. And the feeling is mutual. He dislikes the Jews in general, I think.'

'I meant, is he a man one can rely on?'

I took time to reply, then did so with another question. 'In relation to what?'

Again she hesitated. 'I mean, *domina*, suppose, just suppose he came across evidence enabling him to identify Dio's murderer. Would he act on it?'

'Almost certainly, I should think. Why not?'

'Even if it were someone he had not wanted it to be? Someone who was of use to Rome. An informer, say?'

'The murdered man was a Roman soldier. I think the Prefect would want to arrest the culprit.'

'Dio was but an auxiliary, *domina*. Not a Roman citizen.'

'True. But from what Teutonicus told me, his loyalty to Rome was undoubted. That would count for a good deal.' I paused. 'Can you tell me what this information is?'

Again she hesitated. 'May I think about it, *domina*?'

'Of course.' I made the decision. 'I shall be setting out for Jerusalem tomorrow. If you come with me, it will be convenient for you should you decide to speak to the Prefect. And in any case, we can await the arrival of our Lord.'

Strictly speaking I could have insisted upon her travelling with me, for in order to rescue her from her previous employment I had had to purchase her. Of course I would have freed her any time she asked, but she preferred to remain my slave, arguing that she felt safer under my legal protection. And indeed it seemed to help her on this occasion.

'Thank you, *domina*,' she said, smiling. 'I should like that.'

*

THE INTERVIEW with the Prefect went better than I had feared. My centurion was present part of the time, and gave Salome a good reference. In short, she suspected the man Judas bar-Simon of the murder, on the basis of claims she had heard him make to one of the leading Zealots, a man named Izaak bar-Lavan.

Everyone who knew Judas realized that he was a boastful fool whose word could not be relied on, for which reason I had half-expected Pilate to dismiss the girl's story as worthless. To my surprise he listened with attention throughout, occasionally asking a pertinent question, and at the end promised to look into the matter.

Perhaps I have misjudged the Prefect. When he visited the centre months ago he showed more patience and interest in my work than I had expected. He seems a cold, unfeeling man, but not without some idea of truth and justice.

*

I JOINED my Lord again as he entered into Jerusalem the next day. This time there were no cheering crowds, nor palm leaves. Indeed I had to confess to a feeling of disappointment.

There were but two incidents of note. About the fifth hour we reached the Fig Tree Tavern, in the City of David, and, being a little tired and hungry, our Lord asked for something to eat.

The proprietor, a surly fellow, said that he had nothing left but a few meat pies, whereupon our Lord enquired whether they had been prepared in accordance with Kosher laws. 'Well, how should I know?' demanded the proprietor. 'I just get my meat from the temple, same as everyone else.'

'The temple rules are often administered in slovenly fashion nowadays, you know that.'

'I know nothing of the sort. Meat from the temple is good enough for me, or anyone else.'

'Not for me, it isn't. I'll have some figs.'

'Figs, in spring? You'll have to wait a few months.'

'Surely you've got some dried and preserved.'

'Kept back for regular customers. Now, do you want a meat pie or not?'

But our Lord had turned his back on him. 'I curse this inn,' he said loudly, 'and the fig tree in its yard. May it never bear fruit again.'

Whereat he and his disciples resumed their march to the temple.

*

MY Lord spent most of the day in preaching. I followed him avidly, paying close attention to all that he said, memorizing his comments and particularly the parables, pondering them carefully and trying to interpret them correctly. By the time we reached the temple it was approaching sunset.

I may have mentioned that not all twelve of my Lord's disciples accompanied him during his time in Jerusalem. Simon Zelotes, his son Judas, and Levi the publican were usually missing.

Just as my Lord was about to begin the ascent to the temple building Levi made his way through the crowd, using his considerable bulk to push people out of the way. 'I have a query, my lord.'

Joshua raised a hand. 'Speak.'

Levi brandished a silver coin, a Roman sestertius if I was not mistaken. 'Is it lawful, my lord, to pay tribute to Caesar, or not?'

One or two of those in the crowd gasped at the temerity of the question. It put my Lord in an impossible position. If he said no, he would be liable to be charged with *maiestas*, high treason against the Emperor. If yes, the Pharisees might consider him guilty of blasphemy, the only crime committed directly against Almighty God himself.

My Lord held out his hand in mute invitiation to Levi to hand him the coin. The eyes of all in the crowd were glued to him. His disciples in particular looked apprehensive. A couple of nearby Roman soldiers also evinced an interest.

'Whose picture is this?' he enquired, indicating the graven image of Tiberius on the obverse of the coin.

Levi frowned. 'Why, Caesar's.'

My Lord nodded and handed it back to him. 'Render unto Caesar the things that are Caesar's, and unto God the things that are God's.'

The Roman soldiers, I thought, seemed a good deal happier with this answer than the Jewish faithful. For my part, I decided that I must think about things on my own. It is strange that I do not ask my Lord for his guidance as much as I did formerly. Is that a sign of my increasing maturity, or of the Serpent entering my heart? I wish I knew.

*

IT WAS the late afternoon of the following day, *Yom Chamishi*. My knees were shaking as I mounted the stairs to the upper room belonging to the man Moshe. The building had formerly been a textile warehouse, and its owner was currently engaged in converting the first floor into a set of apartments for him and his family. It looked bleak and undistinguished enough, until I set foot on the stairs.

From then on events seemed increasingly unreal. 'Unreal' is not quite the word I am seeking. They had a dream-like quality, as if I were a playing out a previously rehearsed part, and had no power to alter what had previously been ordained. I tell myself that this is because my Lord is fulfilling the ancient prophecies, and we have no power to interfere with the course of events. I wondered what my centurion would have made of that argument. I would rather that he might have been present, but no doubt his duties required him to be elsewhere.

There might have been a couple of dozen persons there

when I arrived, men and women in approximately equal numbers, but no children. Some were already seated, while others stood about chatting in small groups.

The tables extended around three sides of the room to form a sort of hollow square with one side missing. The centre of the top table was vacant, our Lord and his closest disciples not yet having arrived. Among those present I recognized Judas Secarius, and the Essenes Tomasso and Thaddeus. They were soon joined by Simon Zelotes.

Looking around for a friend, I saw the taxman Levi. Fulsome in his greeting, he invited me to sit opposite him on one of the side tables. This suited me well, as I had no wish to draw attention to myself. Besides, Levi is an easy man to talk to, and whilst I have some misgivings regarding his means of livelihood, I never fear his attempting anything ungentlemanly. He is faithful to his fat, plain wife of many years.

Soon afterward we were joined by the girl I now tended to regard as my best female friend, little Salome. She had also suffered at the hands of men, and was a sinner, albeit to a far lesser extent than me. In view of her age, little more than half of mine, I was inclined to regard her as the daughter I had never had. I was delighted that she was coming to recognize my Lord and the momentous nature of his teachings.

In not taking a prominent position Levi was alone amongst the disciples, who were otherwise occupied in stationing themselves at the ends of the top table. The five centre places remained vacant.

There was a stir, some whispering: 'He's coming! He's coming!' before our Lord's two best beloved disciples, the fisherman Simon Peter, and Jacob the son of Zebadiah, in turn showed their heads through the open trapdoor to the stairs. Next came their respective brothers: Andrew and Johan, before all four stood aside and gestured to the staircase. Those of us who had been seated stood. And finally our Lord appeared, bare-headed as ever, raising his hand, nodding, and smiling faintly. Escorted by the others, he made his way to the top table. The God-given light from the window behind fell across his dear face, illuminating his countenance far more impressively than the artificial haloes which disfigure the icons of the various pagan sun deities.

Our Lord took position and indicated that we also could sit. After blessing the meal he permitted us to eat. It was but a simple repast of unleavened bread, fish, and wine. Occasionally our Lord would answer a question, often using one of his parables to illustrate his reply, but for the most part he talked with his nearest disciples. At one stage his conversation with Simon Peter became animated, Peter shaking his head vigorously.

Judas Secarius sat at the far end of the top table. Once I made eye contact with him. He looked away hurriedly. Was this the mere embarrassment associated with such accidental contact, or was there more to it? Certainly he seemed very ill at ease.

For my part, I mostly talked quietly with my two companions, Salome and Levi. Both, like myself, seemed to feel that we were on the brink of something truly momentous, which we were powerless to prevent or even influence. My main memory of them is that the girl showed herself far more intelligent, and the publican more sensitive, than in my arrogance I had previously been inclined to believe.

As dusk descended, our Lord got to his feet. We all did

likewise as a sign of respect. He said, 'Now I go about my father's business.' Glancing at Peter and Jacob, he continued: 'None shall follow except those closest to me.'

Whereupon he left, together with his two chosen disciples. The others continued talking amongst themselves, often frowning or shaking their heads. It seemed not only that they were worried, but that there was no great measure of agreement between them. After a brief lull in the conversation, Judas Secarius stood and made some furtive excuse, as if he needed to leave the room upon a necessary occasion. He did not return.

The rest of those present had remained silent for a while, before resuming our discourse uncertainly. We were all, I think, rather puzzled. Not only had our Lord's teaching this evening lacked its usual force and confidence, but his intentions were far from clear. Eventually Levi seemed to come to a decision.

'I don't like it,' he said firmly. 'I don't like it at all. And whether our Lord wills it or no, I'm going to follow him. He may be in danger. Whether a middle-aged, overweight and unarmed publican can defend him effectively, I rather doubt, but methinks it's my duty to try.'

A great load was lifted from my mind. This man had shown me the way. 'And I'm a mere woman,' I said, 'but I shall accompany you.'

According to Pilate

TEUTONICUS duly confirmed that following the tumultuous events resulting from his supposedly triumphal entry into Jerusalem Joshua had returned to Bethany without incident. As I recall, it was the afternoon of the *dies Martis* before there occurred anything else worthy of note.

'Forgive me, *domine*.'

A slave was hovering at the door.

'What is it?'

'Two women beg leave to see you, *domine*, regarding the murder of the *dominus* Dio Syrianus. They say it's urgent.'

I laid the papers I had been working on aside. 'I'll see them, then. Send them in.'

He bowed and departed, to return moments later with the Magdalene woman and a slave girl. I indicated to the former that she should be seated.

'You have information regarding the murder of the young centurion Dio Syrianus?'

'Not me, *domine*, but' – she gestured at the slave girl – 'Salome here.'

I could scarce suppress a smile, for the shrinking, frightened creature bore but slight resemblance to her notorious namesake, the stepdaughter of Herod Antipas.

'Is Salome one of the girls from your refuge?'

'She was, my lord, but is now employed at the *castra* in Caesarea.'

'Does she bear a good character?'

'She has worked there only a short time, my lord, but I understand that thus far she has given satisfaction.' The woman hesitated. 'She is known to the centurion Rotgarius Teutonicus, who arranged her employment there.'

His headquarters being in the praetorium next door, I told the slave to summon him. Meanwhile nothing would be gained from the girl by frightening her further. On the other hand I despise the avuncular approach.

'What is it you can tell me?' I asked, addressing her in the Greek tongue.

She swallowed, and replied hesitantly. It soon became apparent that she was not at home in the language. 'I... believe I know the man responsible for the murder, my lord.'

'And who is that?'

'It is a man called Judas bar-Simon, my lord, one of the disciples of Joshua bar-Abbas.'

'And how do you know of his guilt?'

'He admitted it, my lord. I heard him.'

Outside came the sounds of marching feet. A slave escorted the centurion in. He gave the imperial salute.

'At ease, centurion.' As I spoke the words I became conscious of the fact that the women relaxed more than he did. The Magdalene woman's expression made it apparent to the meanest intelligence that she was hopelessly in love with him, while the slave girl looked at him with pitiable gratitude, doubtless as a friendly face among intimidating surroundings.

'What can you tell me about this girl, centurion?'

'She works at the camp at Caesarea, sir, where she has been employed this last three months as a cleaner and laundress.'

'Does she bear a good character?'

'She is a hard worker, sir, and to the best of my knowledge no-one has any complaints about her.'

'Has she resumed her former occupation as a whore?'

'No, sir.'

'Again, to the best of your knowledge.'

Teutonicus allowed himself the ghost of a smile. 'I think I should have heard had she done so.'

I nodded and turned to the girl. 'Proceed.'

'The man Judas is a Zealot, my lord, and calls himself *Secarius*, by which nickname he is beginning to be known.'

'We know of the man, of course. Go on.'

She did so, Teutonicus translating for her when necessary. 'He is known for foolish boasting, *domine*, after the manner of young men. For that reason many do not believe him.'

'So why did you believe him when he admitted it to you?'

'He did not admit it to me, my lord. I overheard him.'

'Explain.'

'I had followed him, my lord, after the arrival of our Lord Joshua on Sunday.'

'Why should you do that? Indeed what were you doing in Jerusalem?'

Again she started to stumble over her words. Teutonicus said, 'She loved Dio Syrianus, sir. They were planning to marry. When he failed to keep a rendezvous with her, she reported him missing. I was with her when the news of his death came through.'

'So this is the girl of whom you told me.'

'Yes, sir.'

'How do you know they planned to marry?'

'He had told me so, sir.'

'Did he know she was a former whore?'

'Oh, yes.'

'What was your attitude to that?'

'I told him that he had obviously given the matter much thought, and that whatever he decided he could rely on my continued support and friendship.'

The slave girl had started to cry silently, and the Magdalene woman to comfort her.

'What is she doing in Jerusalem?'

'She accompanied the First Cohort, sir, as a cleaner and laundress.'

'I see.' I turned to the girl. 'You may continue.'

Again she gulped, then said, 'It was the day before our Lord Joshua entered the city. A man called Simon, Judas's father I think, was leaving the premises of one Moshe, when Judas approached and spoke to him.'

'Where did this take place?'

'In the Essene quarter, my lord, near to the house of the High Priest.'

'How came you to be there?'

'I knew Simon by sight, my lord, and knew that he was reputed to be a Zealot. I therefore followed them.'

'Why?'

'I hoped to discover the man who had killed my... Dio Syrianus.'

Teutonicus intervened. 'I had given her leave of absence, my lord. She told me she was determined to find out who had killed her lover.' He shrugged and pulled a rueful face. 'I judged it useless to try to dissuade her.'

'Just as well you did not, as it happens.' I turned to the slave girl. 'Go on.'

'Judas said that he was high in the councils of the Zealots, and had little time to spare, as he was on his way to meet one of them. I accordingly followed him as unobtrusively as I could. He made his way to a tavern near the theatre, called the Olive Branch. I hung around near the entrance, pretending to ply my former trade.'

'Did any men approach you?'

'Only two, my lord. It was after all the middle of the day. I told them I was waiting for another client. A man entered and made his way over to the corner table where Judas was sitting.'

'Did you know this man?'

'My lord, no. But I heard Judas call him bar-Lavan.'

Izaak bar-Lavan was a well-known Zealot and agitator. I had permitted him to remain at liberty thus far in the hope that he might lead us to others.

'How did you come to hear what they said?'

'Judas speaks rather loudly, my lord. The other man had to tell him to lower his voice more than once.'

'I see. What did Judas say that was so incriminating?'

'He said,' the girl's voice faltered, ' "I stabbed that Roman bastard the other day, you know." '

I frowned. 'Did he just volunteer the information? Surely he didn't blurt it out in the course of normal conversation?'

'No, my lord. It seemed to me that he was trying to persuade the man bar-Lavan to admit him into their organization. When he seemed reluctant, Judas told him what he had done, in the hope, I suppose, that it would serve as some sort of credential.'

'What was bar-Lavan's response?'

'He seemed annoyed, and said that no such action should have been taken without the authority of the organization.'

I considered. 'Is that all?'

She nodded. 'Yes, my lord. The conversation came to an end shortly afterwards, without, it seemed to me, any agreement having been reached between them.'

'You may be required to repeat this under oath. Do you understand?'

'Yes, my lord.'

'Where are you living now?'

'Bethany, my lord. Lodging with the Lady Magdalene.'

'Henceforth she is responsible for you, and ensuring that you attend any enquiry.' I nodded dismissal. 'Very well. You may leave us.'

As she was taking her out, the Magdalene woman turned and said fiercely, 'She is a good girl, my lord. She would not lie.'

'I shall take what she said under consideration. You will hear from us further.'

After they had left, I turned to Teutonicus. 'What do you make of it all?'

'I believe she is telling the truth, sir. The man Judas certainly has some questions to answer.'

Teutonicus had already told me of the man's spying on him and the Magdalene woman the night before last. I nodded.

'His behaviour grows ever more suspicious. What do you know of these women?'

'The *dominus* is aware of how I feel about the Magdalene. I know the girl slightly. There seems no reason for her to lie.'

171

'Perhaps not. But what she said falls far short of proving the Secarius man guilty. All seem to agree that he is a posturing adolescent, pretending to be a dangerous agitator. Or fighter for freedom, as he would doubtless put it. It's not even clear that he's a Zealot.'

'His father is, sir. The lad just seems to hang around on the fringe of the organization.'

'It seems to me,' I said slowly, 'that the response of bar-Lavan may have been significant.'

'I respectfully agree, sir. Had the Zealots been responsible for the assassination, he would have known that Judas was lying. Yet the signs are that he did not. In effect he said: "You shouldn't have done it without our agreement. Don't do anything similar again." '

'See the man bar-Lavan anyway, and find out what he can tell you.'

'Certainly, sir. I was about to suggest that myself.' He smiled. 'I think I can promise that my method of interrogation will be a little more forceful than the *dominus's* questioning of the slave girl.'

I smiled in turn. 'I should certainly hope so.'

*

NEXT day Herod Antipas sent for me. Coming from a mere tetrarch, I decided that this was an impertinence, and returned a message saying that I was busy. As I had expected, he turned up later on in very ill humour, demanding that I take action against the man Joshua, who had attempted to dissuade people from paying their taxes. Having had no report to this effect from my own sources,

I did not believe him. I told him that so far as I was aware the man had demonstrated no hostility towards Rome, and I judged it best to take no action beyond keeping him under surveillance. After much argument to little effect, the Tetrarch left me, in the worst possible humour, saying that the Emperor should hear of my dereliction of duty. He has threatened the same thing before, on more than one occasion. If he has ever carried out these threats, it would seem that neither the Emperor nor his henchman Sejanus are interested enough to contact me. For all that, on this occasion I think it advisable to send immediate dispatches to Capri advising the Emperor of the present position, thus ensuring that he receives my version of matters first.

*

The *Dies Jovis* brought more disturbing news of the man Joshua and his activities. I sent for Teutonicus again. He had a scroll tucked under his arm.

'I see you've brought your latest report.'

'Incomplete, I'm afraid, sir. There are one or two matters to add. I brought it with me as an aid to memory.'

'Summarize it.'

'The man Joshua entered the city again yesterday morning. And yet again he became embroiled in minor disturbance. First there was some sort of pathetic dispute with an innkeeper who either couldn't or wouldn't serve him the food he desired ...'

'Spare me, please.'

'Nearer the Temple there was the coin incident, of which the *dominus* may already have heard.'

'When he tried to dissuade people from paying their taxes.'

'That may have been the version reaching you from other sources, sir, but I was present and can assure you that what he said was precisely the reverse, namely that one should render unto Caesar the things which were Caesar's. I assumed that included lawful taxes.'

'I see.' I took time for consideration. 'What else?'

'My latest information, sir, not yet in my report here, is that the man has booked an upper room in the Essene quarter, not far from the house of the High Priest. He and some fifty of his followers, both men and women, propose to occupy it this afternoon.'

'For what purpose?'

'It seems a meal has been ordered for mid-afternoon, when they will presumably be making further plans.'

'I should like to know what those plans are.'

Teutonicus smiled. 'I dare say that could be arranged, sir.'

'Any idea what they might be?'

He shrugged. 'I doubt if they know themselves yet, and that includes the man Joshua. There seems to be a curious lack of leadership and direction at the moment. One or two of his men are complaining about it.'

'Well, if you're sure you can find out, there's no point in trying to guess in advance. But what of the murder of your friend Dio? Are they involved, or not?'

Teutonicus paused for several seconds. Not, I judged, through evasiveness or indecision, rather to make certain that he expressed himself accurately. 'They are unlikely to have been involved *en masse*, or one or more of them would have talked. Anyway, at the time of the murder only four were even in Caesarea. The others were fifty miles away with their leader, in the Jordan Valley, south of Lake Tiberias.'

'The four in Caesarea being Levi, Barthol, the Zealot Simon, and his son, Judas.'

'Correct, sir.'

'Plus the Magdalene woman.'

He nodded. 'Yes, sir.'

'What is you opinion of the affair?'

'Dio Syrianus was making his enquiries at short notice. It's unlikely that anyone in the district could have known of his whereabouts in advance. So either the killing was a spur-of-the-moment decision, or he had been followed. I think the latter more likely. He was stabbed in the back, which suggests premeditation rather than a quarrel which got out of hand. For the reasons I've given Your Excellency, I don't think the Zealot organization was involved. Which does not prevent one of their members acting on his own initiative.'

'Which of those you've mentioned would you favour?'

'Several of Levi's staff confirm that he was in his office at the time. Barthol has shown no previous signs of extremism. Judas is a weakling. The lady of Magdala – I can't pretend not to be emotionally involved with her, but,' he shook his head emphatically, 'No.' He paused briefly. 'None of them is impossible – Levi may have got his men to lie for him, Barthol certainly had the opportunity, weaklings have committed murder before now, and I might be hopelessly wrong about the woman. But to my mind Simon bar-Cleophas is by far the likeliest. He's a Zealot, claims to have been alone in his lodgings at the time, and didn't report finding the dead body.'

'Did he not?'

'I suspected from the start that the man knew more than he was admitting to us. The other day I took a chance, sent for him out of the blue, as it were, and told him that he had been seen with the body. He caved in and admitted it. Said that he had not dared report it for fear of being suspected of involvement in the crime.'

'I suppose that's possible.'

'Yes,' said Teutonicus, his voice heavy with doubt. 'It's possible.'

'Well, I'll tell you what I propose. Simon is to be arrested and interrogated thoroughly. From the sound of things he should be at this meal they're planning.'

'Very good, sir.'

'And we'll see what Joshua can tell us about him. If he's really the man of peace that some of his followers claim, he may be prepared to help us, as he did up to a point over the issue of taxes.'

'Might I make a suggestion, sir?'

'Of course.'

'Rather than arrest Joshua at the meal, entering the property by force and risking trouble with his followers, it might be possible to detain him quietly later.'

'I'm not sure I understand you.'

'To judge from his past behaviour, sir, after a day's work he likes time in a quiet place, either completely on his own, or with none but his most favoured disciples. I could approach him with a handful of men, explain our business in a more or less friendly, if firm, way and bring him to Your Excellency with a minimum of disturbance. Hopefully any followers with him would see reason.'

I nodded. 'That seems a good idea. It'll mean working into the night, but it can't be helped. The time element is becoming critical. Tomorrow is the *Dies Veneris*, when their Sabbath will begin at sunset. I'm particularly anxious not to take any action after that. Arresting anyone on the Sabbath would be sure to cause trouble.'

'Quite so, sir. I'll try to keep everything as quiet as possible. And Simon could be arrested at the same time.'

'Yes, arresting him is just as important. Like you, so far as the murder is concerned, I'm inclined to think he's our man.'

According to Simon

THE MORNING of the day following our Lord's entry into Jerusalem, I received an unwelcome summons to the praetorium, where I soon found myself before the desk of the centurion Teutonicus.

'I want a word with you, Zelotes,' he said discourteously.

My heart stopped momentarily, but I managed to say: 'Why? What have I done?'

'It's what you haven't done that concerns me. Why didn't you tell me that you'd found Dio's body?'

Thoughts chased one another round in my head. How did he know? Or was he bluffing? I decided to play for time. 'And what makes you think that?'

'We have a witness. Two witnesses, in fact. One of them at the corner of the street, the other looking out of a second-floor window. Both saw you leaning over something lying on the ground. When you moved away they identified it as a dead body. Come now, admit it. You will only make things worse for yourself by continued denial.'

'Who are these witnesses?' I demanded.

'Never mind that. They'll be produced in due course, when you appear before the Prefect charged with murder and *maiestas*.' He smiled in a manner far from pleasant.

I assured him of my innocence, but he would have none of it. 'Why didn't you report finding the body?' he repeated.

'I was afraid of being unjustly suspected.'

'Well, justly or unjustly, you're suspected now. Is that the best you can do for an explanation?'

'It's the truth,' I protested. 'With the victim being a Roman soldier, I knew the Prefect would want to attach blame to someone. He wouldn't be particular who.'

'Nonsense. He considers it all the more important to discover the real culprit.'

'Well, that's what I thought, anyway.'

He was clearly not satisfied, but after further argument let me go on stricter terms, namely that I should report to him daily in future. I was uneasily aware that I stood on the very brink of arrest, and thereafter it would be even more difficult to convince the Romans of my innocence.

*

I SAW my son again a couple of days later. He visited about the fifth hour, and invited me to take drink with him at the Fig Tree Tavern. It is not far from the Hippodrome, and a favourite haunt of those employed in chariot racing, not to mention some of the Zealot leaders. I suspect that hanging about amidst the famous and notorious increases his sense of self-importance. We sat in a corner with drinks before us.

'Is this a mere social outing with your father,' I asked, 'or more serious business?'

'Business.'

'Go on.'

'I have been in touch with your Zealot friends. They are disappointed at not having heard from you for some time. Are you still interested in their work?'

In fact I had made a point of keeping in touch with them, but the Zealots would have had more sense than to disclose the fact to my son. Indeed none but a fool would disclose *anything* to him, unless they were prepared to have it revealed to the Romans. For which reason it seemed advisable to imply that my opinions were decidedly less militant than in truth they were.

'Since you mention it, I begin to have doubts. I have been wondering whether more might be achieved by peaceful means than by taking on the whole military power of Rome.'

'God would defend the right.'

'He shows few signs of having done so thus far.'

Judas looked shocked. 'That is blasphemy.'

'Not at all. God's purpose may best be achieved by co-operation with Rome, rather than conflict.'

'Well, it seems that your associates do not agree with you. If you are intending to continue as one of their number, they require you to demonstrate more enthusiasm for their cause than you have done of late.'

I had no idea whom he had been talking to. None of my Zealot colleagues had suggested any such thing to me. I suspected he was simply attributing his own opinions to them.

'And how am I to do that?' I enquired without interest.

He shrugged. 'Commit some act of opposition to Roman rule. Covert, if you prefer it.'

'Such as?'

'Damaging some of the facilities they have provided. Roads, building works, aquaducts.'

'Thus inconveniencing or endangering our own people.'

'Or more direct action against the Roman military.'

'Like killing that auxiliary the other day? That's caused enough trouble already. Who was responsible, by the way?'

'The *Secarii* don't confide in me to that extent.'

It would have surprised me had the *Secarii* confided in Judas to *any* extent. As with the Zealots, he was boasting of a familiarity with them which he did not in fact enjoy. Either group might have amused themselves by feeding him false information.

'I must see if I can do better,' I said sarcastically.

The irony escaped him. 'They'll be pleased to hear that,' he assured me. 'Elias bar-Abel drinks here most afternoons. Why not have a word with him and explain yourself?'

Bar-Abel was leader of the Zealot cause in south Jerusalem, and as it happened I had intended speaking to him anyway. But by now I had had enough of explaining myself to Judas, and turned his question back on him.

'Do they know you're in the pay of the Romans?'

'I am scarcely in their pay,' he said huffily. 'I've simply agreed to co-operate with them on an informal basis. Precisely how I take advantage of the situation I have not yet decided. Conveying false intelligence to them would be one way of furthering our cause …'

My son has always imagined himself far cleverer than in truth he is. Reneging on an agreement with the Roman authorities struck me as insane folly, and I said so. Our potential dispute was forestalled by a commotion from outside.

'Now what's up?' I demanded of a servant who was hovering about.

'An awkward customer out front, sir,' he suggested, 'from the sound of things.'

I was about to dismiss the matter as of no moment when I recognized one or two of the raised voices. So apparently did Judas. We left our drinks half-consumed and hurried to the front courtyard.

It was as I thought. The difficult customer was none other than Joshua bar-Abbas. 'I'm hungry,' he said angrily. 'By the terms of your licence, you're bound to serve any traveller who calls at your tavern.'

The proprietor, Aaron bar-Nahum, as I knew from experience, was not a man to avoid a quarrel if he considered himself in the right. 'Then I'll serve you,' he said, albeit in a far from servile manner. 'You can have one of my meat pies.'

'And how do I know they're Kosher?'

'Because I say so, for one thing. And it's difficult to get anything in Jerusalem that isn't.'

Which was true enough, for the priests guarded their slaughterhouse jealously and effectively controlled all sales of meat.

'I don't want meat, anyway,' said Joshua peevishly. 'I want figs.'

'Figs in Nissan? You'll have to wait another four or five months. Everyone knows that.'

'Dried figs.'

'I haven't got any. Except for regular customers,' the innkeeper added as an afterthought. 'I've offered you refreshment, which is all I'm bound to do. You've no right to decide the menu. Report me to the Romans if you're not satisfied.'

'Do you know who you're talking to?'

'Yes. Joshua bar-Josef, a joiner's son from a back-of-beyond place in Galilee, who's got too big for his boots.'

He laughed heartily. 'Can any good thing come out of Nazareth?'

Joshua cast his eyes up to heaven. 'Lord, I curse this Fig Tree Inn. Let none ever obtain figs or refreshment here again.'

At which he took himself off, together with the handful of disciples accompanying him. I felt no inclination to follow. It occurred to me that for the second time in four days Joshua bar-Abbas had shown himself to be very far from perfect.

*

I SPOKE to bar-Abel an hour later, when he called in at the Fig Tree for a drink, as was his custom. A hatchet-faced man with an occasional mad gleam in his eye, rather as I imagine the prophets of ancient time, he holds strange visionary ideas of how a holy war should be waged against the Romans, and has no time for my more practical attitude to the question. It was particularly disappointing to discover that he was not prepared to authorize me to take any action on their behalf, either diplomatic or more militant. Indeed, he as good as said that so far as he was concerned my membership of our Lord's chosen twelve meant that I hardly qualified as a Zealot at all.

He also mentioned that my son had been making a nuisance of himself by falsely confessing to his colleague bar-Lavan of having killed the Roman, Dio Silvanus. Whilst sharing his irritation in this respect, I saw no reason why it should have so prejudiced bar-Abel against me.

For a while now I have been considering my position

with the Zealots. It may be that the time has come to sever connection with a group which clearly has no sympathy with any but those who share their own bigoted ideals. I must give the matter further thought.

*

THAT same afternoon, Nisan 12, I was present at the incident which more than any other seems likely to determine our Lord's fate. I had visited the upper room in the Essene quarter to confirm the booking, only to discover that Joshua and his men had already done so. Moshe believed that that they were now on their way to the temple. I hoped, but did not say, that I hoped Joshua would perform there better than he had earlier in the week. These last few days he had seemed to be in an unpredictable mood, to say the least.

As I neared the temple he was there indeed, though surrounded by a crowd much smaller than that marking his progress the previous Sunday. Not for the first time he was in dispute with a number of scribes and Pharisees, waving his arms and hands in animated fashion as he made his points. And not for the first time he was resorting to *ad hominem* arguments, calling them judgmental sinners and hypocrites.

It was one of the disciples, Levi the tax-collector, who aggravated the trouble by producing a coin, as I now recalled he had threatened to do. 'Tell me, master,' he said, 'is it lawful for men to pay tribute to Caesar, or not?'

That, surely, was the question. There could be no further equivocation or dissembling. Either he supported Judaean independence, or the rule of Caesar. He had no other choice.

'Hand it to me,' he said. Looking puzzled, Levi did so.

Joshua held it up. It was, I perceived, a silver Roman sestertius, bearing on the obverse a portrait of the present Emperor. Some of the Pharisees winced. It is well known that they strongly disapprove of the display of any image, especially in the vicinity of the temple.

'Whose picture is this?' he asked.

'Caesar's,' Levi replied, still seeming puzzled.

'Then render unto Caesar those things that are Caesar's, and unto God those things that are God's.'

This was not what had been expected, certainly not by me. One of the Pharisees gasped. A couple of others shook their heads. A Roman auxiliary standing nearby – there is always one nowadays – smiled. Evidently the reply had suited him far better. I glimpsed someone furtively making haste to leave the crowd. I should have guessed. It was Judas, probably to convey a garbled version of the incident to the Romans.

Joshua flipped the coin back to Levi, and continued unperturbed up the staircase to the outer court of the temple, that of the Gentiles. Following him was a crowd of perhaps a couple of dozen people, including three or four of his chosen twelve. Most of the rest were women, amongst whom I noticed that most fanatic of his followers, Mary of Magdala.

I remained with them about an hour, listening to our Lord's preachings and parables, including an intriguing one about talents, which I confess I did not entirely comprehend. It seemed to me that the servant who hid his talent so as to be certain of returning it to his master without risk had done nothing very wrong, yet his master was angry with him, telling him that he should have loaned it to money-lenders at interest. And for not so lending them the money the servant was cast into outer darkness, and eternal punishment. Yet these money-lenders are the very same persons that our Lord scourged and reviled the other day. I must ask him to explain his meaning. The meal tomorrow, to which I have naturally been invited, should provide the opportunity.

The other teaching I remember clearly concerned wise and foolish virgins, and obviously meant that we must prepare for the coming of the Kingdom of God on earth without delay, at which time all persons shall be separated into sheep and goats, namely those to be saved, and those to be damned for all eternity.

Our Lord has said that this generation shall not pass away before these things take place. I have the strong suspicion that he expects the great day to arrive much sooner even than that, possibly this same weekend. Which is very disturbing. For like all men, I am a sinner, and have done things difficult to excuse. I must make confession to him. Meanwhile I decided to make my way back to my lodgings to bring my notes up to date.

*

AS I sit writing these notes in my chamber, I cannot help but speculate about tomorrow's meal. It seems clear that our Lord intends to give us further instruction regarding his teachings, perhaps with a view to our spreading his word independently. What a prospect that would be! For in that way the Holy Word of God would reach more people more quickly. Even our Lord cannot be in two or more places at once. But it is vitally important that we understand him correctly, rather than risk spreading false doctrines.

What a privilege to be amongst those chosen to convey the news of the forthcoming apocalypse, and needless to say to do so as a matter of extreme urgency. For like the wise and foolish virgins, we know not when the great day will be upon us.

My account of our Lord's latest entry into Jerusalem and his teachings there is now almost up to date. There is just one other matter about which I will speak to him after the meal, and hope to obtain his advice. This time tomorrow I shall add it to these notes, with more detail than I have provided hitherto.

The candle is burning low, and about to gutter. Shadows flicker around the walls. The rest of my notes I shall postpone until writing them up in full tomorrow evening. I take a final glance around the darkling room before turning in.

*

HERE the manuscript of Simon bar-Cleophas of Canaan, known as Zelotes, comes to an end. His body was found in the woods near Gethsemane in the early hours of Nisan 14, or by the Roman reckoning, the seventh day before the Ides of April. It bore multiple stab wounds.

According to the Centurion

IN ACCORDANCE with the terms of his release, Simon Zelotes had to report to military headquarters every other day at noon. The meant that he was due to visit on the *dies Martis*, but being far from satisfied with his account of matters I decided to have him brought before me the previous day. I judged that the unexpected arrest might disconcert him to the extent of loosening his tongue, and so it proved.

'I want a word with you, Zelotes,' I said brusquely.

'Why? What have I done?'

'It's what you haven't done that concerns me. Why didn't you tell me that you'd found Dio's body?'

He made incoherent noises of expostulation which made his guilt so apparent that he could then hardly deny it. My bluff had succeeded.

'I… er… how… What makes you suggest such a thing?'

Avoiding the lie direct. A familiar reaction. Lacking any such scruples, I said confidently, 'We have a witness. Two, indeed. One walking down the street like yourself, the other looking out of the window of an insula block. Both saw you leaning over something, which on closer inspection proved to be the body of Syrianus. Come, now, admit it. You will only make things worse for yourself by continued denial.'

'Who are these witnesses?'

'Never mind. They will be produced in due course, when you appear before the Prefect charged with murder and *maiestas*.'

By now his demoralization was virtually complete. 'I… I didn't do it. I didn't do it.'

'Then why didn't you report finding his body?'

'I was afraid I'd be unjustly suspected.'

'Well, justly or unjustly, you're suspected now. Explain yourself more satisfactorily.'

'With the victim being a Roman soldier, I knew Pil… the Prefect would want to attach blame to someone. He wouldn't be particular who.'

'Nonsense. All the more important to discover the real culprit.'

'Well, that's what I thought, anyway.'

I did not disclose the fact that the physician had given his opinion that the deceased had been dead between one and two hours when he examined him, whereas Zelotes had come across the body a mere half hour before. After further threats and intimidation I let him go, on condition that henceforth he reported to us every day.

As for Judas, he was due to report on the morrow anyway. I decided to leave seeing him till then.

*

NEXT day I received further information regarding the widow Eunice. My duties in Jerusalem had made it impractical for me to see her again before leaving Caesarea, but I had left instructions that she be interviewed once more, in the hope that additional matters might have occurred to her in the meantime.

As it happened, it was as well that I did. By shortly after midday it had become clear that a further visit from Joshua bar-Abbas was unlikely, and having stood most of my men down, I made my way back to the praetorium of Herod's Fortress.

A young auxiliary was awaiting me. He had been amongst those I had left as a skeleton force in Caesarea. He looked tired and dishevelled. As I arrived he stood and saluted. 'Sir.'

'Yes, Darius, what is it?'

'The result of further enquiries of the woman Eunice, sir. I thought it best to notify you forthwith.'

'Go on.'

'She's a verbose kind of person, sir …'

'I discovered that for myself.'

'Quite so, sir, forgive me. But eventually, amidst all the chaff, certain facts were elicited which might prove relevant. It seems Syrianus mentioned that the reason he had called was that he had suspicions regarding a man he believed to be a *Secarius*.'

'Why did she not mention this before?'

'It seems he made it clear that the man in question was one of the followers of Joshua bar-Josef. Being in sympathy with the group and their leader, she was not prepared to mention the fact before. But on thinking things over, she realized that regardless of religious or political factors, the murder of Syrianus was a despicable and cowardly act, and she would like to see his killer apprehended.'

I raised my eyebrows. Was the solution going to be as easy as that? 'And the killer is?'

'She cannot say, sir. Another reason she would not speak out before is that she feared her nephews, Philip and Barthol, might be suspected. But she says she is sure that neither of them could have done such a thing.'

'Philip was in Capernaum at the time, along with most of the other disciples.'

'Yes, sir. That has since been confirmed.'

'Which leaves us,' I said, thinking aloud, 'with four main suspects: Zelotes, Judas, Barthol and Levi. It always comes down to the same four. You've done well, Darius. Go and clean up, then have a well-merited rest.' I rang the bell on my desk. 'I'll arrange a room for you. And you must be my guest for supper tonight.'

*

LATER the same afternoon Pilate sent for me again. The slave girl, Salome, was with him, together with her owner, my Lady Mary of Magdala. The Prefect later commented to me drily that it was glaringly obvious how the Magdalene woman and I felt about one another. Evidently I had been less successful in hiding my feelings than I cared to imagine. On the other hand his comments about Mary pleased me mightily. From her stiff and formal demeanour I had thought something of her former hostility to me might have returned.

It seemed that the girl Salome had been pursuing enquiry of her own, notwithstanding the obvious dangers involved for a lone woman. She alleged that whilst posing as a tavern wench in the Olive Branch Inn she had overheard the youth Judas in conversation with a Zealot leader, Izaak bar-Lavan. According to her, Judas had claimed to have committed the murder of Dio Syrianus. For his part bar-Lavan had seemed less than impressed, and told him that no such action should have been taken without the appoval of their leadership..

She was in a very emotional state. Pilate enquired of me regarding the girl's reliability, and I gave her a good reference. He had already seemed inclined to view her evidence favourably. Indeed I thought Pilate handled the affair well. Had he shown either hostility or sympathy he would probably have reduced her to hysterical tears, and her testimony would have been rendered worthless. As it was, his demeanour was strictly neutral, and whilst she wept a little, her account was perfectly coherent.

We agreed that the next step was to interview the man bar-Lavan, and as a result I was sitting opposite to him in the Fig Tree that same evening, alongside my deputy, young Publius Vulpino. The man had been accompanied by some cronies. We took their names before telling them to clear off.

'Now what do you want?'

'There are two ways we can do this,' I informed him. 'You can answer my questions in a co-operative manner, or you can accompany me to my headquarters, which I remind you form part of the Prefect's fortress. He has methods available which both he and I would prefer not to use, but we will do so if necessary.'

'Am I supposed to be afraid?'

'Two days ago,' I went on as if he had not spoken, 'you were sitting in the Olive Branch Tavern talking to a youth called Judas bar-Simon. Fortunately for our purposes, but unfortunately for you, he has a rather loud drawling voice.'

'Fucking young idiot,' he said. 'The landlord told you, I suppose. Or that young whore who was hanging around in the doorway.'

'Never mind who it was. He admitted to killing the auxiliary Dio Syrianus in Caesarea a few days ago.'

He shrugged. 'Was that his name?'

'Yes, that was his name, and he was a good friend of mine. I don't like people who refer to his death lightly. Did Judas admit to killing him?'

'As you already know. But like I said, he's a young idiot. Thought it would impress me. He wanted to join the Zealots.'

'And what did you say?'

'Apart from persistently telling him to keep his voice down, I said that if he had done anything of the sort, we strongly disapproved. Any militant action can be taken only with the agreement of our committee, and does not include cowardly murder.'

'What about the *Secarii*?'

'They're a terror group. Nothing to do with us.'

'Who's in charge of them?'

'I don't know, and don't care. Nobody, probably. They're individual thugs and criminals, who often commit their crimes for money. They don't care who they kill. Seem to do it for fun, a lot of the time.'

'Why didn't you report the conversation with Judas?' asked Vulpino.

'Why should I do your job for you? Anyway, I didn't believe him. He calls himself Secarius, but he'd faint at the sight of blood.'

*

'OF course,' said Vulpino on our way back to headquarters, 'weak, cowardly men have committed murder before now.'

'I agree. In my view most random acts of violence are committed by the weak rather than the strong, because the weak lack self-control.'

'And of course killing might make a weak man feel big and strong.'

'You're right again. We certainly can't rule the man out. But I think we *can* rule out the Zealot leaders. Bar-Lavan's account agreed with that of the girl, and if I'm not mistaken he's no more idea who did it than we have.'

*

THE MAN Joshua entered Jerusalem again the following day. To have attempted a repeat of his supposedly triumphal progress would have been ridiculous. Indeed it had been far from an unqualified success the first time. On this occasion he was content to bring a handful of disciples with him, including my lady Mary. Yet again his behaviour comprised a strange admixture of wisdom and absurdity. I heard that he had got involved in a stupid row with the keeper of the Fig Tree Tavern, and cursed either the inn or the eponymous tree in its courtyard, I know not which. Neither subsequently seemed any the worse for it. He told some parables, two of which I had heard before, and a new one which appeared to suggest that the Kingdom of God was coming very shortly.

I reasoned thus. In the unikely event that their god intended to make his entry into Jerusalem in person, trailing clouds of glory, and with a heavenly host behind him to overthrow all temporal power, there would be nothing I or anyone else could do about it. On the other hand if Joshua meant to help matters along by raising the Judaean people against Rome, that was a different matter.

But it seemed to me unlikely. As he neared the Temple one of his disciples, the tax-collector Levi, brandished a coin and asked him if it was lawful to pay tribute to Caesar. I feared the worst. But he handled the situation well, indeed gave what so far as I was concerned was the ideal answer, namely that one should render unto Caesar the things that were Caesar's. A garbled account of the incident made its way to Pilate, courtesy of the priests, no doubt. When I saw him the next morning I put the record straight, and he clearly preferred my version. Curiously, I seemed to be about the only man in Jerusalem in whom he had complete confidence. I told myself that I must try to be worthy of his trust.

The last time I saw the Prefect before the meal Joshua's disciples took to calling the Last Supper, we agreed that the evidence against the man Zelotes was now sufficient to justify his arrest and detailed interrogation, notwithstanding his son's extremely dubious claim to have committed the murder. Joshua ought also to be questioned, not only about his own intentions, but the possible activities of his disciples, particularly the Essenes and those known to have links with the Zealots.

As the man seemed to be suggesting that greatly significant events would take place during the next few days, there was no time to lose. Our taking any action on the Sabbath would be almost certain to lead to trouble, so the arrests should be carried out immediately after conclusion of the meal. If his previous behaviour were any guide, Joshua would then spend time alone in a secluded place, to seek the guidance of his god before embarking on his next step. This would provide the opportunity to approach him in a neutral, non-hostile manner, and invite him to meet the Prefect to explain himself.

Pilate asked me how many men I would need. I said a dozen should suffice, half to arrest Simon the Zealot, the other half to approach the man Joshua, while being prepared for possible trouble from the more hot-headed of his disciples. The former task being the simpler, I entrusted it to my lieutenant, young Vulpino. The interview with the man Joshua was likely to call for skilful diplomacy. Whether this was a quality I possessed in sufficient measure, I knew not. But it was a task I ought not to shirk or delegate.

To this day, and I write many years after the event, I cannot decide whether I was guilty of the greatest mistake of my life, or whether the disastrous outcome was inevitable in any case.

Book V

Arrest

According to Mary

IT WAS the night of the full moon of Nissan. It shone brightly, low in the east, casting dark shadows across our path. On such nights *Secarii* are most likely to be abroad. The foreboding silence was broken by the hooting of an owl. Some hundred paces ahead we glimpsed our Lord and his followers making for the city wall and the Essene Gate.

Whilst breathing heavily, Levi was showing a fair turn of speed for one of his bulk, anxious not to lose sight of our Lord and his friends even for a moment. The gate led into the ill-omened Gehenna, known by some as the Valley of the Damned. Thence he and his companions turned left, skirting the southern stretch of the city walls, continuing past the Water Gate into the Kidron Valley, where my centurion and I had walked and talked together but four days earlier. It seemed much longer.

Neither of us spoke. On a silent desert night the sound would have been audible for miles. So far as I could tell, our Lord and his friends were silent too. We dared not join them, for fear our Lord would be displeased. Passing the Temple Mount on our left, opposite the more distant Mount of Olives, I found myself thinking again of that time when my centurion and I had come to know one another so well, not carnally, but spiritually.

I stopped. In an unwelcome echo of that night, we were being followed. I was sure of it. Levi had likewise come to a halt. We exchanged glances, and nodded. No need to speak.

Ahead to our right lay the Garden of Gethsemane. Of course. That would be the place chosen by our Lord for his meditation and prayer before re-entering the city to fulfil his appointed purpose. As to what that purpose was, I remained ignorant.

At this time of year the garden was full of pilgrims during the day, but at night it was dark and sinister, ill-tended pathways and overhanging bushes and undergrowth providing plentiful concealment for evildoers. In the distance we saw our Lord turn and speak briefly to Simon Peter before disappearing into some straggling olive bushes ahead.

Levi stepped forward and spoke.

'*Shalom.*'

'*Shalom,*' Peter replied. 'We thought we heard you back there.' He and Jacob turned to me in salutation. 'Our Lord wishes to be alone to prepare himself.'

'Very good,' said Levi. 'But we felt we had to be here.'

Peter smiled. 'You need not explain yourselves to me. Our orders are to remain here until our Lord returns. It could be a few moments, or several hours, I know not.' I shivered a little. 'But you are cold, Mary. Let us light you a fire.'

'Perhaps,' said Jacob, 'our Lord would not like us to draw attention to ourselves in that way.'

Peter nodded. 'You may be right. Take my cloak.'

'Thank you, but that is unnecessary,' I said. 'If we sit close together in the shade of this cedar, we shall be warm enough.'

So that we did, quietly talking a little from time to time. I sensed that the others felt as I did; that we were on the eve of an event that would resonate for all eternity. Yet could such a thing happen to an ordinary person such as myself? Or the others, for that matter. Levi was an important man locally, but the world had not heard of him. Peter was a prosperous fisherman and Jacob a scholar, both well-respected men, but far from famous even in Judaea.

'Were you followed?' asked Jacob.

So he had sensed as much, too. 'I thought we might have been,' said Levi. 'But we could not be sure. I saw nothing.'

I nodded. 'I felt the same, but did not like to say anything. For women are prone to imagine things, or so many men believe.'

Levi shook his head. 'I don't think you imagined it this time.'

Peter's eyes were sharper, or his powers of observation more acute, than those of the rest of us. 'Don't turn, but there is someone in those bushes over to our right, some thirty paces distant. I'm sure of it.'

Despite what he said, I turned my head slowly. The grasses and fronds of the bushes were moving, perhaps in a breath of wind, though it was a still night. 'Of course,' said Levi in his down-to-earth manner, 'couples do come out here …'

'If there's any fornication going on,' said Peter with a grin, 'they're keeping very quiet about it.' At this we all laughed a little to relieve the tension.

But then there came a sound indeed, near, and quite distinct, splitting the silence as if it had never been. Of a sudden the light of the moon was supplemented by that of half a dozen lanterns. Men were talking, and orders were being shouted. Moments later those responsible burst upon the scene, a score of heavily armed men headed by a huge brute of an officer. Rayshan, captain of the Palace Guard.

'Right,' he demanded angrily, 'where is he? The blaspheming wretch who claims to be the son of God.'

It was Peter who first recovered himself. 'I know not what you mean,' he said, standing. 'We have come to the gardens as a convenient place for prayer and meditation on the eve of the Passover …'

Then I noticed him. The odious little wretch Judas, self-styled Secarius, worming his way between his protectors, the guardsmen. Otherwise I swear Peter would have struck him dead.

'I knew he'd be here!' cried Judas triumphantly. 'These men are his disciples, and doubtless are awaiting him. What did I tell you?'

Whereupon our Lord emerged from the bushes, his glorious face shining pale in the moonlight. 'Oh, master!' cried Judas with sickening facetiousness, 'I greet you with a kiss.' And incredible to relate, he actually made his way forward and attempted an embrace.

Our Lord ignored him. 'Here I am,' he said to the guardsmen. 'What is your business?'

'Are you Joshua bar-Josef, calling himself bar-Abbas?' asked Rayshan.

'You know I am.'

'Joshua bar-Josef,' said the guard, placing a hand on his shoulder, 'you are under arrest for blasphemy, having taken the holy name of the Lord God in vain. Under Mosaic Law, as set out in the holy Book of Leviticus, that is punishable by death by stoning. You will this night be tried by the Sanhedrin …'

'I don't think so,' came a calm familiar voice.

My heart leapt into my mouth as I turned. For my centurion stood there, three of his men beside him, one carrying a lantern. Truly it lightened my darkness. But my joy was only momentary. For what could four men achieve against twenty? Besides, they would have been sent to arrest our Lord too.

'Stand aside, centurion. We have our duty to do.'

'And I have mine. The Prefect wishes to question this man, to ascertain whether he intends any harm to Rome.'

The guardsman turned and gestured towards his men, giving voice to my own thoughts. 'I'll put it bluntly, centurion. What can four men achieve against five times as many?'

'What can Judaea achieve against Rome? If the Palace Guard kill four Roman soldiers, within a week there will not be one stone of your temple left standing on another. An interesting fulfilment of this man Joshua's prophecy.'

The guardsman jerked his head. 'Seize him, men.'

I took this ambiguous order to refer to our Lord, who stood calm as a tree to the axe which cuts it down. But not surprisingly some of the guardsmen seemed uncertain, making half-hearted gestures of hostility towards Romans. A couple made for our Lord, whereupon Simon Peter, who had been restraining himself with difficulty, lashed out with his sword and laid open the face of one of them. He howled with pain. Blood flowed freely, though it was to prove but a superficial wound.

'Put up your swords,' said my centurion, stepping

forward. He did not deign to draw his own. His men stood stolidly awaiting orders.

'Joshua bar-Josef,' he said. 'The Prefect has ordered me to detain you with a view to questioning. His object is to discover whether you intend, or are likely to cause, any harm to Rome. You will now accompany me.'

'He will not,' blustered the giant oaf who commanded the guard. 'He will come with us to the house of the High Priest.'

'I'm not going to argue about it,' said my centurion. 'But since the High Priest's house lies not fifty paces from the Prefect's palace, the point seems academic.' He turned to my Lord. 'Come with us.'

'What of my followers?'

'I have no orders about them. They may accompany you if they wish, so long as they do not attempt a rescue.'

'Arrest them! Arrest them!' squealed Judas. 'Filthy traitors against Rome!'

'I think I know a traitor when I see one,' said my centurion. He nodded in Judas's direction. 'Arrest him, men. He can explain himself to the Prefect.'

Judas gazed around wildly. 'Are you going to permit this?' he shrieked at the guardsmen.

'I think we might,' said Rayshan drily. 'You're scarce worth fighting over.' And for a moment I believe that everyone there, from our Lord down to the meanest guardsman, was united in contempt for the miserable creature.

'Very good,' said my centurion in a more placatory tone. 'We'll be off to the Prefect's palace. And if your High Priest wants to accompany us for the last few yards, of course he would be perfectly within his rights.'

Rayshan nodded. 'So be it.'

*

AS we were leaving, my centurion turned to me for a moment.

'If you get a chance to speak to Joshua before the Prefect sees him,' he said quietly, 'tell him to be frank and friendly. As things stand, Pilate is not ill-disposed towards him. Methinks the advice would come better from you.' Not trusting myself to speak, I nodded.

A moment later a young Roman officer scrambled out of the bushes, careless of the briars whipping back into his face. 'Centurion!' he gasped.

'What is it?'

'The man Simon Zelotes.'

'Have you arrested him?'

'Arrested him, sir? Oh no.' The man seemed on the verge of hysteria. 'Not arrested him.'

'What's happened, then? Has he escaped?'

'No, not escaped.' The young soldier drew a deep breath. 'He's dead. By violence.'

All present glanced at one another in bewilderment. 'How?' asked my centurion.

'Stabbed to the heart, and belly.'

'How long has he been dead?'

'A few moments only. He was but briefly out of our sight.'

Fear took me by the throat. There was but one present who could have done such a thing. Again the demons had entered my heart. My craven, vicious heart. I stifled a cry.

'Return to his body,' said my centurion, 'and prepare a full description of all that you see. Search for the weapon, make a note of any footprints, draw sketches if you think they might help. Here.' He offered the young soldier a slate.

'I have one, thank you, sir. So have a couple of my men.'

'Good. I'll send some stretcher-bearers for the body. Remain here meanwhile.'

'Sir.' The man saluted and withdrew.

By now my Lord and his escort were some twenty or thirty paces ahead of us. Before following them, I touched my centurion's arm to draw his attention.

'There is no need for enquiry,' I whispered. 'I did it. Vile tool of the Evil One that I am.'

He drew a deep breath as if to control himself. 'You can be a very difficult woman sometimes.'

' "Difficult"?' I shrieked. 'Yes, I suppose I am "difficult." Liable to commit murder at any moment. Not many people are more "difficult" than that.'

'I mean, that you talk the most arrant nonsense. For one thing, you have not been out of our sight this last half hour. You have spent most of the time on your knees praying, and the rest gazing after Joshua bar-Abbas with an expression of moonstruck infatuation on your face.'

'How dare you say that! How dare you!'

'Furthermore, if you persist in your absurd claim, I shall have to arrest you for making false statements impeding our enquiry.'

By now I was so angry I could hardly speak. 'Pig!' I managed at last. 'Pig!'

'Stop acting like a spoiled infant. I've grown-up matters to attend to.'

With that he stalked off after my Lord and the guard. I collapsed in a sobbing heap of anger and self-pity. I was the more furious because I knew he was right.

*

AFTER I had pulled myself together I hurried to catch up with the convoy. Peter and Jacob were no longer to be seen. I was ashamed of them. The shrinking figure of Judas was closely guarded by the centurion's men. Amongst the crowd of soldiers and guardsmen our Lord stood straight and tall. He looked a very lonely figure, none the less. I at least would not desert him.

I caught up with the centurion outside the Essene Gate. 'I have come to apologize,' I said. 'I hope you're not going to make it difficult for me.'

'Of course not,' he said briskly. 'These devils, as you call them, are naught but your own sense of guilt and lack of self-belief.'

'Whence do they come, then?'

'From within yourself, of course.'

'I'm not convinced. Tell me again that you never let me out of your sight.'

'I can't. We agreed always to tell one another the truth. You were out of my sight from time to time, albeit briefly.'

'So. You lied to me.'

'I apologize. But it's inconceivable that you could have committed murder in the time available. If you still insist that you're guilty, what was your motive? What did you do with the weapon? Why aren't you covered in blood?'

'It doesn't make sense, I know that. But the devils …'

'There are no such things. The human mind is quite capable of deceiving itself, without any need for devils. Why did you show no sign of distress until you heard Vulpino tell me the news? Because you didn't know of the man's death, that's why.'

I said uncertainly, 'The devils hide what I have done from me until it suits them to reveal it.'

'You actually believe that, do you?'

'I'm not sure what to believe,' I confessed. 'I'm so afraid.'

'You need not be,' he said. 'At least, not on account of your own behaviour. But you should be worried about your Lord. The high priests are determined to have him executed. Pilate is the only man who can save him. Make sure he realizes that. The Prefect is not the most popular of men, but he is amenable to reason.'

We passed through the gate, and glanced up at the room where my Lord had hosted his followers but a few hours before. How much had changed since. Once more I became conscious of being followed, and turned. I was right. The complement of Roman soldiers had increased to a dozen, reinforced by some of those guarding the gate. I glanced again at my centurion, who smiled and nodded.

As we reached the house of the High Priest the guardsmen stopped and moved in front of the Romans. 'We will now enter,' said Rayshan.

'That is not what we agreed,' said my centurion.

'There was no agreement,' lied Rayshan. 'And it is my duty to convey this blasphemer before the High Priest for trial.'

'I could prevent you,' said my centurion, unruffled as ever. 'For a dozen Romans are more than a match for your twenty guards.'

'Be reasonable. Does your prefect want a disturbance, and casualties amongst the forces of law and order?'

'No, he does not, for which reason I will allow a brief interview between this man and bar-Caiaphas. I shall be present throughout, together with my men, and matters will be brought to an end when I say so.'

'A dozen men is far too many,' said Rayshan sulkily. 'The courtroom would be overcrowded.'

'Very well. Half my men will remain out here on guard. The remainder will accompany me to Caiaphas.'

There was further argument and compromise at the gate to the priest's house, but matters were ultimately agreed. My Lord and Judas would be admitted, but not allowed to speak save to reply to the priests' questions. 'I wish to be present too,' I said.

My centurion nodded. 'Certainly.'

'Impossible,' said Rayshan. 'Women are not to be admitted.'

'This woman will be. She is under my protection.'

'Oh, I see,' jeered one of the guards on the door. 'So that's the way things stand, is it?'

'You will apologize to this lady at once,' said my centurion.

'Or what?'

'Or I will knock you down.'

The man laughed offensively. With a lightning punch the centurion was as good as his word. The guard scrambled to his knees, where he remained, wiping the blood from his face, shaking with fear and rage. Some of the others placed hands on their swords, albeit uncertainly, and looked to their commander for guidance.

He hesitated, then grinned reluctantly and said, 'Maybe that'll teach you to watch your tongue in future, Rafael. It's not worth fighting over.' He jerked his head at us. 'Go on in.'

As we did so it occurred to me that my Lord had not said

or done anything throughout. I was uncertain whether this was a sign of weakness or of strength. All I knew was that my centurion had knocked a man down for insulting me. And I gloated inwardly, vain foolish creature that I am.

*

CAIAPHAS sat enthroned between two other priests who sat on slightly less elaborate sieges. A score of others were perched on seats and benches throughout the room. Our Lord stood before them, flanked by two of the Palace Guard, with two of the centurion's men close behind. The remaining Romans surrounded Judas, and partly supported him, for he seemed likely to faint. I had never seen a man in such a state of panic fear.

'The Court of Sanhedrin is now in session,' announced an aged acolyte in the Hebrew tongue, brandishing a scroll.

'Correction,' said my centurion, in Greek. 'This is not a court, but an informal interview.'

'There you are in error, centurion. This is a formal Sanhedrin, with powers of trial, life and death.'

'The Sanhedrin needs to convene a court of seventy-one. You have scarcely a third of that number.'

'We have three-and-twenty, which is all that is required.'

My centurion shook his head. 'Three-and-twenty suffices only for the Lesser Sanhedrin, which meet in provincial cities. The Great Sanhedrin, which alone has power of life and death, requires seventy-one. It meets in the Temple, in the Hall of Hewn Stones, not in the house of the High Priest. And it cannot convene after sunset, which occurred over an hour since. Apart from that, you may well be right.'

Caiaphas seemed beyond speech with suppressed fury, but his deputy, one Jethro, said: 'You claim to know a lot about the Sanhedrin, Roman soldier. May I remind you that it is a Jewish institution, and that our revered High Priest, Josef bar-Caiaphas, is the earthly representative of Almighty God.'

Caiaphas tried to look suitably modest. 'If we are to swap titles,' said my centurion, 'I am a local representative of Tiberius Claudius Nero, second Emperor of Rome, whose cohorts control this city.'

'The cohorts of Almighty God control both heaven and earth.'

'I can only observe,' said my centurion drily, 'that those of Caesar are more immediately apparent.'

In the silence that followed I heard one of the Sanhedrin whisper the words: 'Cohorts of the damned.'

'I heard that remark,' my centurion continued, 'and can only say that in my view it comes close to *maiestas*. I shall of course have to report it to the Prefect.'

'What remark? I heard none.'

'My men heard it, I think. And who is the Prefect likely to believe?'

Caiaphas tried another tack. 'These proceedings, whatever they are, will be conducted in the local tongue.' He smiled sanctimoniously. 'That is the custom, and indeed must be so, in fairness to the accused man, whose knowledge of Greek is, I understand, but limited.'

'By all means,' said my centurion. 'I fancy I know enough of the Hebrew and Aramaic languages to follow the proceedings in outline at least, and convey their meaning to this man.' He turned to me with a smile. 'No doubt this lady will help me if need be.'

'A woman has no right to be present.'

'She is a witness.' This was the first I had heard of such a thing, but I said nothing.

'If you allege that she is a witness,' said the High Priest, an oily smile beneath his moustache, 'you accept that this is a court, with the right to call witnesses.'

'On the contrary. It is you that claim it is a court, and therefore accept that witnesses can be called. In other words, by your own argument, you are estopped – yes, estopped, no less – from excluding her. I, on the other hand, say that this is not a court. If you accept that fact, I agree she has no right to be present, and will order her to depart.'

Caiaphas turned to confer with his two closest advisors. 'The Prefect will not be pleased by further delay,' said my centurion. 'I suggest that you let the man Joshua know of what charge he is accused, and leave it at that. There is no time for a fair trial, even if this were a properly convened court.'

Eventually Caiaphas said, 'The Prisoner is accused of blasphemy, by taking the name of the Lord God in vain, the punishment for which is death by stoning.'

'Thank you,' said my centurion. 'Now he knows where he stands. And I now propose to execute my original purpose by taking him before the Prefect for examination. If he allows a trial to take place before a properly convened Sanhedrin, which I take leave to doubt, a date will be fixed in the near future.' He turned and nodded to his men. 'Take the man Joshua out.'

'He's a blasphemer!' screamed Judas, finding his voice at last. 'I heard him! He claimed to be "the Son of Man," who would come to earth trailing clouds of glory, to usher in the time of Har-Mageddon, the ultimate battle between good and evil, and the establishment of the Kingdom of God on earth. In other words, he says he is the earthly manifestation of God himself.'

My centurion jerked his head at Judas. 'This man is a cowardly hysteric,' he said, 'who will say anything he thinks you want him to say, in the interests of saving his own skin.'

'His skin is in no danger from us,' said Caiaphas. 'None accuses him of claiming to be divine.'

'True. But he stands accused of the murder of a Roman soldier on duty, which constitutes *maiestas*, that is, treason against the Empire, Caesar, and the senate and people of Rome. So he needs all the help he can get, and seeks to find it from you and your so-called court.'

Caiaphas glanced briefly from side to side. His associates nodded. 'We find the prisoner Joshua bar-Josef guilty,' he said. 'This court finds him guilty, and sentences him to death by stoning.'

'This court,' said my centurion, 'could not try a beggar off the street. Take him away.'

Some of the acolytes made to block his way, but faltered and moved aside. And so we left the self-styled court of the Greater Sanhedrin. As we did so I finally realized what I had been refusing to face for so long. I loved my centurion. If my future were to lie with any man, it would be with him.

*

I SAW little of my centurion after that. He arranged quarters for me at Herod's Palace, where he and his men were billeted. If they thought I was his whore, I cared not.

The next hour I spent on tenterhooks, imagining our dear Lord's interrogation by Pilate. Time passed more slowly than any snail moved. Several times a man entered the doorway for one reason or another, and I caught my breath. But always it was a false alarm. At long last my centurion came to me. I stood eagerly. But a glance at his face told me all.

He shook his head. 'Things did not go well.'

'In what way?'

'Joshua repeated what he has already said, but I feel that he failed to explain himself to the Prefect's satisfaction.'

I drew a few deep breaths. 'Then it means… death?'

'Not necessarily. If it were Pilate's decision alone, I think he might be merciful. But he needs to appease the priests and the Tetrarch, who are for death. As it is, he has ordered a whipping, thirty lashes, as punishment for the incident in the temple forecourt the other day, and for Joshua to be then released.'

'Surely that is good news? Or at least, not the worst.'

'As you say, it could be worse. But he advised – advised, mark you, not ordered – Joshua to leave Jerusalem at once and return to Galilee. Otherwise he said he could not guarantee his safety.'

'I am not familiar with politicians' language,' I said impatiently. 'What did he mean by that?'

My centurion paused for thought. 'I think he meant, that if he stays in Jerusalem his enemies will foment disorder until he is sentenced to death. As a last resort, Pilate will condemn him.'

'The man's a coward!'

'Not according to his military record.'

'A man who is a hero in certain circumstances can be a coward in others.'

My centurion nodded. 'That is a wise remark. Let me put Pilate's case. He simply has not enough men to defend Jerusalem against rebellion. Not immediately.'

'There are legions in Syria.'

'Exactly. In Syria. They are needed here.'

According to the Centurion

THE FIRST part of my task presented little difficulty. The man Joshua attended the meeting with his followers in the upper room of the merchant Moshe. It was well-conducted, and there was no disturbance. Waiting outside, I and my men faced no problem worse than that of boredom.

An hour after sunset Joshua left, accompanied by two of his closest disciples, Peter the fisherman, and Jacob, one of the sons of Zebadiah. Simon Zelotes was not with them. I accordingly ordered Vulpino and his troop to maintain their position, whilst I and three of my men set out after Joshua and his companions.

They left the city almost at once, by way of the Essene Gate. My first thought was that they intended to make for Bethany, which the man had effectively used as a base for his Passover operations thus far.

In the clear moonlight it seemed almost as bright as day. We should not follow them too closely. As they turned to the east we let them go.

Someone was following us. Hastily I moved my men against the wall, hoping to hide behind the buttresses. It seemed unlikely that the *Secarii* would tackle a group of Roman soldiers, but the signs were that they had become bolder of late, the savagery of some of their recent atrocities amounting almost to insanity. Either that or their activities had attracted murderously deranged mimics. And it is widely believed that lunatics are more active at the time of the full moon.

My fears were groundless. For who should emerge from the gate but my lady of Magdala, accompanied by the comfortably prosperous tax-collector Levi. They also turned to the left, following Joshua and his companions at a distance of perhaps a hundred paces. I gave them almost as much start on us, then nodded to my men to maintain the pursuit.

It ocurred to me that should the man Zelotes leave the upper room shortly, the affair might take on the appearance of a bizarre game of follow-my-leader. First Joshua and his men, then Levi and Mary, ourselves, Zelotes and any he might take with him, and finally Vulpino with my remaining men. It would also become increasingly difficult to conceal from our respective quarries the fact that they were being followed.

We passed through the Kidron Valley without incident, until the Mount of Olives reared its head to our right. Here I expected Joshua to make the turn for Bethany, but he did not. Neither did he approach the Temple Porch, instead making his way straight ahead. And it was here that he finally left the road, turning off into the Garden of Gethsemane. Unsurprisingly Levi and Mary did the same. In the moonlight, concealment amidst the sparse vegetation would be a problem, so I halted my companions until those we followed had disappeared into the gardens on the trail of their lord.

I was about to order that we set off again, when we perceived a score or so of guardsmen making their way down the Temple Mount, which they left by the Golden Gate, immediately opposite the gardens. Whether they had seen us I knew not, but they were unquestionably on a similar mission.

We resumed tracking our quarry. A path had been trodden through the shrubs and grasses at the entrance to Gethsemane, so it was no very difficult matter to follow the route they had taken. Soon we glimpsed them in a moonlit clearing amidst the trees: Peter and Jacob were engaged in low conversation, while Joshua made his way, alone, into a dark corner characterized by caves and ancient decaying stone monuments. Levi emerged ahead of us and strode across to his friends. After momentary hesitation Mary joined him.

Before them the gardens were bounded by a sheer rock face. It was impossible to scale, so they would have needed to emerge by the path whereby they had entered. Joshua could not escape us.

I spoke to my men quietly. 'I hesitate to arrest a man when he's at prayer, but we can't wait for ever. We'll give him half an hour, then move in.'

Even as I spoke I realized that we were too late. From within the glade there came a sound of disturbance, and rough voices. Above them all I heard a youth squeal: 'Arrest him! Arrest him! I told you so!'

'Judas bar-Simon,' said my batman Gnaeus wryly.

'Who else?' I agreed.

We stepped forward into the clearing. A dozen or more of the palace guard were present, some carrying lanterns. They were headed by their commander Rayshan, whom I knew slightly. A huge fellow who could be a bit of a bully, and none too bright. But there were plenty worse.

Judas chose to draw attention to himself. 'Oh, master,' he fawned, 'I greet you with a kiss.' Which he attempted to do.

The man Joshua looked at him as if he had crawled from under a stone. 'Here I am,' he said to the guardsmen. 'What is it you want?'

'Are you called Joshua bar-Josef?'

'I am.'

'Joshua bar-Josef,' said Rayshan, 'you are under arrest for blasphemy, having taken the holy name of the Lord God in vain. Under Mosaic Law, as evidenced by the holy Book of Leviticus, this is punishable by death by stoning. You will this night be tried by the Sanhedrin …'

'The Sanhedrin never meet at night,' said Joshua.

'Well, they're making an exception for you.'

'Allow me,' I said as politely as I could manage. 'This man is my prisoner, sir, and I shall convey him to the Roman Prefect for interrogation.'

Rayshan seemed somewhat at a loss. Eventually he said without much conviction, 'I have a score of men, centurion, and you but four.'

'And Rome has a million. How many have your priests? Lift your hand against me and my men, and within a week this man's prophesy will be fulfilled. There will not be one stone of the temple standing on another.'

Still Rayshan seemed uncertain. A couple of his men made a half-hearted move towards Joshua. Whereupon Simon Peter swung his sword and laid open the face of one of them. The man howled with pain and clasped his ear.

'Put up your swords,' I ordered. 'Joshua bar-Josef, I have orders from the Roman Prefect of Judaea, Q. Pontius Pilatus, to detain you with a view to questioning. He intends to discover whether you intend, or are likely to cause, any harm to Rome. You will accompany me.'

'He will accompany us,' said Rayshan sulkily, 'to the house of the High Priest.'

'Since the High Priest's house lies within fifty paces of the Prefect's praetorium, the point hardly seems worth arguing about.' I turned back to Joshua. 'This way, please, sir.'

'And my friends? What of them?'

'There I have no orders. They are not under arrest. They may accompany you if they wish, so long as they do not attempt to interfere with my task.'

Again Judas intervened. 'Arrest them! Arrest them in the name of Almighty God! Filthy traitors!'

'Methinks I see a sort of traitor here.' I turned to my men and jerked my head at Judas. 'Arrest him. He can explain himself to the Prefect.'

Judas, who seemed to be suffering from an advanced form of hysteria, worse than any woman, shrieked madly at the guardsmen, 'Will you permit this?'

'Yes, I think so,' said Rayshan blandly. 'For it seems to me that you have betrayed everyone, from Caesar and Almighty God down to these deluded rogues. Perhaps the Prefect can determine whose side you truly support. None, I suspect.'

'Quite right,' I said amiably. For his part Judas whimpered and seemed close to tears. I'd never met anyone so lacking in *virtus*. Truly the fellow hardly qualified as a man at all. 'So, we'll be off for the praetorium. And if your High Priest wants to accompany us for the last few yards, of course he will be within his rights to do so.'

Rayshan nodded. 'So be it.'

We trooped out of the gardens, myself and my men

escorting the man Joshua, who appeared fairly composed, if a little nervous, which in the circumstances was understandable. We were surrounded by the Palace Guard, headed by Rayshan, who walked beside me in what was by now a comparatively amicable manner. The disciples seemed to have abandoned their leader, but my lady Mary followed in the rear.

*

THAT was not the end of the affair. Just as we quit the gardens and set foot upon the road to the south, young Vulpino came hurrying up to me in as near to a state of panic as I had ever seen that usually imperturbable youth.

'Centurion!' he gasped. 'Sir.'

More formal than usual, but perhaps the presence of Rayshan was responsible. 'What is it?' I asked.

'The man Simon Zelotes.'

'Have you arrested him?'

Vulpino gave a rather mad little laugh. 'Arrested him, sir? Oh no. Not arrested him.'

'Well,' demanded Gneius, 'what's happened? Has he escaped you?'

'No, not escaped.' Vulpino drew a deep breath and controlled himself. 'He's dead. By violence. Stabbed to the heart. With multiple other wounds.'

Judas gave a spectacular howl, and burst into tears. 'Not your day, is it?' said Rayshan. 'Arrested for blasphemy and *maiestas*, facing both stoning and crucifixion, and then your old man gets himself done in. By you, for all we know.'

At this the tearful wretch began to protest his innocence,

with much tiresome humbug about how much he had loved his dear father, which all knew to be far from the truth. It took the threat of a smack in the chops from one of Rayshan's men to shut him up.

I ordered Vulpino and his men to stay with the body, while making any notes about the scene which might help identify the perpetrator. And just as I thought things could hardly become more complicated, my lady Mary hurried over to me. 'I heard what was said, centurion. You need look no further for the culprit. I did it.'

My heart stopped. Surely this could not be true. Not my lady. Yet I knew from experience that almost anyone could be guilty of murder given the right circumstances. What could have been her motive?

'The demons have re-entered my heart. My black, corrupted heart, vicious tool of Eve's Serpent that I am.'

She was fantasizing again. The relief was so great that I was almost angry with her. 'You can be a difficult woman sometimes, you know.'

'Yes, we murderesses are "difficult," I dare say.'

'You have not been out of our view this last half hour.' That was not quite true. There had been moments when she had been out of our line of sight, or gone ahead into the undergrowth, once for a period during which one might have counted slowly to two hundred. From that point of view it was remotely possible that she could have committed the crime. But I knew better.

'During that time,' I continued, 'you were either praying or looking after your lord with a foolishly infatuated expression on your face.'

'How dare you!'

'If you persist in your absurd claim, I shall have to arrest you for making false statements, and thereby impeding our enquiry.'

'Pig!' she said tearfully. 'Pig!'

It caused me great pain to hear such pitiful nonsense from the woman I loved and so greatly admired. The vile bonds of superstition instilled into her by religion – the thing that binds – caused her to behave like a foolish child. I said something of the sort, and hurried after my men.

Some quarter of an hour later she appeared beside me again. 'I am come to apologize,' she said, her voice shaking. 'And I hope you are not going to make it difficult for me.'

'Of course not. The "devils," as you call them, have no power to make you kill, or do anything else. They do not exist.'

'Where do evil thoughts come from, then?'

'From within men's hearts and minds.'

'And women's.'

'And women's.'

'But I was out of your sight for a while. I remember now.'

'You are right. We agreed it should always be the truth between us. I apologize in turn. I lied to you. You were out of my sight for the period of a count to two hundred, if that. It's inconceivable that you could have committed murder within that time.'

'A few moments would be all it took.'

'Very well. If you want to argue about it, I'll try to be logical. What was your motive? How did you know he'd be there? What did you do with the weapon? Why did you show no signs of distress until Vulpino told me the news? Why do your clothes show no sign of blood?'

She was silent for a while. 'I know it doesn't make sense,' she said eventually. 'But I am so terribly afraid. If not of the devils, of the evil within myself.'

'If anyone is incapable of evil, it is you. I have never mentioned this before, Mary of Magdala, but you have more *virtus* than any man I have ever known. There is so much goodness, love and courage deep in the very heart of you, and yet you cannot see it.'

She started to cry quietly. 'I am still afraid.'

'Be afraid for your Lord,' I advised. 'Pilate is the only man who can save him now. Tell him that.'

*

BY far the shortest way to the Prefect's praetorium was through the Essene Gate in the south of the city. Unfortunately this led straight past the house of the High Priest, Caiaphas. It would not be difficult for the Palace Guard to stop outside and deliver their prisoner there. Outnumbered by five to one there would be little I could do about it. Should I order my men to put up a fight, there would be casualties on both sides, the very thing Pilate wanted to avoid. Whatever the outcome, I should be subject to prefectorial displeasure. The alternative was to enter by the Water Gate and trek through the lower city, avoiding the Essene Quarter altogether. This would also have its disadvantages, taking far longer and bringing us close to the temple, where the guard might pick up further support.

I took the simpler option of the Essene Gate. For one thing it was remotely possible that Rayshan would keep to the agreement we had reached. And as we passed through I took care to obtain reinforcements as unobtrusively as possible. By the time we arrived in the neighbourhood of Caiaphas's house, I had a dozen men under my command, admittedly of indifferent quality, but too good for the riff-raff from the Palace Guard. If it came to all-out conflict we should prevail militarily, but at much political cost.

Throughout our journey I had of course kept our prisoner under observation. He differed greatly from the assured figure he had presented when delivering his sermons, or the dangerous rebel of the Court of the Gentiles. Most criminals under arrest on a capital charge affect a sort of defiant swagger. This bedraggled wretch shambled, head down and apparently resigned to his fate. From beginning to end he spoke not a word, save to mumble to himself in the manner of a harmless lunatic, or as some would have put it, one possessed by devils.

As we reached the house of the High Priest, Rayshan stopped. 'We will now enter,' he said with a smirk.

I should have been angrier had I not foreseen this, but I was still angry. I choked back my inclination to make a scene, and said simply, 'That is not what we agreed.'

'There was no agreement,' Rayshan lied. 'And it is my duty to convey this blasphemer before the priests for trial.'

I tried the obvious argument first. 'I could prevent you. A dozen Romans are more than a match for your guards.'

'Be reasonable,' he said. 'Does your prefect want a disturbance, and casualties amongst the forces of law and order?' He spoke confidently, but I sensed the man's unease.

'No,' I agreed. 'Wherefor I will allow a brief interview between your High Priest and this man. I insist on being present, together with my men, and matters will be brought to an end when I say so.'

Rayshan objected to the number, saying that a dozen men were far too many. I was content to have made my point, and we settled on half a dozen. My lady Mary then stated that she wished to be present also.

'Women are not to be admitted,' said Rayshan firmly.

'This one will be,' I said. 'She is under my personal protection.'

One of the guards on the door leered. 'Oh, so that's the way things stand, is it?'

I could not let that pass. 'You will apologize to this lady at once,' I said.

'Or what?'

It wasn't worth killing for. Few things are. 'Or I will knock you down,' I said.

The man gave a filthy laugh, so I knocked him down. As he sprawled on the cobbles, some of the guard placed hands on their swords. I saw Rayshan hesitate, then decide to be reasonable. 'Watch your tongue in future, Rafael.' He jerked his head. 'Come in.'

*

THE MAIN room was laid out as a court, with three thrones for the judges, and tables, benches and lecturns for advocates and witnesses. The tiled floor bore a gorgeous mosaic of Moses and the burning bush, or some such barbaric legend. I wondered how the High Priest managed to reconcile that, and the other splendid sculptures and works of art adorning the place, with Jewish teaching forbidding the making of graven images.

He sat on the central throne, two other of the chief

priests beside him. A score or so of lesser judges sat on benches. It was clear that the whole place had been prepared in advance. Rayshan's visit had been no snap decision. For my part, I had ordered my men to remain close to Judas at all times. Yet again I remarked on his total lack of *virtus*. If a man has not that, he is nothing.

Joshua bar-Josef stood before what for want of a better word I shall call the tribunal, though in my view it possessed no legal powers. He stood straight and tall, albeit clad in a torn and dirty white robe. His features were gaunt, with lank dark hair descending to his shoulders. He did not constitute my idea of a military leader.

An aged acolyte moved forward and read from a scroll, in Hebrew: 'The court of the Sanhedrin is now in session.'

I stepped forward in turn, hoping that I appeared more confident than I felt. 'Nothing of the sort,' I said in Greek. 'This is not a court, but an informal interview.'

'You are in error,' said the aged one sourly. 'This is a formal Sanhedrin, with powers of life and death.'

'The Sanhedrin requires a court of seventy-one. You have not half that number.'

Caiaphas took up the argument. 'We have three-and-twenty, which is all that is required.'

I shook my head. 'As you well know, Chief Priest, three-and-twenty suffices only for the lesser Sanhedrin, which sit throughout the various provinces of Judaea. The Great Sanhedrin, which alone has powers of life and death, requires seventy-one.'

I spoke as confidently as I could. My understanding of Hebrew law was based on nothing more substantial than a few informal conversations I had had with certain

Pharisees with whom I had become friendly, and who had been prepared to discuss their beliefs with me. But it would seem that I was right, for as Caiaphas turned to consult with his fellow-judges, he looked decidedly uneasy. In an attempt to press home my advantage, I continued, 'Furthermore it meets in the Hall of the Hewn Stones, and cannot be convened after sunset. The sun set some hour and a half ago. Add to that the fact that the Prefect has to be informed in advance of any capital proceedings, and give permission for them to take place. So far as I am aware this has not occurred.'

'You are a Roman soldier,' said the High Priest's deputy, one Jethro, 'and as such cannot be expected to know details of the Jewish religion and courts.'

'I know pretentious humbug when I see it,' I replied.

Some of those present gasped, and made signs to heaven. 'I remind you, Roman soldier,' Jethro continued, 'that our High Priest is the representative of Almighty God, creator of all things, whose heavenly cohorts command all time and space.'

'And I act for Tiberius Caesar, Emperor of Rome, whose earthly cohorts control Judaea. To rather more effect than those of your god, it would seem.'

'You blasphemous wretch!' said Caiaphas. 'I wonder you are not struck dead on the spot.'

I remained standing and gazed around, especially to heaven. Quite frankly, a thunderbolt was the last thing I was worried about. A period of some ten heartbeats passed without incident, save that one of the Sanhedrin broke the silence by whispering the words: 'Truly this man represents the cohorts of the damned.'

'I heard that remark,' I said, 'and shall report it to the Prefect. In my view it comes close to *maiestas*.'

'What remark? I heard none.'

I glanced around. 'My men heard it, I think.' Whether they had or not, they knew what I required of them, and nodded. 'And whom is the prefect likely to believe?'

Caiaphas changed tack and decided to pose as one seeking justice at all costs. 'These proceedings will be conducted in the Hebrew tongue.' He smiled. 'That is the custom, and indeed must be so, in fairness to the accused man, whose knowledge of Greek is, I understand, but limited.'

'By all means,' I agreed. 'I fancy I know enough Hebrew and Aramaic to follow the proceedings, in outline at least, and translate them.' I turned to the Magdalene. 'No doubt this lady will help me if need be.'

'A woman has no right to be present.'

'If this is a court, she is entitled to be present as a witness. If you concede that this is not a court, I shall order her to leave. This is after all your private residence, and in that capacity you have the right to decide whom you entertain.'

Again Caiaphas turned to confer with his two closest advisors. 'The Prefect will not be pleased by further delay,' I said as firmly as I could. 'I suggest that you let the man Joshua know of what charge he is accused, and leave it at that. There is certainly no time for a fair trial, even if this were a properly convened court.'

Eventually Caiaphas said, 'The prisoner is accused of blasphemy, by taking the name of the Lord God in vain, the punishment for which is death by stoning.'

'Thank you. Now he knows where he stands.'

'He is a blasphemer!' cried Judas, so suddenly that

all present were taken unawares. 'I heard him say only yesterday, that he would soon descend upon Jerusalem in clouds of glory, to execute his father's will.'

'So he claimed to be the son of Almighty God?' said Caiaphas with a thin smile.

'He did, High Priest. He did.'

'This man,' I said, waving my hand at him dismissively, 'is a cowardly hysteric facing trial for *maiestas* and killing a Roman soldier on duty by stabbing him in the back. He now seeks to defend himself on that charge by recruiting this tribunal, or whatever it is, to his cause. And I now propose to execute my original purpose by taking the prisoner Joshua before the Prefect for examination. If he allows a trial to take place before a properly convened Sanhedrin, which I take leave to doubt, a date will be fixed in the near future.' I nodded to my men. 'Take him out.'

'We find him guilty,' said Caiaphas quickly, after a glance at his two deputies, who nodded. 'This court finds the man Joshua bar-Josef guilty of blasphemy, and sentences him to death by stoning.'

'This co-called court,' I said, 'could not try a drunken beggar off the street. Take him away.'

Some of the acolytes made to prevent our departure, but faltered and moved aside. And so we left the self-styled court of the Greater Sanhedrin. I congratulated myself on the fact that I had just got away with what amounted to the greatest bluff of my life.

*

I REPORTED to Pilate immediately. Although none too

pleased to see me – it was a couple of hours after sunset, after all – he agreed that the man Joshua should be questioned without delay. Two of my men brought him in. The prisoner was half-naked, drenched in sweat, and shaking in every limb. Again he struck me as a character more worthy of pity than of awe.

'Are you Joshua bar-Josef?'

No-one at the so-called Sanhedrin had thought to ask this simple preliminary question, which was yet another reason to doubt the legality of its proceedings.

The prisoner nodded, which action Pilate ordered to be recorded as assent. He continued, 'Do you travel the province of Judaea teaching that you are the Messiah, who will free the land from the Roman yoke?'

The prisoner remained mute, whether through fear or malice I could not determine. Another explanation occurred to me. 'The man is not conversant with the Greek tongue, sir,' I said, 'save for a few words. He speaks Aramaic, and a dialect of Hebrew. May I act as interpreter?'

'Do so.'

I repeated the question in Aramaic. The prisoner hesitated, then replied, 'The words are yours.'

I translated. 'What on earth does that mean?' asked Pilate.

This time the man replied to me. 'By whose authority do you ask?'

'That of Tiberius Claudius Nero, second Emperor of Rome.'

'The Prefect has no authority over me besides that given to him from above.'

'Don't be impertinent.'

The man said nothing further. I translated our exchange for the Prefect's benefit.

'Will he now reply to my question?' he asked.

This time Joshua deigned to respond, saying that his kingdom was not of this world. Again I conveyed his speech to the Prefect.

Of a sudden Pilate smiled. 'This man is a Galilean, is he not?'

'Yes, sir.'

'And has preached his message mainly in Galilee?'

'Yes, sir.'

'It seems therefore that jurisdiction should fall within the province of Herod Antipas, Tetrarch of Galilee. Take the prisoner to his palace, and inform the Tetrarch of my decision.'

At this time of night, Herod would not thank me or Pilate for disturbing him. 'I know it's late,' said the Prefect. 'But I don't see why I should be the only one inconvenienced. Tell Herod to try the man without delay, and report the result to me in person for my ratification.'

'It shall be done, sir.'

'Report to me tomorrow morning, that is. I'm going to bed.'

*

'WHAT'S the meaning of this?'

It had needed a mixture of threats and cajolery, and expenditure of well over a quarter of an hour, to obtain audience with the Tetrarch. He was in night attire, and bleary-eyed.

'Sire. I come from the prefect, Q. Pontius Pilatus.'

'I know that, damn you. Get to the point.'

'The man Joshua bar-Josef was arrested by the Palace Guard earlier this evening and brought before him to answer allegations of *maiestas*. Since the man's alleged offences took place in Galilee, the Prefect considers that jurisdiction in the case rests with your good self.'

'I'll try the bastard tomorrow. Have him here by the second hour.'

*

IT wanted less than half an hour until midnight. There would be little sleep for me. Vulpino stood before me in the praetorium courtyard and saluted. 'Sir. My report on the murder of Zelotes.'

He handed me a thin sheet of wood paper. I glanced at it. It bore a simple representation of the positioning of the man's body. He lay on his face amidst tangled brush and long grasses. I nodded.

'Cause of death?'

'Three stab wounds to the left of the thorax: one in the chest, two in the back. One deep in the belly. Also several more superficial. The mortal wound seems to have been one of those in the back, puncturing the heart, but several of the others would in all likelihood have been fatal eventually. The physician's report should clarify the matter. There was a defence wound on the outside of the pronated left hand.'

'So the course of events seems to have been that he was attacked from the front by a right-handed assailant. He may have managed to strike the first blow aside, but was stabbed

by the second and third. He then turned away, and was struck
by two more blows in the back, one of which was fatal.'

'That's how it seems to have happened, sir.'

'Don't bother with the "sir" when we're alone, we know
one another well enough. Was the deceased armed?'

'No. Nor was any weapon found at the scene. But in the
darkness and undergrowth it might have been missed. I've
ordered a full search of the area by daylight.'

'Good man. Footprints?'

'None. There's been no rain for over a fortnight. The
undergrowth has been disturbed a little here and there, but
there may be no significance even in that. A small animal
could have done as much.'

'So. We've nothing much to go on, apart from the time of
death, which was shortly before he was found, and the fact
that the only persons known to have been in the region were
the man Joshua and his disciples.'

'That's right.'

'What was the deceased doing there, anyway?'

'We don't know. Certainly not accompanying his son.
The Palace Guard never saw him.'

'Any ideas who the culprit might be?'

Vulpino shook his head. 'Not really. The man called
Simon Peter is a hothead, and wore a sword. But I can't see
him butchering an unarmed man like that.' His lip curled.
'Then there's Judas Secarius. According to the guards he was
out of their sight for about an eighth of an hour. Sufficient
for the purpose.'

'Is he capable of patricide, do you reckon?'

'Hard to say. But he's the only man, apart from the
deceased and Joshua himself, who's known to have been in

the vicinity and whose movements are not accounted for for more than a few moments.'

'I take it he had no weapon?'

'That's right. The guard made sure of that.'

I nodded. 'That's not conclusive, of course. Especially if you find the murder weapon tomorrow.'

One of Vulpino's men dashed in. 'Forgive me, sir, but ...'

Vulpino frowned. 'I gave orders that you stay at the scene, with Festus.'

'It seemed urgent, sir. We searched as best we could by lamplight, and found this ...'

He produced a curved knife, perhaps six inches in length. There was blood remaining on the blade, already congealed in the crack where it joined the wooden handle. 'You did well,' said Vulpino. 'Now return to your post.' The man saluted and withdrew.

'Check with the physician that this weapon could have caused the fatal wound,' I said. 'If so, I think we have sufficient to charge Secarius. What of motive?'

'An only son, so he inherits everything. Zelotes was a farrier, with a modest amount of money. Plus a little farming land. And the tools of his trade, of course.'

'Murder has been committed for less. And the man's known to have been on poor terms with his father. Then there's his self-awarded nickname, which shows that he likes playing around with knives. I think we've got enough.'

*

I WAS at Herod's Palace well before the second hour. As I had feared, the Tetrarch chose to assert his authority by keeping us waiting. This was doubly inconvenient, as I was receiving reports from my men that people were pouring into the city for the Passover, some, it would seem, in ugly mood. Eventually he condescended to see us.

The palace of Herod Antipas put that of the High Priest to shame. The walls were decorated with classical scenes in the Roman style, red and orange being the predominant colours. The floor mosaic showed a giant Star of David in blue, against a golden background, surrounded by a quote from the Torah in the Hebrew script. Evidently he was asserting his Jewishness in an attempt to offset the contempt he had demonstrated for their ban on imagery.

Two of my men brought the prisoner in. He looked as bedraggled and pitiful a figure as ever. 'Is this him?' Herod demanded.

'Yes. Sire.'

'Are you Joshua bar-Josef?' he asked in Hebrew.

The man nodded miserably. Antipas sneered. 'You don't look much like the King of the Jews to me. Are you?'

'The words are yours.'

'Whatever that means. I say again, do you claim to be the King of the Jews?'

'My kingdom is not of this world.'

Herod scowled. 'Do you know what he means?' he demanded of me.

'I think he claims to help God rule heaven and earth in the afterlife, Tetrarch.'

'Is he mad?'

'That's not for me to say, sir. He has an unusual personality, to say the least.'

Herod grunted. 'Well, I've no time for the fellow now.'

He turned to some of his slaves. 'Dress him in finery. If he's king, he must have befitting raiment.'

'Er, sire?'

'The finest robes, I said.' Antipas smiled disagreeably. 'Then he must have a crown. Twine some briars and thorns into his hair and send him back to Pilate for a good whipping. I've other things to attend to.'

The significance of this last remark did not occur to me until later.

*

WITHIN the hour I was back before Pilate, the prisoner and his guards alongside me. Observing the bizarre dress and appearance of the prisoner, the Prefect frowned.

'What does this mean?'

'An idea of the Tetrarch, sir. Presumably he intended to hold the prisoner up to ridicule. I did not feel justified in intervening.'

'So the Tetrarch found him guilty of some venial offence against Jewish law?'

'He didn't say so, or not in so many words. He seemed to me, sir, to be more concerned about his status as a client king. He said that you should give the man a whipping.'

'Did he, now? Well, that might not be a bad idea, if only for that business with the money-changers the other day. I can't find any evidence of *maiestas*.' Pilate turned to the prisoner again. 'Why came you to Jerusalem? To bring peace, or a sword?'

Joshua made an effort to pull himself together. Then he replied, 'I was sent by God as a witness to the truth.'

'Do you intend any action against Rome?' asked Pilate.

'Heaven and earth shall pass away, but the things I teach will not. Those who are interested in the truth will listen to me.'

I translated all this for the Prefect. He said, 'What is the truth?'

'It is that which I have spoken.'

Pilate sighed and shrugged. 'I've no more patience with the slave. He's had a fair hearing. Give him a good whipping and let him go. Thirty lashes should suffice. And advise him to return to Galilee forthwith. I can't answer for his safety here.'

I translated. Joshua made no reply. Pilate shrugged again, and returned to his quarters.

*

I SPOKE briefly to Mary, advising her of Pilate's decision, before resuming my duties. As I left the praetorium Vulpino came hurrying up to me. 'Disturbing news, sir.'

'Not more. Go on.'

'Our men report that a mob, or number of mobs, are advancing upon the Essene Quarter from all sides.'

Even as he spoke, I could hear shouting from the neighbouring streets. 'Notify the Prefect at once,' I said. 'I'll see what can be done to control them.'

The first cohort, by now down to little more than four hundred men, were awaiting me outside the praetorium. I marshalled them as best I could before departing to the south to speak to the Second Cohort and its commander.

Before I was halfway there I realized the task facing us would ultimately prove hopeless. I had under my command no more than eight hundred men in all, to deal with a crowd which must already have numbered five thousand, and was rapidly increasing. This was no spontaneous uprising, consisting of persons of both sexes and all ranks of society. These were mostly young aggressive men, and had been organized after a fashion, in many cases bearing weapons. True, they were an undisciplined rabble, but there comes a point when numbers outweigh discipline.

I duly mobilized the Second Cohort, sometimes euphemistically known as all-purpose troops. That meant they got the dirty, undemanding jobs which any oaf could do as well as a soldier. To put it mildly, their military quality was extremely variable. Most were recruited locally, so that their loyalty might have been open to question, though to be fair they had not thus far shown any sign of disaffection.

Half an hour later the situation had deteriorated. Serious violence was still rare, but matters stood on the brink of outright rebellion. There was much shouting of treasonable slogans, while placards and billboards expressed anti-imperial sentiments, often in the crudest terms. I could not criticize my men; they were doing a good job, meeting force with proportionate retribution, whilst not overstepping the mark.

Again Vulpino was at my side, saluting. 'All centuries in position, sir. But …'

'Well?'

'It's everywhere similar to the way it is here, sir. Once the mob break through …'

'Which they will. Prepare to order all centuries to retreat to the tower. I'll give the word when. Mark, I say retreat, which means *en masse*, and in good order.'

Once they broke and fled, it could mean a massacre. Again Vulpino saluted and left.

The Prefect was at my side. Someone threw a stone, which struck him what must have been a painful blow on the left shoulder. He did not deign to rub it, but pointed to the thrower, and to the wrath of the crowd, one of my men dealt with him.

'How long can you hold out?'

'No longer than an hour, sir. Probably not half that time.'

'How many men have you?'

'Just under four hundred, sir, after allowing for casualties, none fatal yet. That's in this cohort. There are perhaps as many again in the second.'

'This is Herod's doing,' he said. 'You were right about him. What's your military advice?'

I shook my head. 'The position can't be held, sir. Not for long. We shall have to take refuge in the tower, and abandon the streets to the mob.'

'Hold out as long as you judge you can, then retreat to the tower. I've sent messengers to Syria demanding reinforcements, but even if they get through I can't see any arriving in much less than a week.'

'Your Excellency and your staff will have to join us in the tower,' I pointed out.

'Of course. I'll arm them as best I can. Meanwhile I'll make one last effort to reason with the Tetrarch. It goes against the grain to give him what he wants, but if I don't we could have a disaster on the scale of the Teutoburg Forest. And I've no ambition to become another Quinctilius Varus.'

Pilate was no coward. But he had Rome to consider. If it became necessary to bargain away the life of the obstreperous Joshua bar-Josef, he would do so.

*

THE NEXT quarter of an hour was one of the longest of my life. At last we could hold out no longer. I was about to pass the order, when Pilate appeared on the wall above the forecourt to the praetorium, and raised his hands for silence. The noise abated somewhat, and the fighting died away into an uneasy truce.

'Citizens of Jerusalem! I order you to depart about your lawful business, in the name of Tiberius Claudius Nero Caesar, Emperor of Rome.'

This was greeted with obscene remarks and gestures, and not a few in the crowd made farting noises with their lips and tongues. Many of my men wanted to react violently, but I succeeded in keeping them in check.

'What are your demands?'

'Death!' cried one or two. 'Death to the usurper!'

This was taken up in a chant, in the Greek language. Evidently they had been rehearsed. A Jewish mob would have spoken Hebrew.

'For whom?'

'For the usurper! He who calls himself King of the Jews!'

There came a great roar of assent. 'Do you mean the man Joshua bar-Josef?'

'Yes! Yes! Death! Death!'

Again Pilate raised a hand for silence, and again succeeded to the extent of subduing the noise somewhat. 'I sentence the man Joshua bar-Josef, calling himself Joshua bar-Abbas, to death by crucifixion, the sentence to be carried out at Golgotha forthwith.'

There came a great roar of appreciation. Pilate rubbed his

hands together, then spread them in a gesture of dismissal, and the danger was over, or at least much reduced.

It was of course a humiliation for Rome, and for the Prefect. But the alternative was full-scale revolt, with heavy casualties and ultimate consequences impossible to predict.

Would I have done the same? I know not. The man had been a nuisance, but meant well, and had done nothing to deserve death. Ever since becoming a Roman citizen I had held their motto '*Fiat justitia, ruat coelum*' in the greatest respect. But was his life worth more than many thousand lives, and a province drenched in blood? As a moral coward, I was glad not to have had to make the decision.

According to Pilate

IT WAS NEARLY two hours after sunset, and I sat in my favourite chair, while my wife, Ursula, massaged the back of my neck. I find this practice tends to rid me of tension prior to going to bed. There is much to be said for marrying a freedwoman. Eternally in one's debt for freeing her, she is docile and obedient as a wife should be. The recalcitrant and faithless creatures who were my first and second wives were always demanding attention and constantly complaining, especially about the lack of a social life.

And that was in Thrace, and Galatea. The gods alone know what they would have thought of Judaea, where the only intelligent and educated persons have their minds addled with all sorts of religious taboos. Remembering what they can and can't eat is one of countless problems involved in entertaining them. I'd held but half a dozen dinner parties since arriving in the place, for which I imagine my cooks at least were grateful.

In contrast to her predecessors, Ursula is a model consort. I regret that she is not the mother of my childen, who despite being adult still cause me almost as much trouble as my former wives. Every day I thank the gods for sending her to me, though not in her hearing of course.

A slave appeared in the doorway. 'Excuse me, *domine*.'

'What is it?'

'The centurion Teutonicus wishes to see you, *domine*. He says it is urgent.'

I sighed. 'Send him in.'

He entered and saluted. 'Forgive me for troubling you at this hour, sir, but I knew you would wish to be kept informed of the latest developments.'

I waved Ursula away. She disappeared, obedient and unobtrusive as ever. 'Go on.'

'The man Joshua was arrested an hour ago in the Garden of Gethsemane, by the Palace Guard. They took him to the house of the High Priest, where there was a form of trial convicting him of blasphemy and sentencing him to death.'

'I gave no permission for such a thing.'

'Quite so, sir. I know a little of their law, and the alleged trial was also deficient in several other respects. As a result I brought the man here, in case you wish to interview him tonight.'

If he was guilty of anything in Roman law, it was *maiestas,* which meant that I had to prioritize it. 'I suppose so. Anything else?'

'Yes, sir. I've arrested the man Judas for *maiestas* and the murder of Syrianus. Whether he's guilty or not, I judged it time to put more pressure on him. What's more, his father, Simon, was found stabbed to death in the Gardens of Gethsemane about the same time that the man Joshua was arrested. It seems to me that Judas has some questions to answer there too.'

I sighed and shook my head. 'Patricide? There seems no limit to his infamy. But anyway, that can wait. I'm sure I needn't tell you to ensure that he's kept under close guard. Meanwhile, I'll see the man Joshua.'

*

TWO burly legionnaries brought him in. Teutonicus stood to one side. The prisoner was a man in the early thirties, tall and thin, clad in a loin cloth and torn woollen robe. He was drenched in sweat, and shaking either from cold or fear.

'Are you Joshua bar-Josef?'

He nodded. I turned to Silvius. 'Mark that down as a yes.' To the prisoner I said, 'Do you travel the province of Judaea teaching that you are the Messiah, who will free the land from the Roman yoke?'

He made no reply. 'The man is not conversant with the Greek tongue, sir,' said Teutonicus. 'He speaks Aramaic, and a dialect of Hebrew. May I translate your words to him?'

'Do so.'

The centurion spoke a few words in what I recognized as one of the Semitic tongues. The prisoner hesitated, then replied shortly. Teutonicus turned to me.

'He says, sir: "The words are yours." '

'What does that mean?' I asked irritably.

Again the centurion spoke to the man, who replied after a short delay. Further words were exchanged, of which I caught the Emperor's name, before their speech was translated.

'He wants to know, sir, by whose authority you ask the question. I told him, by authority of Caesar. Whereupon he said you had no authority over him apart from that given to you by others.'

'Deuced impertinence. Tell him so.'

The faintest of smiles crossed the centurion's face. 'I have already done so, sir.'

'Will he now reply to my question?'

Again the centurion spoke to him. 'He now says, sir, that his kingdom is not of this world.'

I was tired and irritable, and had neither the time nor energy to argue with the man about religious dogma. An idea now struck me, so ingenious that it almost restored me to good humour. 'This man is a Galilean, is he not?'

'Yes, sir.'

'And has preached his message mainly in Galilee?'

'Indeed, sir.'

I smiled. 'It seems therefore that jurisdiction in this case falls within the province of the Tetrarch Herod Antipas. Take the prisoner to his palace and inform Herod of my decision.'

For an instant Teutonicus hesitated, then came to attention and saluted. 'Sir.'

'I know it's late,' I said. 'But I don't see why I should be the only one to be inconvenienced. Tell Herod to try the man without delay, and report the result to me in person for my ratification.'

'It shall be done, sir.'

'Report tomorrow morning.' I yawned. 'Now I'm going to bed.'

*

BY the third hour of the next day the man stood before me again. This time he was decked in gorgeous if ill-fitting robes of purple and gold. Some briars had been twisted into his long dark hair, and he was unsteady on his feet. A rivulet of blood was running down his face.

'What means this?' I demanded.

Teutonicus stepped forward. 'Forgive me, sir, but it was none of my doing. The Tetrarch Herod ordered the man to be decked in this way as a form of mockery, and crowned with what he called a crown of thorns. I did not feel justified in intervening.'

I had after all passed jurisdiction over to Herod. 'So, he has found him guilty of some venial offence against Jewish law?'

'It would seem so, sir. I thought – '

'Yes?'

'I thought the Tetrarch seemed more concerned about his status as a client king than any of the man's religious teaching. Hence the mockery of his claim to be King of the Jews, if indeed he has made any such claim, which seems doubtful. Herod insisted that you, sir, were the appropriate authority to try the man on the charge of *maiestas*.'

'So I shall be, if he's ever charged with that. I haven't yet decided.' I turned to the man again. 'Why have you come to Jerusalem?'

The centurion translated. The man seemed to have recovered his poise somewhat, and replied coherently. Teutonicus turned back to me.

'He says, sir, that he was sent by God as a witness to the truth, and that anyone interested in the truth will listen to him.'

'What is the truth?' I asked.

Again the centurion translated for me. This time the man made no reply. The centurion spoke to him again. At last he made some sort of response.

'He says again that what he speaks is the truth. I asked him if his truth included any action against Rome.'

'And what did he say to that?'

'He said, sir, that heaven and earth should pass away, but the things he teaches will not pass away.'

I came to a decision. 'As I thought. The man's nothing but a religious crackpot, with a following of gullible persons from all classes of society, more than half of them women. No evidence of any military following at all.'

'For what it's worth, sir, that coincides with my own view.'

'Tell him that I expect him to be less of a damned nuisance in future. Give him thirty lashes for that stupid business in the temple grounds the other day, then let him go. And advise him to return to Galilee forthwith. If he remains in Jerusalem, I can't answer for his safety.'

Teutonicus duly translated. The man made no comment or response of any kind, and was marched away.

*

I HAD assumed that to be the end of the matter, at least for the time being, but within half an hour I was informed that Herod and the Chief Priest wanted to see me.

I had just broken my fast, and laid the last of the food aside. 'I'll see them shortly, in the tablinum.'

The slave departed. 'Whatever now?' asked Ursula.

I sighed and shook my head. 'No doubt they want me to have the man Joshua crucified.'

'Will you do so?'

'Not if I can help it. The important thing is to avoid trouble at all costs. But the main difficulty in this god-dominated place is that whatever I choose to do seems to make matters worse. These people simply ask for trouble the whole time.'

The slave reappeared. 'What is it now?'

'Messenger, *domine*. From the centurion Teutonicus.'

'Send him in. Yes?' I demanded of the newcomer.

He saluted. 'P. Vulpino, sir. From the centurion Ti. Rotgarius …'

'I know, I know.'

'He apologizes, my lord, for not reporting in person as is his wont, but he is engaged in trying to conrol an unruly mob assembled before the temple and extending into both the Upper and Lower Cities. He estimates the number at five thousand, increasing rapidly.'

'Ye gods.'

'He wishes me to say that the assembly does not appear to be spontaneous, but has been organized. He is endeavouring to find out who is responsible.'

'I think I can make a good guess.'

The man seemed to come to a decision. 'Yes, my lord. King Herod Antipas, aided and abetted by the chief priests. Forgive one of humble rank for speaking so candidly.'

'Say what you like about the bastards so far as I'm concerned. How many men has Teutonicus?'

'Two cohorts, my lord, and to speak frankly, one is of very unreliable quality. Less than a thousand men in all.'

'This mob. I assume they are hostile to the prisoner Joshua?'

'My lord, yes. For the most part, that is. There are some who support him, mostly women and family groups. Some scuffles have broken out, which we are attempting to quell.'

'I'll come and see for myself.'

'Very good, my lord.' The man saluted again and left.

As I strode out on to the balcony above the street a slave muttered unhappily, 'King Herod and the chief priests wish to see you, my lord.'

'They can wait.'

The scene below was on the verge of degenerating into anarchy. I judged the crowd to number between five and ten thousand, stretching from the theatre in the south to Antipas's palace to the north-east. And indeed beyond that, into the very grounds of the temple. Soldiers were trying to marshal the crowd into some semblance of order, intervening directly only to suppress violence. In command, to the extent that that could be claimed for anyone, was the ubiquitous centurion Teutonicus, now shouting orders to his men to intercept a section of the rabble as it advanced on the praetorium, now calming an hysterical woman, now fetching a huge rioter a smack in the jaw with his fist which rendered him senseless. The man's cronies made as if to respond in kind, then noting the Roman's drawn sword, thought better of it.

As if sensing my presence, Teutonicus turned and saluted briefly before resuming his duties. I acknowledged, and re-entered the tablinum.

I snapped my fingers at a slave, and ordered him to send Silvius. The scribe appeared within moments. 'Take this down: "Pilate to Lamia." You know all the titles, and so on. "Be advised as a matter of extreme urgency that Judaea is on the verge of revolt. I require a minimum reinforcement of one whole legion, five thousand men. Immediate." Usual valediction. Send it to Damascus by three separate couriers, to ensure that at least one gets through.'

Silvius completed his scribblings. '*Domine*. Should I add by whom the revolt was instigated?'

'No. For one thing, I'm not entirely sure. For another, I suspect those in high places. Need I say more?'

'No indeed, *domine*.' Some men perform better than expected in a crisis, others worse. I have to admit that old Silvius fell into the first class. He saluted and hurried away at once, a more purposeful figure than his usual pettifogging self.

Now at last I was ready to see those responsible for the mayhem below. I drew a few deep breaths. I must at all costs keep my temper. It would not be easy.

Another slave entered. 'Yes?'

'The High Priest Josef bar-Caiaphas begs audience with you, *domine*. Alone.'

'Is not the Tetrarch with him?'

'My lord, yes. But it seems,' the slave shifted his feet awkwardly, 'that he would prefer to speak to you alone first.'

I frowned and took a moment for thought. 'Very well. We are not to be disturbed save for matters of extreme urgency.'

'*Domine*.'

From Caiaphas I had expected the usual mixture of self-importance and sychophancy. Instead he looked decidedly worried.

I gestured him to a seat. 'This must be quick, High Priest. You can see that I have other matters to attend to.'

'So I observe.' He hesitated. 'I hope that Your Excellency does not think I have had any hand in this riotous assembly.'

'The possibility had crossed my mind.'

'There, Excellency, you do me an injustice.'

'Yesterday the citizens of Jerusalem seemed, if not docile, at least no worse than usual at the time of the Passover. And most of them were respectable women and family groups. This assembly, as you call it, seems unlikely to be spontaneous. The majority are loutish young men, looking for trouble.'

He shifted in his seat. 'There I fear I have to agree with Your Excellency.'

'You surely do not blame the Zealots? They number but a couple of score, and have no power to raise a crowd this size.'

'I do not blame the Zealots,' he said uneasily. 'And whereas Joshua is a blasphemer and …'

'Yes, I know all about that. But I can see that there is something else you wish to impart to me, Chief Priest, and I implore you to be quick about it.'

'Despite Your Excellency's suspicions, and the fact that your Excellency and I have not always seen eye to eye on certain topics, I can assure Your Excellency that I have always had the interests of the Empire and Your Excellency at heart. Consistent of course with my duty to God and the Children of Israel.'

This was more like the sanctimonious knave I was used to. 'I accept that,' I said mendaciously. 'Go on.'

'The rabble out there are for the most part hostile to Rome. I doubt if the followers of Joshua bar-Josef account for more than a tenth of them.'

'Less than that, if my information is to be believed.'

'Ah. I am glad to find your Excellency in agreement with me. I… I'm sure Your Excellency remembers the lunatic Johan the Baptizer, executed some eighteen months since.'

'Of course,' I replied, wondering where this was leading. 'Come to the point.'

'Executed on the orders of King Herod Antipas.'

'At the instigation of his wife and stepdaughter, as I understand it. As a result of some imagined insult to a couple of vain and vindictive women.'

'Whilst I respectfully agree with Your Excellency's asssessment of the ladies in question, my information is that the King intended to have him executed anyway. He alleged that Johan had proclaimed the man Joshua to be the Messiah, and King of the Jews.'

'I begin to understand. Herod wants him killed, and will incite a revolt if he does not have his way.'

Caiaphas essayed a thin smile into his beard. 'I doubt if he would put it as bluntly as that, my lord.'

'Does he know,' I said, 'that reinforcements are on their way from Syria? And that any insurrection will be put down without mercy?'

Caiaphas did not seem impressed. He obviously realized I was bluffing. I should be lucky to see any reinforcement within a week, by which time the damage would have been done. And that was assuming there was a legion stationed near Damascus. If Labia had to send to Antioch, three hundred miles away and more, I might as well not have bothered. Against the might of Rome no Jewish revolt stood the least chance of ultimate success, but every chance of causing sufficient mayhem to ensure that I was recalled to Rome in disgrace and required to open my veins.

The noise from without was increasing. How much longer could a few hundred men of variable quality keep the murderous rabble at bay?

'And what are you inviting me to do, High Priest?'

He shrugged and spread his hands 'There appears but one thing Your Excellency can do. Order the man Joshua to be crucified. By claiming to be the son of Almighty God he has forfeited his right to live.'

There was no sense in arguing with the fellow. By all pragmatic standards he was right. The trouble caused by the man's adherents if he were executed would be as nothing compared with that which Herod could bring about. From what I had observed, over half of Joshua's following were women, the majority of the rest men without military experience or inclination. And the man deserved little sympathy. I had given him the chance to explain his teachings and he had failed to do so, so far as I could see, though sheer contumacy.

'I hope,' said Caiaphas in his oiliest manner, 'that Your Excellency does not think me guilty of any disloyalty to Rome and her great Emperor. I am making no threats of any description. Indeed, I wash my hands of them.' He suited action to his words by rubbing his hands together in feigned humility. 'I have made it clear that any such threats emanate from elsewhere. All that concerns me is the avoidance of a conflict which would result in many deaths, and profit no-one. But methinks it were well that your Excellency see King Herod now.'

'I'll see Herod,' I said firmly, 'when I am good and ready. Meanwhile I have someone else to see.'

*

I SUCCEEDED in getting a word with Teutonicus in the

forecourt to the praetorium. He would not have thanked me for removing him from his duties by inviting him inside.

'How long can you keep things under control?' I asked.

He shook his head. 'An hour at most, sir. You can see what things are like.'

And indeed the Antipas mob were growing in size all the time – men streaming in from the Essene Quarter, the Lower City, whence they swamped the theatre grounds, from the Temple itself, and even further north. A human wave without limit, stretching as far as I could see.

'How many men have you?'

'I started with four hundred three-and-twenty, sir. Plus about as many again in the second cohort, under command of Maximinus. A dozen have been wounded seriously enough to put them out of action, none killed yet.'

'You were right about Herod,' I said. 'It's his doing. The high priests will co-operate with him for their own purposes, but are anxious to avoid falling out with me. What's your advice? Militarily, I mean.'

'In less than an hour's time,' he said, 'I and my men will have to take shelter in the northern towers of the Palace, and abandon the city to the mob.'

'Suppose I were to order you to stand against the mob at all costs, and fight it out to the end if need be?'

'You represent Caesar, my lord. Your orders would of course be obeyed.'

'Faithful unto death. Good man. Hold out as long as you judge you can, then retreat to the tower. I've sent couriers for reinforcements from Syria, but Zeus knows how long it will take for them to arrive. If indeed the messengers get through.'

He nodded. 'I ought to mention that from the tower we should not be able to defend Your Excellency. It would therefore be well for you and your staff to join us there.'

'Don't you worry about that,' I said drily.

*

HEROD looked slightly less pleased with himself than I had feared. Something of the enormity of what he intended may have struck him. My report to Rome would make his role in the affair perfectly clear. And yet… he was known to have the backing of the imperial prefect Sejanus, whom the Emperor now seemed to rely upon in all things.

I write the final few sections of these memoranda some years later, during my retirement, and having the benefit of hindsight now realize that at the time in question the sun of Sejanus was already low in the sky. He fell from power eighteen months later, and was executed for *maiestas*, along with most of his family. Which fact I have to admit gave me far more satisfaction than the condemnation of a harmless lunatic from Galilee.

Herod waved his hands. 'You can see how things stand out there, Excellency. I cannot control the people. Indeed I doubt if anyone could control them.'

'A Roman legion could control them,' I said. 'Or even a couple of decent cohorts, but as you know I lack such things. What have you to say to me?'

'The man Joshua. He threatens the peace of Rome and the Empire by falsely claiming to be King of the Jews. Our loyal subjects out there strongly object to such treason.'

'He said to me,' I replied, 'that his kingdom was not of this world. And his followers seemed to be peaceable, if deluded.'

'When I interviewed him, he said he was King of the Jews.'

'I see. And what role did he assign to you?'

'This is no laughing matter,' said the Tetrarch querulously. 'Judaea is on the verge of revolt, and you make light of things. Caesar would not be pleased.'

'Neither would he be pleased to learn of the actions of those who claim to be loyal subjects of the Empire, but store illegal caches of arms, and incite their followers to sedition and affray.'

'Do you accuse me of such a thing?'

'I have not said so. Only you and the gods know the truth of the matter. But rest assured, I shall do my best to discover it, and advise Caesar of my findings.'

With Sejanus in charge of Rome, this was an empty threat, as Herod well knew. 'He would not believe you.'

'Well, we shall see. I shall make my own decision about the man Joshua, and you will be advised of it, as will the people out there, whom you claim are so dear to you.'

There came a knock, and a slave entered. 'Forgive me, Excellency. The centurion …'

I stood. 'Good day, my dear tetrarch. I have work to do.'

Herod departed with very ill grace. Teutonicus saluted him perfunctorily. 'I must now order my men to the towers, sir. And for your own safety …'

'I shall go out on to the balcony and address the people. After that, if need be, I will accompany you to the towers.'

'As you will, sir.'

'I am about to make a decision you will disapprove of,' I told him. 'I do so in the interests of Rome.'

He nodded. 'I understand.'
'It may be an injustice, or it may not.'
Teutonicus shrugged. 'Who knows?'

Book VI

Crucifixion

According to Pilate

I BRACED myself, and walked out on to the balcony. Behind their shield-wall the soldiers below were making a valiant attempt to keep the mob at bay. I raised my hands for silence, and partly succeeded. At least the noise abated somewhat.

'Citizens of Jerusalem! In the name of Caesar, I order you to depart in peace.'

Someone made an obscenely offensive remark about Caesar, to general amusement. One or two of the soldiers surged forward, threatening to break ranks, and a few heads, but Teutonicus managed to keep them in order.

'What is it you want?'

'Death for the usurper! The one who calls himself King of the Jews!'

This demand met with almost universal approbation. 'Do you mean the man Joshua bar-Josef?'

'Yes! Yes! Death! Death!'

There was nothing for it. I judged it a choice between bad and worse. Indeed as a rule it would not have occasioned me much grief. I do not particularly like passing sentence of death, but never before had I hesitated to do so. Normally the welfare of Rome, and to be frank that of myself, would have been the only factors to affect my decision. I leave debates about right and wrong to those interested in such matters, philosophers and the like. Yet something had thus far stopped me confirming the death sentence. All I can think of is an abstract belief that what I was doing was in some sense morally repugnant. Strange.

But it had to be done. Once I had spoken the word 'Crucifixion,' the mob first roared approval, then quietened down. Some say, I moved my hands as if washing them clean of the matter, but all I remember is raising both hands in dismissal. Then I turned away, and made for my own quarters. It took some time for the crowd to disperse, but Teutonius and his men were able to maintain order with less difficulty than before.

Now that the decision had been made, there was no point in delay. Next day was the Sabbath, when a crucifixion would result in all sorts of problems with the Jews. I gave orders that the execution be carried out at once. Two other condemned men, convicted brigands, were likewise taken from the cells.

On impulse I grabbed a piece of papyrus from Silvius and scribbled on it in Greek the words: 'JESUS OF NAZARETH, THE KING OF THE JEWS.'

I summoned a member of my personal bodyguard. 'Make sure that this is affixed to the headpiece of the cross.'

He looked at it dubiously. 'What's the matter?' I asked.

'Should it not say, *domine*, "Jesus of Nazareth, who *said* he was the King of the Jews"?'

'What I have written,' I said, 'I have written. *Stet.*'

To this day, and I write some ten years later, I know not why I acted as I did. I must have had some vague idea of annoying the Jews, a people I always loathed, and at the time in question had good cause to resent deeply. The implication might have been: 'Is this wretched creature the best you can do for a king?' And yet at the back of my mind I swear there was some obscure sense of lodging a form of protest against what I had been forced to do. That just possibly this strange, deluded man might indeed have had some special role to play in the affairs of Jewry, and the world.

Be that as it might, less than a quarter of an hour later the supposed prophet Joshua was marched out into the street, guarded by half a dozen men from the Second Cohort. He was followed by the two brigands, similarly escorted. To my relief, most of those hostile to him had dispersed, and paradoxically those now lining the route to Calvary seemed in sympathy with the condemned man. Twice he stumbled under the weight of the beam he carried, and was whipped to his feet. Someone in the crowd cried: 'Joshua! Messiah!' Someone else, 'Bar-Abbas! The Son of Man! Bar-Abbas!' Yet another, in Greek: 'Jesus bar-Abbas! Save him! Free bar-Abbas!' and this curious chant was taken up by many in the crowd, who otherwise showed no sign of causing trouble or disaffection. Typical of the Jews, I reflected. Whatever I chose to do was wrong.

I watched the small convoy until it reached the Gennath Gate, beyond the Tower of Hippicus, its embattled summit pointing the way to the heavens. The prisoners passed through it, and were lost to sight. I never saw the man again.

*

NEXT day was the Sabbath, when the Jews are supposed to do no work. Would that I could afford such idleness. I decided to make my move against those Judaeans guilty of *maiestas*. If their priests saw fit to complain about my having profaned the Sabbath, they could do so. They would be too late.

Acting on information received, several of the Zealots were arrested at their homes, offering little resistence. None were Roman citizens, and therefore they were not entitled to a trial. I spent much of the day interrogating them. The majority were convicted. Those found guilty of disorder only were flogged and pardoned with a severe warning, those convicted of *maiestas* sentenced to crucifixion.

It being the Sabbath, the executions would not take place until the morrow or the day following. Those not condemned would be retained in gaol for the time being, released in ones and twos during the following week, and kept under close surveillance. Deprived of leadership, any remaining malignants could easily be dealt with. I judged the threat to Rome to be barely a quarter of what it had been eight-and-forty hours earlier.

*

IN late evening Teutonicus, who of course had been called to give evidence and had done so admirably, came to see me about a matter relating to the man Secarius, who had been amongst those I had condemned, and the murder of his father, the Zealot Simon bar-Cleophas.

It seems Teutonicus and his woman were concerned about an aspect of the affair which in a formal document such as this I shall not write down. It would serve no useful purpose. Suffice it to say that I may have bent the law a little in the interests of what I perceived to be justice.

Judas Secarius was crucified early in the afternoon of the following day. Apart from those carrying out the sentence, no-one attended.

According to Mary

TODAY they crucified my Lord. I am distraught. So sick at heart that I can barely write. Everything is blotted with tears. How can Almighty God, perfect and omnipotent, allow such a thing to happen?

I cannot blame my centurion. He did his best. From what he has said to me it seems that the man mainly responsible was Herod Antipas, who had previously murdered Johan the Baptizer, aided and abetted by his evil wife and daughter. The chief priests were also to blame, nor can I find it in me to forgive Pilate.

Shortly after noon, gangs of youths began to make their way towards the praetorium where my Lord had been arraigned. From an initial few score, their numbers soon swelled to hundreds, then thousands. Some were fanatical in their hatred of my Lord, others merely brutal louts looking for trouble at any cost. Yet others I suspect had been bribed by Herod or his agents. A few of our Lord's followers, mostly women, managed to line the streets in his support, but we were heavily outnumbered, and no match for Herod's thugs.

I was in the crowd when the Prefect made his announcement. Never one to shirk an unpleasant task, my centurion sought me out to tell me the news, unnecessarily of course. He expected me to blame him, but I could not. He may be employed by the forces of evil, but I am convinced that he is fundamentally a good man. I pray to Almighty God that when those responsible for this heinous deed are called to account, as assuredly they will be, my centurion will not be amongst them. If only I could get him to recognize the truth.

A quarter of an hour after Pilate's announcement our Lord descended the steps from the praetorium, bearing on his shoulders the heavy cross-beam to which his dear hands were to be nailed. Wearing a bright purple robe, in which I later learned he had been arrayed by Herod as a cruel jest, and with blood running down his face from a crown of thorns, he looked a pitiful sight as he staggered under the load. Behind him came two bandits arrested during the recent disturbances and likewise sentenced to death. They were both young fellows, heavily built, but even they had difficulty supporting the beams they bore.

Alongside them marched a guard provided from the Second Cohort, headed by a centurion whom I partly knew: one Maximin, an ignorant and boorish man, much prone to brutality and foul language. He yelled constantly both at his men and those condemned. They set off to the north, through the Gennath Gate, barely a quarter of a mile from the site of the abomination, a place called Golgotha, or head-bone, from the domed shape of the hill on which it stood.

Three times my Lord fell, crushed under the weight of the beam, and twice he struggled to his feet. The third time he failed to rise. After whipping him proved of no avail, the centurion Maximin ordered a member of the crowd to pick up the beam and carry it. Needless to say he selected one of those in sympathy with our Lord, a sturdily-built middle-aged man who I later learnt was called Simon of Cyrene. He was a good man, who willingly took up the burden to save our Lord the additional ordeal.

As we neared the site of crucifixion I could see the upright stakes being lowered to the ground for the cross-beams to be affixed. By now a greater proportion of the crowd were sympathetic to our Lord, many of the troublemakers having dispersed, their work accomplished. The godly section of the crowd even managed to raise occasional cries of: 'Joshua! Messiah!' or even 'King of the Jews!' Above all they kept chanting the title which he preferred to apply to himself: 'Joshua, Son of Man!' Many called upon the Romans to free him, crying: 'Free Joshua bar-Abbas!' in the Greek, 'Jesus bar-Abbas!' or simply: 'Free bar-Abbas!'

Fortunately the soldiers refused to allow me and my Lord's other followers to approach the scene of crucifixion, so we had to watch from afar. Had we been any closer I believe the sickening sight would have driven me mad. With me by now was my friend little Salome, in silent tears, and a namesake of mine: Mary, the widow of one Zebadiah, and mother of our Lord's disciples Jacob and Johan.

By the time my Lord arrived at the scene, the two criminals had been laid on the ground beside their stakes, and the crossbeams were being affixed. Then they were tightly bound by ropes around their wrists and ankles.

It is the Roman custom to nail prisoners to their crosses in addition to the ropes only if the victims have been convicted of particularly grave offences. This included banditry. I could no longer look. The screams as the nails were driven into position, particularly that through the ankles, were terrible to hear. The centurion and his men merely laughed.

The stakes were then raised into position, one on either side of the brow of the hill. By now the victims' screams had subsided into a low moaning. One of them seemed to have lost consciousness.

Intent upon watching the sufferings of my Lord, I had not been aware of the presence of a man who had come to stand beside me. I glanced up. It was my centurion.

'Take courage,' he murmured.

'I had thought you would have been deputed to this work,' I said, trying to keep the bitterness out of my voice.

He shook his head. 'There was never any question of that. Crucifixion work is given to all-purpose troops from outside the First Cohort. Front-line combat men are seldom called upon for such tasks.'

He meant the elite, but was too modest to use such an expression. He winced. 'And men who show a dislike for it are usually transferred to other duties.'

'So those men …?' I gestured to the soldiers involved.

'The dregs,' he said shortly.

The nails were going in. I could not watch. I thought the hammering would drive me mad. My centurion held me. I heard a low moan from my Lord.

'That's the worst over,' said my centurion softly. 'He took it well. And he was so weak from the scourging and beatings that methinks he may not survive for long.'

As his cross was raised into position I noticed a legend in the Greek language attached to the top of the stake. It read: 'JESUS OF NAZARETH, THE KING OF THE JEWS.'

At length the cross reached the vertical. Soon afterward

came the worst moment of all. My Lord cried out in the Aramaic tongue: 'My God, my God, why hast thou forsaken me?'

He had believed all along that Almighty God would intervene in miraculous fashion to save him from imminent death. He now knew that was not going to happen. And so did I.

The soldiers were playing dice at the foot of the cross, the prize being my Lord's rich raiment. My centurion muttered something under his breath which I did not catch. With what passed for a smile, little Salome, whose ears were sharper than mine, whispered: 'He said, my lady, that any of his men who behaved like that at a crucifixion would find themselves cleaning the latrines for a month.'

Clouds were building up from the west, darkening the sun despite the fact that it was but two hours since noon. The heavens were about to weep. There came a blinding flash of light overhead, as the ominous silence was shattered by a crash of thunder. Thus did Almighty God show his grief and rage.

Then came the rain – a few heavy drops at first, before they multiplied and hammered down hard as a hailstorm. Finally, a cloudburst. Impossible to see through the cataract of solid rain. Most onlookers fled for whatever cover they could find. We had been soaked to the skin within moments, but refused to move. The bandits were shouting something at our Lord, but again I could not hear.

At last our Lord's head, which had been gazing to heaven, dropped suddenly, and his arms stretched out above him. I prayed that his sufferings were at an end.

The bandits were still struggling to raise themselves

to breathe, their chests heaving with the effort. Our Lord remained still. The storm abated into steady rain.

'Surely,' said my centurion softly to himself, 'this was a son of God.

'I don't think there's much point in your remaining longer,' he continued quietly. 'You will distress yourselves further to no purpose. Tomorrow being the Sabbath, the bodies will be removed before sunset. You and his other friends can then arrange for burial. A man called Josef of Arimathaea has arranged something with Pilate, or so I understand.'

'A good man. I know him.'

'I expect you'll wish to attend the burial. You're welcome to stay at headquarters meanwhile.'

'What of Salome?'

'Of course the same applies to her.'

'Thank you, *domine*,' said the little slave.

With a last glance at my dear Lord, our sad little convoy moved off, clothes steaming in the rain. 'Will you be at the burial?' I asked my centurion.

He shook his head. 'I've too much to deal with. Besides, I think any such ceremony better confined to those who believed in your Lord.'

'I heard you call him the Son of God.'

'Are not all the righteous sons and daughters of their gods?'

*

WE buried my Lord by moonlight that same night, for works of necessity and mercy may be carried out upon the Sabbath.

Josef of Arimathaea and Simon of Cyrene had removed his body from the accursed cross, that epitome of everything that was evil. The body had been laid out, anointed with unguents and wrapped in linen by the remaining women of his family, that is, his kinswoman Mary, wife of Zebadiah, and two of her serving-maids.

I arrived in time for the committal. No priest would attend, so there was no ceremony, but alongside Josef of Amimathaea and Simon Cyrene, Salome and I stood with bowed head, as we remembered all the good that had been said and done by our Lord, now so cravenly deserted by his followers.

Josef and Simon then took our dear Lord's body and interred it in a cave forming part of the city wall. Not without much effort, they rolled a large stone before it for protection. A narrow gap was left, in case any wished to pay their respects within the tomb itself, away from prying eyes.

This, then, would be the last I should ever see of my dearest Lord.

*

I HAD been so wrapped up in my own grief that I had failed to observe that Salome seemed at least as distraught, and more nervous. '*Domina,*' she said on our way back, 'what kind of a man is the Dominus Teutonicus?'

'I don't think anyone quite knows that,' I said thoughtfully. 'Why do you ask? Have you information which might help him trace the murderer of your lover?'

'Yes, *domina*. That is why I asked.'

The recent access of formality had taken me by surprise.

'There is no need to keep calling me *domina*. Mary is my name. We are friends, are we not?'

'Thank you, *d*... Mary. You see, I know the murderer.'

I turned to her in surprise. 'Tell him then, by all means. What has stopped you?'

'I am afraid.'

'Of the murderer?'

'Oh, no, *dom*... Mary.' She gave a hysterical little laugh. 'Not of the murderer.'

'Of his friends, perhaps? Has he friends in high places?'

'No. No, it's not that.'

She stopped suddenly, a small frail figure, her shadow blurred in the light of the clouded moon.

Then she told me.

*

WHAT she said was of such momentous nature that I could scarce believe it. I begged her not to say anything to anyone else, but she insisted that she must tell Pilate, or at least my centurion. Eventually we compromised, she promising not to do anything until the morrow. And she did not, though I kept a careful eye on her all day.

In the evening, the Sabbath now being over, I sent her to prepare a light supper. Of course I should have known. She went straight to my centurion.

I soon guessed what she had done, and hurried after her, but was too late to prevent her talking. Throughout the interview with him I begged her to desist, but she would have none of it. Truly such disobedience ought to have earned her a whipping, but I had not the heart.

Again I was proud of my centurion. He listened carefully, asked thoughtful questions, and was totally free from bigotry, condescension, or any attitude save that of humanity, and resolve to learn the truth. I left his room in a far more tranquil state of mind than when I had entered, convinced that despite everything, all would be well.

A subsequent meeting between my centurion and Pilate finally put my mind at rest. My centurion emerged from the Prefect's tablinum to inform me that no further action was deemed necessary. Yet again he had put me eternally in his debt. Remembering our Lord's words, I even began to think less judgmentally of the Prefect.

On the way back to our chambers Salome said, quite firmly, 'May a slave offer you advice, *domina*?'

'Do not call yourself a slave. A friend may do so, of course.'

'Very well. Rotgarius Teutonicus is a good man. You are lucky to have met him. Do not let the chance of happiness escape you because you think differently about certain things.'

'Very important things,' I said, after a pause.

'Maybe. But I repeat, he is a good man. You surely no longer believe him to be an agent of the Evil One?'

'No,' I said slowly. 'I have not thought that for some time. I now believe that he is a man sent by God, but does not know it.'

'Well, that's all right, then,' said Salome placidly.

I now recognize that little Salome, who in my foolish pride I used to treat in a patronizing manner, possesses a courage and strength of character I can only aspire to. And not before time I am convinced that she is right. As I sit to make these final notes of the day the light is fading, and moonlight gleams between the shutters. The candles will soon gutter and die.

But hope has started again in my breast. Yesterday was the worst day of my life. Today has thus far turned out better than I had any right to expect. I thought the hideous events at Golgotha might have poisoned my relationship with my centurion, but now I am confident that they will not. I shall tell him so.

Before then I shall visit the tomb of my Lord, and tell him what I have decided. The morning would be the best time, methinks, during the first or second hour. That will be the best chance of being alone.

According to the Centurion

HALF an hour later the danger of revolt was over. The mob had dispersed, if not in good order, at least with minimal casualties and damage. I was now free to follow my own inclination. I had performed my duty to Rome. Now I had to do my duty to my woman. Whether she realized it or not, she needed me.

She would blame me as an agent of Rome, and probably of the powers of Evil. In her eyes I would be one of those who had crucified the man she worshipped. But I had to face her. It was now or never. If in cowardice I could not face her now, I should lose all right to her love.

The convoy making for the place of execution had passed through the Gennath Gate some time before. In the distance, faintly, I could hear Joshua's supporters chanting in the Greek language: 'Jesus bar-Abbas! Free Jesus bar-Abbas!'

I turned to young Vulpino. 'Take over. I must see this through to the end.'

He nodded. 'Leave it to me, sir.'

Once through the gate, I could see the band of condemned men and their guards. Joshua was lagging behind, so weak from the floggings and torture that he could hardly stand. Another man, just dragged out of the crowd, was carrying the cross-member for him. Some of these lining the route greeted me with boos and catcalls, as a representative of hated Roman authority, but none offered me violence. In similar circumstances I have often found that the best policy is not to retaliate. I accordingly looked sad and serious, trying to regard those in the mob without hostility. To some small extent I suppose I was following the teachings of the man Joshua. Certainly I avoided the poisonous gloatings of the so-called soldiers from Maximin's Second Cohort. And I succeeded beyond my expectation, for I swear I heard a voice from the crowd cry, 'Never mind, centurion, you are not to blame!'

I reached the hill called Calvary, or by the locals Golgotha, which in the Hebrew tongue means the main bone of the head. I imagine it derives from the domed shape of the hill. As I arrived I heard the screams of one of the prisoners being nailed to his cross. The other brigand had accepted his lot more stoically.

A small crowd had gathered some way from the scene of execution, Maximin's men preventing them from approaching more closely. Amongst them I saw a group of three women: My lady Magdalene, the little slave Salome, and a middle-aged woman whom I later learned to have been my lady's namesake: Mary, distantly related to Joshua. Otherwise no members of his family were present. I assume they did not learn of his fate until later.

Of the nailings of Joshua's hands and feet I will not speak. His cross was then raised into position between the others. To my surprise the headboard bore a message in Greek: 'JESUS OF NAZARETH, THE KING OF THE JEWS.' At the time I assumed it was a cruel joke by the soldiers, but later learned that it was a whim of Pilate's.

I approached my lady and stood behind her. 'Take courage,' I murmured.

She turned. To my infinite relief, she smiled sadly. 'I had thought you would have carried out this work.'

I shook my head. 'Not that, at least. Crucifixion and other non-military tasks are seldom given to front-line troops. And men who demonstrate dislike for it are transferred to other duties.'

She gestured to the soldiers, some of whom were squatting to play dice for his robes, while making crude jests. 'So these men …?'

'Scum,' I said simply.

As the cross reached its final position I said, 'He is so weak from the scourging and beatings that methinks he will not long survive.'

Even as I spoke, Joshua raised his eyes and screamed in the Aramaic tongue: 'My God, my God, why hast thou forsaken me?'

One of the soldiers jeered, 'He saved others. Himself he cannot save.' The others agreed with coarse laughter. I muttered curses on them.

Shortly afterwards the skies darkened and the rains came in a sudden flood. Most of the crowd left the scene, but our group remained, soaked through yet determined to see the affair out to the end. One of the brigands cursed Joshua, who by now seemed but semi-conscious. He had been gazing up into the rain, but of a sudden his head dropped. He might have died, or just lost consciousness. In the latter case he would be unlikely to regain it. Surely, I thought, this had been a righteous man.

'I think it's over,' I said softly. 'To remain would be to

distress yourselves further to no purpose. Tomorrow being the Sabbath, the bodies will be removed before sunset.'

'What about burial?' My lady's face was drenched with rain and tears, but her voice was firm.

'His friends can arrange for burial then. A man called Josef of Arimathaea has arranged something with Pilate, or so I understand.'

'I know him slightly. He is a good man, who helps with our work sometimes.'

Salome spoke next. 'What will happen to the man Judas, my lord?'

'His arrest has been ordered on a charge of *maiestas*. Also murdering his father, Zelotes.'

'Is the evidence against him strong?'

Evidently she and Mary would be glad to see him condemned, if only for having betrayed the man Joshua.

'It is, I think, sufficient to obtain a conviction,' I said. 'He was on bad terms with his father, stood to inherit on his death, and he is the only man known to have been in Gethsemane at the relevant time whose movements are unaccounted for long enough to enable him to do the deed. Add to that the blood-stained knife found at the scene, his own self-styled title of *Secarius*, and... yes, there is sufficient for a conviction.'

For some reason this answer did not seem to satisfy her.

*

NEXT evening I sat alone in my quarters mulling over the day's events prior to turning in. The immediate threat of insurrection had been averted. Pilate had avenged his humiliation of the previous day by acting swiftly against those he judged to be enemies of Rome, mostly Zealots and their associates. Arrests had taken place soon after dawn, the prisoners being taken unawares and offering little resistence. Much of the day had been spent in his questioning and judging them.

Several times I was called upon to give evidence, and tried to do so as fairly as I could. Amongst those condemned to death was Judas Secarius, who apart from killing his father was proved to have committed several acts of *maiestas*. True to form, he had sobbed, blubbered and protested his loyalty to Rome even as he was dragged out to await execution.

Herod and the priests could complain all they liked, but the initiative had passed to Rome. For the time being at least the threat of rebellion was over.

Despite that, my spirits were depressed beyond measure. For all her attempts to be generous, I knew that my relations with the Lady Magdalene had suffered serious damage. I could only pray that it was not irreparable.

I was four-and-thirty years old, and had been a soldier since early adolescence, so there had of course been women in my life before. And there had been times when I had felt enough for a woman to have dreamt of a future with her, and been disappointed when such dreams had come to naught.

Yes, I had felt the same way before, but not to the same extent. I remembered her tear-stained face, hopeless, helpless despair written into every line of it. I felt sick at heart myself, but in a few days I should feel better. She would probably be worse. Her whole reason for living had collapsed around her.

For the first time it occurred to me that her happiness meant more to me than my own, and for some reason this encouraged me. I felt myself to be a better man than I had previously thought. And if I were, perhaps all was not yet lost. Maybe I came somewhere near being worthy of her. If so, conceivably I could make her happy.

I had already made a tiny start in that direction. I had reported to Pilate on the conduct of the men at the foot of the cross, and their commander Gaius Maximinus. I had ordered them thirty lashes each, and that Maximin be reduced to the ranks. In addition all got a spell of latrine duty. The Prefect was something of a martinet when it came to military discipline. Not only had he confirmed my decision, but increased the period of latrine duty, and ordered that the robe they had diced for be confiscated.

I was beginning to feel a little better. Tomorrow I should speak to my lady again.

There came a barely audible tapping at my door. 'Come in!' I cried.

To my surprise it was the little slave, Salome.

'Yes, what is it?'

'I have something to tell you, *domine*.'

'Go ahead, then,' I said in a friendly manner. 'But sit down.'

She shook her head and remained standing. 'Tell me, *domine*. Is it usual to crucify women?'

'Most unusual. For one thing they hardly ever commit serious crime. Though I have known it. Why?'

She took a deep breath. 'I am a murderess, *domine*, and so deserve to die.'

Bearing in mind that her mistress had confessed to such a thing without cause, I was inclined to be sceptical. 'Are you confessing to the murder of your lover, Dio?'

'Oh, no, *domine*, not that at least. I have killed his murderer, Simon Zelotes.'

*

I WAS considering this for a few moments in silence, when the door burst open, and my lady Mary tore in breathlessly.

'I don't know what this girl has told you,' she gasped, 'but it is not true.'

'If you don't know what she's told me, how do you know whether it be true or not?'

'Oh, very clever,' she said angrily.

'Please, no, *domina*,' said Salome, 'I must confess the truth.'

'Don't listen to her!'

I raised my hands. 'Ladies, please. There is no-one else here, so if you subsequently deny what you have said, I cannot prove it. But in view of what you say, Salome, I am put on enquiry. I am going to ask you to think quietly and carefully before you reply. Do you stand by what you have said, or do you wish to withdraw it?'

She paused, then said, 'I will explain it, *domine*.' Mary started to interrupt, but I raised my hand.

'I have always loathed the man Zelotes, *domine*. Like his son, he assumed a *cognomen* for himself based upon wanting to be a hero. In fact he was a coward. I knew one of the Zealots slightly; he used to visit the house where I was employed. He said that Simon Zelotes was always something of a joke among the other Zealots, talking big but never volunteering to match actions to his words.'

'From what I know,' I said, 'that description might equally apply to his son.'

'Indeed, my lord, they were much alike. That day, that dreadful day when we learned of Dio's death, I noticed Zelotes. Most of those present, even Judas, were bewildered. You and I grieved. But not Zelotes. For an instant he positively preened himself. Then he remembered to look shocked like everyone else.'

'That's not much to go on.'

She shook her head impatiently. 'Of course not, *domine*. But listen. From that time onwards I determined to find out whatever I could about him, even followed him at times. One day – it was the day before the meal in the Upper Room – I was lucky. It was in the tavern called the Fig Tree. He met a man called Elias bar-Abel, whom I also knew from my time as a whore. He stands high in the councils of the Zealots.'

I nodded. 'He was amongst those convicted of *maiestas* this afternoon.'

'I dressed similarly to the serving wenches, my lord, and had contrived to make myself look as plain as possible. No-one notices a serving wench unless she is pretty.'

'True,' I agreed. 'Go on.'

'After preliminary remarks to no consequence, he said: "I gather you and your men are under suspicion for the killing of that Roman bastard." Elias just grunted. Zelotes continued: "I know you are innocent. Guess how?" Elias said, "Don't tell me. Your son did it. He's already admitted as much to bar-Lavan, but we don't believe him. He's nothing but a bag of wind."

'Simon then said, "I know that as well as you. No, it was I who stabbed the bastard. I can give you details if you like." Elias just nodded, and Simon continued, "I found his body, certainly. What nobody knew was that I'd stabbed him an hour earlier, and gone back home. Miriam was visiting her aged mother that afternoon, so I was alone. None could prove that I had not been there all the time. When setting out for the inn I came across his body again. Strange that none had reported it meanwhile, but that suited me. The longer it took the better.

' "I'd followed him as he went to see the woman Eunice. She gave him short shrift, and refused to admit him to the house. I was hiding behind one of the buttresses to the city wall. He turned away, and glanced up and down the street. There was no-one else about. He walked a few paces, then stopped, looked down at a scrap of paper he was carrying, and began to make a scribbled note. That was my chance. I emerged from my hiding-place, and stabbed him deep in the back. Then I stabbed him again as he fell. I've done it once or twice before, you know. But never a Roman. It felt good. Really good." He then said,' Salome's eyes brimmed with tears, and her voice faltered, ' "As he lay dying, the bastard breathed the name of that little whore of his, Salome."

'I was shaking with fury and hate, *domine*. Never had I felt like that before. And Zelotes sat there so smug and pleased with himself. Until Elias said, "So you did it. You stupid bastard. I've a good mind to turn you in." He went on to say that Zelotes had put the whole movement in danger by alerting the Romans, and making it more difficult to organize an uprising. He also said that killing a man in combat was one thing, but stabbing him in the back like a coward was no part of God's plan.'

It never ceases to amaze me how Jews are always so

certain of their creator's opinions and intentions. I simply said, 'I see. Go on.'

'There then followed a bitter argument, carried on perforce in an undertone. Eventually they went outside together. Having learnt what I wanted, I didn't risk discovery by following them.'

I frowned thoughtfully. 'Why did you not tell me this at the time?'

'I was not sure what to do for the best, *domine*. Above all things I wanted revenge. I was afraid that I might not be believed, or at least that my evidence be deemed insufficient. Eventually I decided to deal with things myself.'

'Don't say any more, Salome,' said Mary hurriedly.

Again I raised my hand. 'At this stage, Salome, I must remind you that I am an official of Rome, and shall have to report what you say to the Prefect. You don't have to say anything further. Do you really want to?'

Again she drew a deep breath. 'Yes, *domine*. Our Lord Joshua said that he was the way, the truth and the life. I must therefore tell the truth. The following evening, if you remember, I was late arriving at our Lord's last evening meal.' Mary nodded. 'Zelotes was rather late too. I accosted him in the street, and got into converse with him. I said I was bored with my life with the Lady Mary – forgive me, my lady, that was not true – and I should appreciate a little masculine attention. We agreed a fee, and that we should meet that evening in the Gardens of Gethsemane, which are of course often used for such purposes. I stole a knife from your kitchen, my lord.'

I raised my eyebrows and nodded. 'I wondered what had happened to it.'

'I followed him there. We met in one of the depressions in the rock, known as the Caves.'

'I know them,' I said quietly. 'Go on.'

'I wanted to stab him there and then. He was everything I hated in men – smug and self-righteous, looking down on those less fortunate, especially women like me. And he had killed the man I loved, a man whose boots he wasn't fit to lick. I wanted to kill him so much. I wanted to kill …'

'But you couldn't.'

She gaped. 'How did you know?'

I smiled and inclined my head. 'It's not easy to kill a man. Especially the first time.'

'He realized there was something wrong, and asked what it was. So I told him. He just laughed. He laughed and said, "Well, fancy that! It'll be fun to screw his little whore after having killed the bastard." He reached out and grabbed me …'

'Don't say any more!' screamed Mary.

'… I grabbed the knife from his belt and stabbed him, deep in the gut. I can still see the look of surprise on his evil face. Then I stabbed him again and again. I was full of fiendish joy. I gloried in it. I kept stabbing and stabbing… There was blood all over me. As I looked down on him he convulsed and said, "You've killed me, you bitch." Then he coughed up a torrent of blood, shuddered and died.'

'What did you do with your bloodstained clothing?'

'I went back to your quarters, *domine*, reckless of whether anyone saw me or not. Dio had been avenged, that was the main thing. Then I calmed down a little. I took off my tunic, washed myself at the pump, and donned my only other dress. I squeezed much of the blood from the tunic into the gutters near the abbatoir, and threw the tunic itself into a well. Then I went back to your quarters, and returned the knife I had stolen to your kitchen. Soon after that you returned with my Lord and Judas ...'

'Yes, I know the rest.'

'Shall I go to the land of the damned for ever, *domine*? Our Lord spoke of outer darkness, weeping and wailing and gnashing of teeth. You are well educated, *domine*, and know about such things. Am I damned for ever?'

I shook my head. 'I know nothing of the afterlife, Salome, if there is such a thing. And nor in my view does anyone else, whatever they may claim.'

'You are not damned!' said Mary fiercely. 'No! No! No!' It crossed my mind to wonder whether she was rebelling against the teaching of her faith, which in truth seemed to me in some respects very far from humane.

Salome raised her chin. 'I should like to be taken before the Prefect immediately, *domine*. Before my courage fails.'

'Your courage will not fail,' I said. 'And I speak as one who has had some experience in such matters. But whether it will be necessary to appear before him I rather doubt.'

Mary looked puzzled. Salome said, 'I don't understand.'

'First let me say that my own enquiries had brought me to the same conclusion as yourself. We had someone listening to the conversation you describe, and we subsequently interrogated the man bar-Abel, who confirmed it. In other words Zelotes had treacherously murdered a Roman soldier, who incidentally was my best friend.

'As for what you have confessed to, there is no evidence besides your own. On that basis, it seems to me that a clever lawyer could persuade the Prefect that you acted in self-defence. The man was attempting to violate you, so in desperation you grabbed his dagger and struck out blindly. We subsequently found the bloodstained weapon, and it was his, not yours. The probability is that it was the same one which killed Dio, your lover and my friend.' I shrugged. 'I can't see that there's sufficient evidence to justify conviction for murder. Nor I think will Pilate. You have saved him the trouble of crucifying the man, with possible further trouble from the Zealots.'

'But …' she hesitated, 'an innocent man will be crucified for what I did.'

'Hardly. Judas was condemned not alone for the murder of Zelotes, but for *maiestas,* which I can assure you the Prefect takes far more seriously. He was betraying Rome to the Zealots, and vice versa. But as you rightly said, there's no point in delay. I'll see the Prefect at once.'

*

IT was the third hour of the night, but Pilate still sat behind a desk strewn with his scribes' reports of the trials, which he had been checking tirelessly. I had put the facts to him, without naming Salome, though no doubt he was aware of whom I was speaking. 'What you've told me is interesting,' he said. 'But methinks, hardly of great moment.'

'Sir, I respectfully agree.'

'Quite apart from the question of self-defence, you say that in your view the young woman in question is over-emotional and an unreliable witness.'

I nodded. 'Yes, sir.'

'Add to which the fact that this man not only was no

loss, but a positive danger to Rome, guilty of at least one blatant act of *maiestas,* and would undoubtedly have been crucified in any case.'

'Quite so, sir. Whilst she is clearly of no danger to Rome whatever.'

'As you say.' Pilate returned his attention to the heap of papers and scrolls on his desk. 'You may tell your little friend that I find the evidence insufficient to justify proceedings, and that I am not to be pestered about the matter further.' He looked up and gave one of his rare smiles. 'But tell her it would be inadvisable to do anything like it again.'

Book VII

Aftermath

According to Mary

I WRITE these lines with trembling fist. For this morning I have seen something so dreadful, so monstrous in its Evil, that it has made me doubt the ultimate goodness which hitherto, even at the worst of times, I always believed to lie behind all things. I shake with terror as I prepare to cast my mind back to the events I have witnessed. And yet I must record them.

I rose well before cock-crow, and set out alone, taking with me a bunch of early wild-flowers which I planned to leave in the burial chamber beside our dear Lord's body. Then I should kneel in prayer and ask for his blessing on my union with my centurion. I was confident that my Lord would consent. When they met, had he not said of him that he had not found so great a faith in all Israel? Truly he had recognized in him a man of God.

The crows and ravens, birds of ill-omen, were in flight across the sky, a dark cloud of them gathered around Golgotha. And small wonder, for the bodies of the malefactors crucified with my Lord still hung from their crosses, minus their eyes, the first things to have been pecked out. Some of the vile creatures were at work upon their bodies, the open wounds being torn still further as they feasted greedily upon the entrails, pausing only to squawk and flap wings as they threatened one another.

My Lord's cross lay on the ground, without its beam, which had been returned to Herod's Fortress. It would be borne back here this afternoon by our Lord's betrayer Judas. The man whose treachery had led to our Lord's crucifixion would himself suffer ignominious death. The thought gave me but little comfort.

It was a cold clear morning in early spring. Shivering not only for that reason, I gathered my cloak around me and hurried onward. The tomb lay on my right, beyond the hill, with the boulder in position where Josef and Simon had placed it. I approached. And here my courage almost fails. But I must set it down.

The stone still stood where it had before, leaving a small gap through which most persons of normal build could enter and leave. Now that I was here, I felt curiously loath to proceed further. But I steeled myself, gripped my flowers more tightly, and entered our Lord's burial chamber.

At first I could see nothing. Then, as my eyes became accustomed to the darkness, I could make out the recess in the wall where the body had been laid.

It was not there. The linen and the winding-cloth were crumpled and unrolled, and the dust of the surface had been disturbed. But my Lord's body was not there.

My first thought was that some malefactors had removed it, though for what purpose I could not imagine. It had borne nothing worth stealing. I burst into tears. The last of my Lord's dignity had been taken away, the decent burial of his body.

I remained a few moments in prayer, and remembered to leave the bunch of wild-flowers which was all that would now commemorate my Lord. Then I stood and left, without looking back. For now there was nothing to see. I stood outside, breathing the cold air deeply into my lungs, and trying to decide what to do. I supposed I should seek out Simon Peter and the other disciples, and advise them of what had happened. Not that I felt very kindly towards them, after the cowardly way they had deserted my Lord in his hour of need.

Then I saw a man squatting with his back to me. My eyes were still blinded with tears, so I could not see him clearly, but he seemed to be wearing some sort of white linen garment, similar to that in which my Lord had been buried. Maybe it was one of the gardeners who tended the shrubs and flowers bordering the city walls. If so, he was at work very early.

The man stood and turned. And the horror struck me like a physical blow.

For this was my Lord. And yet it was not my Lord. The Thing that stood before me, not five cubits distant, was his height and size, and wore his burial clothes. But it was not he.

The Thing's face was drawn down into a hideous mask, an obscene parody of the way my Lord had looked in life. Its chops were fallen, the jaw sagging loosely, and smashed teeth were visible within. Worst of all, its eyes were dead. Those of my lord had been full of wisdom and compassion.

I say again, it was not my Lord. It was an insane mockery, a foul shell covering something inconceivably Evil. It began to stumble toward me.

I backed away, my mind numb with fear. 'Don't touch me!' I screamed. 'Don't touch me!' for surely to be touched by this creature meant certain death, and far worse, eternal damnation. Was that what had happened to my Lord? Was the Serpent after all mightier than God?

At last I managed to move. Wrenching my eyes from the sight, I turned and fled. A hundred yards distant, I forced myself to look back. The dreadful revenant stood gazing after me, motionless in the morning mist.

*

I WROTE the above this morning, in the uttermost depths of terror and despair. There have been times during the last few hours when I seriously considered destroying myself, prevented only by the fear that the powers of Evil would ensure that sufferings after death were even worse than those in life: a nightmarish twilight existence of indescribable fear, pain and confusion from which I could never awake, not for all eternity.

Yet little by little I began to see glimmerings of hope. The sun had risen that morning, as it always did. Birds still sang in the trees. Jerusalem still stood. Women gossiped on their doorsteps, and men were drinking in the taverns. Even the sight of an occasional Roman soldier on patrol was a welcome sign of normality. Outwardly the world seemed no different from usual. The powers of darkness had not yet taken over. And I was, I confessed it, a woman with serious problems affecting her mind and spirit. Had I in some bizarre fashion imagined things, creating a world consisting of my worst fears? Less drastically, could I indeed have seen something very strange, but misinterpreted it?

My other hope centred around my centurion. When things seemed worst, I had tried to think of him. How would he have dealt with the matter? Certainly he would not have turned and fled in blind panic, as I had done. He would have stayed, and if necessary faced death and destruction with his usual equanimity. Unmoved.

It helped a little. Then a little more. By early afternoon I was feeling sufficiently in control of myself to impart what I had seen to him.

He saw me at once, though I observed that his desk was littered with papers. As I entered, he stood. For some reason this small courtesy moved me. His face changed.

'What's the matter?'

I stretched out my hands to him in mute appeal. As he took me in his arms I began to shake and sob. He conducted me gently to a seat.

'Tell me when you feel like talking.'

I made a couple of incoherent false starts. All he said was, 'There's no hurry. Take your time.'

'I have seen… Oh God, what have I seen?' Again I found myself unable to continue.

'Nothing good, from the look of things. Has something befallen your friend Salome?'

It was a reasonable assumption, for her death would have distressed me more than that of any, save his own. 'No,' I gasped, shaking my head wildly. 'Not that.'

Ninety-nine men out of a hundred would have said, 'What, then?' but he just waited until I was ready to continue.

'I… this morning, early, I attended the tomb of my Lord to pray and leave some flowers. When I got there, I found the tomb empty.' Again I paused to gather myself. And again he remained silent.

'All I could think of was that some of his followers had

removed it for reasons of their own. There was nothing to have attracted grave robbers, who in any case would have had no reason to take the body. I knelt in prayer for a time, and left the flowers where his body should have been.

'Then I left. And as I did I saw a man, or what I thought was a man, squatting on the ground with his back to me. I took him for a gardener. At my approach he rose, and turned …' Again I had to stop, as the demoniacal moment repeated itself in my memory. 'And it was dreadful. An obscene shell. I cannot find the words. A hideous mockery of my Lord in life. His eyes… his eyes were dead …'

'You saw your Lord? Alive?'

'No, no. Not my Lord.' I gave a screech of insane laughter. 'Not alive. The Thing I saw was dead. Dead, but walking about.'

'What did you do?'

'At first I stood transfixed. Then I turned and fled. As I glanced back, the Thing was gazing after me. With those dead eyes …'

Again I gave way. 'I'm sorry. Of course you think you're listening to the ravings of a deranged woman. Or hysterical, at least.'

'Neither. I'm sure you saw what you've described.' He paused. 'What construction do you put on things?'

'I think, oh God, I would it were otherwise – I think that the Serpent himself has in some foul way taken possession of my dear Lord's body, and turned it into a sort of diabolical revenant. A creature which will wander the earth spreading evil throughout. I now doubt, what all my life I have believed to be the fundamental truth – the ultimate triumph of Good over Evil.'

'I see.' Again my centurion paused. 'Let's think for a few moments. Quietly and logically. Let us consider all the possibilities.'

By now he had dragged the bench from his desk and was sitting next to me. 'Don't speak until I have finished,' he warned, 'however much you may disagree.

'The first possibility is that you have somehow imagined this nightmarish creature. That it was an hallucination. Second, that you are right, and it is indeed some appalling revenant belonging to the grave or the spirit world, and not to this earth. Thirdly, that you saw what you have described to me, but have in some way misinterpreted it. That covers every possibility, I think. One of those three must be the correct explanation.'

I bowed my head in assent. He had mentioned the very three possibilities I had considered myself. Unlike me he had set them out logically, with a view to considering them calmly one at a time, instead of his mind careering chaotically from one to another. 'I suppose it must be so,' I whispered.

'Let's first consider hallucination. It is possible, I think, but only just. You were under extreme stress, first having witnessed your Lord's death, then finding that his tomb had been desecrated and his body removed. Yes, it is possible. But unlikely.

'Second, that what you saw was indeed a supernatural being of supreme evil. Here I have to confess my own beliefs, or prejudices, if you will. I don't believe there are any such things. What you have told me does not alter that belief.

'Finally, that you saw what you say you saw, but have somehow misinterpreted it.'

'How could I possibly …? You think I might have seen our Risen Lord, returned from the dead for the final judgment… But it cannot be. What I saw was foul beyond belief. Neither human nor divine.'

'Suppose it was neither a creation of your own mind, nor a supernatural being, but a mortal man. A mortal man who was neither dead, nor evil, but very, very sick.'

'So you think I deserted our Lord when he most needed me. That the poor mutilated creature was asking me for help, and that through my stupidity and cowardice I failed him. But how can that be? We saw him die.'

'No, we saw him pass from consciousness. Judging that he would never regain it, I suggested that we leave rather than distress you further.'

'He was dead when we buried him. And I told you, his eyes were dead.'

'You thought he was dead. I have known men remain comatose for many hours, in extreme cases even days. As for his eyes, he may not have been conscious. Sleepwalkers have their eyes open, but unseeing.'

I considered this, trying to pacify my unquiet mind. 'Are you sure?'

'No, but it's the best explanation I can think of.'

'Then I have deserted him. Just like his disciples.'

'What could you have done? He wasn't even conscious. You said his eyes were dead.'

'Will he… do you think it possible that he might recover? And live to preach his holy message once more?'

My centurion paused yet again, then said simply, 'No.'

*

THAT night I forced myself to return to the tomb. No doubt my centurion would have accompanied me had I asked him. But it was something I had to do myself. Face my fears alone, as in the end we all must do.

It was again a bright moonlit night, the type beloved by the *Secarii* and other evildoers. I made my way through the old city to the Genneth Gate, where I explained my business to the sentries. I half hoped that they would turn me back, coward that I am, but they permitted me to proceed. I forced my steps toward Golgotha, and onward to the tomb.

It lay in deep shadow, for in the east the moon had scarcely risen. I saw and heard nothing. Would I have the courage to enter?

'Mary, is that you?'

I almost fainted with relief. A down-to-earth artisan's voice, speaking in the blessed tongue of Galilee so familiar to me. And I recognized it. Simon Peter. So he had thought better of his abandonment of our Lord.

'Peter! Oh, Peter!'

'Not so loud,' he urged softly. 'What we intend is most secret, for all the glorious news we bear.'

'You mean?'

'Our Lord is risen! He has conquered death and the fiends of hell, and is returned to us.'

His tone of voice did not match the words. Andrew came out of the tomb to stand beside his brother. Then Jacob and Johan, the sons of Zebadiah. All looked troubled and uncertain rather than joyful.

I knew what to ask, but not how to put it. 'Is he… himself?'

'Well,' said Peter uneasily, 'naturally he bears the scars of his ordeal. We shall convey him to Jerusalem tonight, to the Upper Room, and have him tended by a physician.'

The room had been reserved for a whole week. And Moshe was an incurious landlord. They should escape discovery for a day or two at least.

'We did not recognize him at first,' Jacob admitted, 'but surely his having been spared in this miraculous fashion means something. At any rate, we must keep the faith.'

The others nodded. 'The sentries on the gate will stop you,' I said.

'We thought of that, of course,' said Peter testily. 'We shall proceed outside the city until we reach the Serpents' Pond. It's less than a mile. Then we plan to enter the Essene Quarter by the eye of the needle. They are but seldom guarded.'

The eyes he referred to were small breaches in the city walls where merchants and others with legitimate business may enter at all hours without let or hindrance, save the ordeal of squeezing themselves through the gap.

'What can I do to help?'

'Nothing,' said Peter brusquely. 'This is men's work, and we have the four stretcher-bearers needed. You may walk behind us if you wish.'

They disappeared within the tomb, to emerge shortly with the stretcher upon which lay our dear Lord. I was struck by the fact that one of his arms hung down, as they say Caesar's did when they took his body from the Capitol. But I must not think like that.

The journey seemed timeless, though in view of the distance involved I suppose it must have taken no more than half an hour. Once again the great city revealed itself in the moonlight. Yet this time, its outline black against the sky, it seemed ugly and sinister.

For much of the time I could not take my eyes from the stretcher. Was it the promised Messiah who lay there? Who would arise and smite his foes from Israel? Or a man-God who had miraculously conquered death? Surely not, for the Torah teaches us there there is but one God, not two.

There remained a third possibility: that Joshua bar-Josef was a man, mortal and fallible as other men are. And strangely enough I was no longer so reluctant to admit this as I would have been a week earlier. In a way I was quite unable to explain, it would have been a relief.

*

NEXT morning I went to the Upper Room in the hope of encountering those of the disciples who had not dispersed in cowardly panic. No action had been taken against any of them, either by the Romans or the priests, so possibly some might have returned to the fold.

At the door I was met by the publican Levi. Of all of them he was the one I had judged least likely to abandon our Lord. No doubt he had repented of his behaviour. But he did not seem overjoyed to see me.

'Oh, it's you, Mary,' he said rather obviously.

'Yes,' I said with equal inadequacy.

'Matters have indeed... ah... taken an unforeseen direction. Glorious news, in a sense.'

Even without the last three words I could tell that he was far from unreservedly delighted.

'I know.'

'I will show you,' he said grudgingly. 'But remember, nothing must yet be said to anyone. I know how women talk.'

I followed him up the stepladder. Our Lord lay on a bed at the far side of the bleak room. Several of his disciples were gathered around him, two in tears. Alongside stood a physician, looking helpless. And then I knew. Our Lord was indeed the man I had seen beside the tomb. And this time there was that in his face which was neither Good nor Evil, but simply Death. There was death in his face. And I had only just arrived in time. He looked at me, but whether he recognized me I know not.

A quarter of an hour later he sighed gently and relaxed. His face was calm at last. 'It's over,' said the physician. 'Nothing could have been done. The spear wound in the side was fatal. Surprising that he survived so long.'

'Will you tell the Romans what we have done?' asked Andrew.

'I'm no informer,' said the physician shortly. 'Good day, gentlemen. Madam,' he added as he left, noticing me for the first time.

'Our Lord,' said Peter determinedly, 'rose miraculously from the dead. Having demonstrated his conquest of death and hell, he has now ascended into heaven, to sit on the right hand of Almighty God.'

The others for the most part seemed to accept what he said, and nodded. Levi and Tomasso looked doubtful.

After that they discussed at length what they should do. Eventually they decided to re-bury the body by dead of night. Then they would spread the word of their Lord's resurrection. None of them consulted me, or paid me the least attention. Considering that over half of our Lord's followers had been women, I thought their proprietory attitude shameful. Then fat old Levi caught my eye, smiled, and came over to me.

'I don't think you belong here, my dear,' he said quietly. 'And come to think of it, I'm not sure I do either.'

I cast one last look at our Lord's disciples, clustered around his bed and debating earnestly. Joshua bar-Abbas, the Son of Man, was no longer a man. He had become a religious commodity. Levi was right. There was nothing there for me. We descended the ladder.

'So that is that,' I said, trying to keep the bitterness out of my voice.

'In a sense, yes,' said Levi. 'And yet, I cannot say that I have learned nothing from this dead man. Before I met him, I was the most hated man in Galilee. Since listening to Joshua bar-Josef, I have become a different person.'

'I think I perceive your meaning,' I said.

'I started to wonder what my parents, both long dead, would have thought of me, their little boy and only child, of whom they had had such high hopes. I used to imagine that they would have been proud of me, a bricklayer's son, who had become one of the richest men in Judaea. But now I fear I would have disappointed them.'

'You believe that a rich man cannot enter into the kingdom of heaven?'

He shook his head. 'Methinks there is nothing wrong with being a rich man, or a tax collector. Neither is there anything wrong in being a bricklayer, or an emperor, or a slave. All play their appointed part. What is important is to deal justly with all men.'

'And women,' I said.

He smiled acknowledgment. 'And women. I am now a much gentler person than I was. And I believe I am under an obligation to make some sort of amends for the moneys I have obtained unjustly, by giving much of my wealth to good causes, particularly helping the poor. You might even persuade me to make a donation to your house for fallen women. Who knows?'

*

THAT night they buried my Lord again. I did not attend. Instead I went for a walk in the Kidron Valley, amongst the stars, alone, recalling the last time I had walked there, with my centurion. How happy I had been then, and didn't know it.

But I was no longer alone. 'I hope,' said my centurion, materializing from out the darkness, 'that you have not been avoiding me.'

I started from my thoughts. 'I have been avoiding everyone. I needed to think.'

'Of course.'

I told him of the events of that morning. He nodded but made no immediate comment.

I was used to his remaining silent, but eventually asked, 'What do you think?'

'What you've told me is much as I expected. I said before that I considered your Lord a righteous man, and I still do. As for what happens to men after death, who knows? We Germans, we pagan Germans, say that human life is like that of a sparrow, who flies from the darkness into the brightly lit and tumultuous banqueting hall for a few moments, and then flies out again, back into the darkness and silence.'

'Life,' I said, 'can be dark and silent too.'

Again we kissed beneath the stars.

According to Pilate

I HAD assumed the death of the man Joshua and subsequent arrests of the Zealots to mark the end of the affair, but it did not. On the *Dies Lunae*, as a result of disturbing rumours I had heard, I sent for Teutonicus, who by now seemed to have established himself as my right-hand man in so many ways.

'You've heard the rumours,' I said, more as a statement than a question. 'Of a resurrection from the dead.'

'That I have, sir.'

'Any comments?'

'They're untrue, of course. The question is what led to their circulation.'

'Quite. Look into it, will you?'

'I have already done so, sir.'

I could hardly contain my surprise. 'What have you discovered?'

He drew a scroll from his jerkin. 'Sir. My report.'

I held out a hand, and he passed it over. In less than five hundred words he had disposed of the whole thing. If I could ever have believed that any man possessed supernatural powers, surely it was him. I passed a comment to that effect. He smiled and shook his head.

'How do you suggest we handle it?' I asked.

'In the short term, sir, for the reasons I've given, I fancy the matter will resolve itself. Whether his followers will be able to continue the pretence further, I know not.'

'Have you taken disciplinary action against the soldiers?'

'I have, sir. Two of the men have been flogged for their part in the dicing incident, and their centurion demoted to the ranks.'

'Quite right. And give them all a spell of latrine duty into the bargain.'

*

A FEW days later Teutonicus informed me that despite the rumours to the contrary, he had indisputable evidence that the man Joshua had died three days after his crucifixion, and his body had been reburied. His followers claimed to have witnessed his ascension into heaven, but no-one believed them, least of all myself.

I judged that to be the end of the matter, but again I was mistaken. A few years later a Jew called Saul of Tarsus, who claimed to be a Roman citizen, allegedly received a message from the dead man, and travelled around the east of the Mare Nostrum preaching that Joshua, or Jesus as he called him in the Greek, had been what he called the Christ, sacrificing his life that others might live. I know little of these religious disputes, and care less. At any rate, Saul's followers have split from Orthodox Jewry, and now call themselves Christians. Unlike the Jews they can eat what they like, and are not required to undergo circumcision, which doubtless is a considerable aid to recruitment. How much of a nuisance they make of themselves in future remains to be seen.

For all that, I am not sure that if I had my time over again, I should make the same decision. Strangely enough I feel that I should like to discuss the matter with the centurion Teutonicus. He left the army a year after the events I have described, and I never saw him again. Nor did I ever have a lieutenant his equal. If I made sufficient effort I dare say I could discover what has become of the man, but it hardly seems worth while.

It may be that in the hereafter I shall be called to account for my actions that day, but as to that I know not. I am no philosopher, and make no claim to understand the intentions of the gods. Last year I became offically *senex*, sixty years old, and being in indifferent health, I suspect I shall not be in this world much longer. And I reckon I shall go where most men go.

According to the Centurion

I STOOD before the Prefect once more. 'I'm disturbed by these rumours,' he said, 'emanating from followers of the man Joshua, to the effect that he has been resurrected from the dead.'

This came as no surprise. My lady Magdalene had visited me the previous day in great distress, claiming that she had witnessed the man Joshua, or something resembling him, and that he, or it, was no longer dead. Presumably others had since seen something similar.

'What do you think?'

'Superstition,' I said.

'Quite so. But look into them, will you?'

'I've already done so, sir.' I produced my report. 'And I believe I have the solution.'

A likely possibility had suggested itself to me straight away, and I still saw no reason to doubt it. Indeed it was difficult to think of any other explanation to fit the facts.

Pilate shook his head and sighed. 'There are times, centurion, when I am almost tempted to believe you possess supernatural powers yourself. Go ahead.'

I attempted a modest smile and handed the report to him. 'I think this must be the explanation, sir.'

He read it through twice in silence. Eventually he looked up and said, as if choosing his words carefully, 'What it amounts to, centurion, is this. Either a couple of Roman soldiers made a mistake, or everything we have ever known about life and death has somehow been miraculously suspended for the sake of one man.'

'That's about the size of it, sir.'

'If you are right – I say if, but there's really no doubt about it – it shouldn't be difficult to prove. Or at least get some evidence in support. See to it, will you?'

'I was just about to do so, sir.'

*

I STOOD at the gate of the headquarters of the Second Cohort in the Tower of Phaesal. The men of the Second Cohort didn't like me. They didn't like me personally, because I made it clear that I thought they were incompetent thugs, and apologies for soldiers. And they didn't like me in my role as *primus pilus*, because my appearance usually meant trouble for them. Young Vulpino was at my side. It would be advisable to have a witness.

'I want to see the former commander of your first century,' I said, trying not to place too much emphasis on the word 'former.'

'Maximin, sir?'

'That's right.'

'Sir.' The man scurried away. Moments later he reappeared, accompanied by the great lout of a fellow who had superintended the crucifixion of Joshua.

'What do you want?' he asked in a surly tone.

'Information. Were you in charge of the party who broke the prisoners' legs?'

He hesitated, as if sensing danger. 'That's right. The Jews didn't want them hanging about dying on the Sabbath. What of it?'

'Who were the others?'

'Sergius and Columbus.'

'Who actually broke the legs?'

'Sergius. Used a sledge-hammer. Made them scream.' He grinned. 'Not for long, though. The bastards soon couldn't breathe, let alone scream.'

'All of them?'

'What?'

'Did he break the legs of all three?'

'Er, yes.' I reflected that the man was one of the worst liars I had ever encountered.

'What did Columbus do?'

'Nothing much, except puke up. He's a mummy's-boy. I thought it'd do him good to see a bit of the dirty work. He couldn't hack it. Not surprised.'

'Send for them.'

'I'll go and fetch them,' he said disobligingly.

'Thank you.' I turned to Vulpino. 'Go with him. Make sure he doesn't brief them what to say.'

Maximin's murderous expression suggested that that had been precisely his intention. He departed with Vulpino, to return moments later with the men in question. I already knew them both, as members of the dicing party. Sergius was in his fifties, so presumably an experienced man on the verge of retirement. Columbus was a wet sort of lad, who looked about fifteen. I suppose he must have been older. They had recently been flogged, and moved awkwardly. I suspected Columbus had been crying.

'You broke the legs of the prisoners?'

'I did,' said the older man.

'All of them?'

He hesitated before replying, and I knew he was about to lie. 'Yes.'

'What about the man Joshua?'

'He was already dead.'

'That's not what I asked. Did you break his legs? The fact can easily be checked.'

'We didn't need to,' said Maximin, intervening. 'Like he said, he was already dead.'

'Did you make sure of that?'

'Yes, I did. Shoved a spear into him, if you must know. He didn't react.'

'He bled all over the place, sir,' Columbus provided eagerly.

Now I knew for certain. 'So. A dead man bled all over the place.'

'I tell you he was dead,' insisted Maximin. 'I know a dead man when I see one. I've been in the army twenty years.'

'Not long enough to learn that a dead man doesn't bleed, apparently.'

'Well, he'd obviously only been dead a few moments.'

'Really? So he died while you were breaking the legs of his companions. And they were screaming. Did he react when they screamed?'

'No. I tell you he was dead.'

'Well, let me tell you something. Thanks to you and your men demonstrating an incompetence so great it amounts almost to imbecility, the man Joshua is still alive. He walked out of his tomb at Golgotha, and as a result his followers are claiming that he has been resurrected from the dead.'

'He'll die soon, anyway,' said Maximin sourly. 'He couldn't have survived the spear-thrust. I shoved it in well and truly.'

'No doubt. Meanwhile the more gullible of his disciples will have persuaded themselves that he defeated death in some miraculous fashion and will subsequently choose to ascend into heaven of his own volition.'

'Stupid bastards. Thinking he was still alive when he was obviously a goner.'

'You appear to have made an equally crass mistake in the opposite direction. Anyway, I'll now have a word with your new commander and tell him to give you and Sergius a month on the latrines for incompetence and neglect of duty. Columbus I excuse on the grounds of his youth and inexperience. And incidentally, Maximin, bearing in mind that I'm now your superior officer, a "sir" or two thrown into your conversation now and again wouldn't have come amiss.'

'There's no need to take it like that,' he mumbled. 'Sir.'

'Oh, but I do take it like that,' I assured him cheerfully. 'And I shall of course report this conversation and your demeanour to the Prefect. Whether he chooses to take further action against you will naturally be up to him. Dismiss.'

*

I HAD told Pilate of my discovery. Now I had to face telling Mary. What would be the effect upon relations between us, I knew not. Would she forever associate me with everything that was painful and destructive in her life?

On my return to headquarters that evening I called at

the apartment where she lodged, to be met by Salome, who told me that her mistress had seemed disturbed, and gone for a walk alone.

'Disturbed? In what way?'

She hesitated, then said, 'She had learned something about our Lord that had upset her.'

'That he had survived crucifixion?'

'Yes.' Again she hesitated, before continuing, 'My lady, I think, would not mind my telling you, for I know she trusts you above all men. Our Lord indeed survived his crucifixion, but died this morning. His followers intend burying him tonight, but she does not know exactly where or when. I expect she has gone to find them.'

'At Golgotha?'

'I suppose so, my Lord. But she did not know for certain.'

I thanked her and left. That was strange. If Mary knew of his death, either she had observed it herself, or been informed of it by his disciples. In either event she would surely have been told of the new arrangements for his burial.

I made for Golgotha. On the way I spoke to the sentries on the Gennath Gate. They confirmed that a small party of men had left not half an hour before, consisting of seven or eight disciples of the crucified prophet Joshua bar-Josef. They had explained that they were going to pray at his tomb. There seemed no harm in that, and in view of the Prefect's orders not to stir up unnecessary trouble they had been permitted to proceed.

'They've not yet returned?'

'No, sir.'

I nodded. If I mistook not, his body would have been secretly conveyed out of the city through one of the needle-eyes. 'I'll look into it,' I assured them, and set out for the north.

*

IT was not far. Atop the hill there stood a cross, bearing on it what was left of the eyeless and ravaged body of the malefactor Judas Secarius, amongst others in similar condition. It was, as the Greeks might have said with their love of litotes, not a pretty sight.

I heard subdued voices. And there in the darkness, scarce fifty paces distant, were a group of men collected around the tomb of Joshua bar-Josef. Six of them knelt in prayer, their backs towards me. The other two stood holding an empty stretcher which doubtless had borne the body of their leader. Mary was not present, nor any other woman.

I remained there silently whilst one might have counted to five hundred, no longer. Then I turned and made my way back.

The sentries on the gate saluted. 'It was as you said,' I assured them. 'They are holding some sort of commemorative religious ceremony around the tomb of their leader. It was quiet and orderly, with no sign of anything amiss. Certainly nothing to indicate disaffection. You did right to let them through.'

'Thank you, sir,' said the senior of the two, looking relieved. 'Good night.'

'Good night.'

*

THERE remained one other place where my lady might be. The Kidron Valley, where I had escorted her that magic night which now seemed so long ago. Had I any hope of success? A Roman, or rather a German barbarian, and a Jewess. One who believed in a creator god, and one who did not.

She was still a rich woman, I a man of but modest means, if no pauper. I had a certain amount to offer. In a little over twelve months time I should have served twenty years with the Romans, most of it as a legionary, and would be entitled to leave the army. I was not a rich man, but I had been careful with money, and taken sound advice. I owned cash and property to a total value of over nine thousand sesterces, which represented ten years pay for a legionary. More important, thanks to Governor Lamia I had been confirmed as a Roman citizen, entitled to a grant of land upon my discharge. Where it would be, I knew not. Could I persuade my lady to leave her homeland to live with me? At least I could offer her a life free from the dangerous instability of Judaea, and the threat of the *Secarii*, those predators by moonlight.

I left the city by the Water Gate. Yet again it was a clear night. The moon was in third quarter, peeping 'twixt the twin peaks of the Mounts of Olive and Offence. Ahead of me, low in the northern sky, shone the Immortals: the constant stars that never set.

A solitary figure stood straight in the moonlight, her shadow stretching before her toward the troubled and dangerous city the Jews considered holy. Hekate, I mused in a flight of fancy unusual for me. Goddess of Magic and the Darkness.

Rapt in her thoughts, she was slow to notice me. If I had

prepared any romantic speech I forgot it, and uttered the first thing to come into my head.

'I hope you have not been avoiding me.'

She gave a start of surprise. 'I have been avoiding everyone. I needed to think. Have you heard of our Lord's death?'

'Yes. I am come from seeing the re-burial party.'

'His disciples plan to teach that he was miraculously resurrected, and has now ascended to heaven by his own choice. But of course you know the truth.'

I could not tell whether she spoke bitterly or not. But I decided to explain further. 'Soldiers often break the legs of those crucified. It causes extreme pain, but shortens their ordeal. They can't continue to push themselves up to relieve the pressure on their lungs, and soon suffocate. As sunset approaches on the eve of the Sabbath, leg-breaking is the invariable practice. It's one of the reasons I took you away. You wouldn't have wanted to see such a thing.'

She nodded. 'So as soon as the crowd were out of the way they broke the legs of the brigands, but when it came to my Lord they thought he was already dead, and didn't bother.'

'That's right. The men concerned have admitted it.'

'Well, that's that, then,' she said briskly. Again I could not determine her thoughts. Would she blame me for ever for disillusioning her?

'I was surprised not to see you at the re-burial,' I ventured.

'I don't think I should have been welcome. The twelve, or ten, or however many of his chief followers are left, insist that our Lord's apostles should all be men.'

'I can't imagine you letting that stop you.'

'I would not, if I still believed.'

'Then… '

'I now realize that Joshua bar-Josef was mortal, as other men are. But I am still a Jewess. I believe in one God, creator of heaven and earth, whereas you do not.'

'The fact that I don't believe in your god doesn't mean I don't believe in anything.'

She looked at me closely. 'Can you explain further?'

'Whether your god, or other gods, exist, I know not. I do not believe that the world is about to end. It will still be here in a thousand years, and many thousand more. But it soon ends for each one of us. Human life is short, and a mystery we are never likely to solve, which perhaps is for the best. According to a German proverb, it is like a sparrow, who flies from the outer darkness into a bright and noisy banqueting hall, and then out again, no-one knows where.

'But I believe I am a better man than I was before I met your Lord. Others have become better men too, and there may be more, as yet unborn. Perhaps that is the only miracle he wrought, and of more worth than all the rest.'

Now was the moment. I should delay no longer. I went down on one knee. 'Will you take me, Mary of Magdala? One whom you rightly called a flawed and mortal man? I never knelt to Caesar, but I kneel to you.'

She smiled and blinked away the tears. 'I feel towards you the same way as I now realize I have always felt. The demons that tormented me no longer exist – perhaps they never did. I still know myself to be a sinner, but I did not kill my husband. And at last I can give you your answer.

'There are many difficulties facing us. You are a Germanic Roman, I am a Jewess. You believe in the pagan gods, I in one God, creator of heaven and earth. But now I know that he has linked my destiny with yours, and it is with you that I shall find happiness, or not at all.'

And so it proved.

Glossary

(All dates are AD unless otherwise stated)

Abrogatio.
Formal adoption under Roman law.

Aramaic.
An archaic Semitic language related to Arabic. Spoken in Syria and Galilee. Believed to be the mother tongue of Jesus of Nazareth. Only distantly related to Hebrew.

Bar-Caiaphas, Josef. (c. 14 BC-c.46 AD).
High Priest of the Temple of Herod 18-36 or 37.

Caesarea.
A city on the northern coast of Judaea, built by Herod the Great about 25–13 BC as a major port and administrative centre.

Caligae.
Open-toed military boots. Singular *caliga*, with the diminutive *caligula,* by which nickname ('Little Boot') the subsequent Roman emperor was known.

Capernaum.
A town on the northern shore of the Sea of Galilee.

Castra.
Military camp.

Centurion.
A Roman officer, of whom there were sixty in every legion, six per cohort. Despite the title, the average number of men he commanded was about eighty. The head of the first century of the First Cohort was called *primus pilus,* and wielded more power in the legion than anyone else.

Cognomen.
The last component of a male Roman's name, and although originally a nickname, often inherited.

Cohort.
Usually one tenth of a legion, numbering slightly less than five hundred men. The *cohors quingenaria* were auxiliary infantry forces existing independently of the legions. Commanded by the senior centurion, who headed the first century of the cohort.

Dies Jovis.
Thursday.

Dies Lunae.
Monday.

Dies Martis.
Tuesday.

Dies Mercurii.
Wednesday.

Dies Veneris.
Friday.

Dominus.
Master, feminine form *domina*. The masculine vocative *domine* was used in speaking to a social superior, and approximates to 'sir.'

Elohim.
One of several Jewish holy names for God, though less holy than the Tetragrammaton, JHWH, (usually transliterated into English as 'Jahweh'), which was considered too holy to be pronounced.

Elui.
Sixth Month of the Jewish year, extending from late August to late September.

Eremos, Mount.
A hill near to Lake Gennesaret, possible site of the Sermon on the Mount.

Essenes.
A Jewish religious group, strict in their interpretation of the Torah.

Falernian.

A white wine grown on the slopes of Mount Falernus. The most prestigious wine of Roman times.

Fiat justitia, ruat coelum.

Latin: 'Let justice be done, though the heavens fall.'

Galilee.

A region in the north of Judaea.

Galilee, Sea of.

See Gennesaret.

Gennesaret.

A lake in Galilee, called Tiberias by the Romans. Later known as the Sea of Galilee.

Germanicus, Julius Caesar. (15 BC-19 AD)

A Roman general of the royal Julio-Claudian house, grandson of Mark Antony. Reputedly a military genius, and immensely popular in his day. Modern scholarship has thrown doubt both on his ability and his ethics.

Gladius hispaniensis.

The Spanish sword, standard issue for the Roman infantry.

Gravitas.

A quality much admired by the Romans. The nearest English translation might be 'integrity.'

Herod Antipas (20 BC-39 AD.)

Son of Herod the Great. King of Galilee from 4 BC-39 AD.

Herodias (c.15 BC-c.50 AD).

Wife of Herod Antipas and mother of the notorious Salome. According to the Gospels, responsible for the death of John the Baptist.

Herod's Fortress.

A building in north-west Jerusalem, constructed on the orders of Herod the Great. It comprised three parts: the palace, the military praetorium, and the towers of Marianne, Phaesal and Hippicus.

Herod's Temple, Jerusalem.

The centre of Jewish religious belief, including the Holy of Holies. Built on the site of the earlier Solomon's Temple, and much extended and refurbished by Herod the Great. Destroyed by the Roman Emperor Vespasian in 70.

Insula.

A block of flats.

Joshua bar-Josef (c.5 BC-c.30 AD).

Literally 'Joshua, son of Josef.' The man known to us as Jesus of Nazareth.

Legion.

The main unit of a Roman army, usually consisting of slightly less than 5,000 men.

Litotes.

A Greek figure of speech consisting of understatement, usually in the form of asserting something by denying its opposite, as in 'a citizen of no mean city.'

Maiestas.

Treason.

Mare Nostrum.

The Mediterranean Sea. Literally: 'Our sea.'

Magdala.

A small town on the west coast of Lake Gennesaret, putative home of Mary Magdalene.

Messiah.

The Jewish leader promised by the Old Testament prophets, who will free Judaea from bondage.

Nisan.

The Jewish month extending from late March to late April.

Nomen.

A male Roman's second name, inherited from his family, and therefore corresponding roughly to a modern surname.

Pharisees.

Experts in the Judaean law and religion, mostly believing in strict observance of the Torah. Political opponents of the Sadducees. Forerunners of the modern rabbis.

Pontius Pilate. (Dates and praenomen unknown.)

Prefect of Judaea from 26-36 or 37. Sometimes called the Governor or Procurator, though neither title is completely accurate. He was in effect a sort of sub-governor, under the authority of the Governor of Syria.

Praenomen.

A male Roman's first name, corresponding to the modern Christian, or given name.

Praetorium.

Military barracks.

Primus pilus.

See Centurion.

Prefect.

See Procurator.

Procurator.

A title applied to a variety of Roman officials with differing powers. Sometimes applied to Pontius Pilate, who in fact never seems to have been known by any title other than Prefect.

Publican.

Tax collector for the Romans. *Not* a tavern-keeper.

Rabbi.

A teacher of Jewish law and religion.

Quingenaria.

A Roman auxiliary force, consisting of five hundred men. Organized on similar lines to a Roman cohort.

Sadducees.

The Judaean priestly class, who administered the Temple of Herod. Non-believers in an afterlife, and for the most part prepared to co-operate politically with the Romans.

Sanhedrin.

Jewish religious court, whose scope and functions were described reasonably accurately by the Centurion in Book V, pp. 210 and 227/8, *supra.*

Scheol.

According to Jewish belief, the grave of oblivion at the end of life. Some schools of thought, but not all, believed that the righteous would be resurrected on the Day of Judgment.

Secarii, or knifemen.

A terrorist group possibly connected with the Zealots, who stabbed those believed to be sympathetic to Rome. They often seem to have indulged in random killing, and in all probability included criminals and cut-throats with little or no political motivation.

Sejanus, Lucius Aelius (20 BC-31 AD).

Prefect of the Praetorian Guard (i.e. Emperor's bodyguard) from 14-31. Became increasingly powerful during the later years of the reign of Tiberius. Very unfavourably regarded by most sources. Accused of *maiestas* and executed in October 31.

Sestertius.

A silver Roman coin, representing one-quarter of a denarius. In Tiberius's time a Roman legionary was paid 900 sesterces a year.

Tablinum.

The main reception room of a Roman house, also usually containing the family records.

Tetrarch.

Ruler of a quarter of a Roman province. Used of Herod as ruler of Galilee, one of the four regions of Judaea.

Teutoburg Forest, Rhineland.

Site of a massive Roman defeat in 9 AD, when three whole legions were destroyed.

Tiberias, Lake.

See Gennesaret.

Tiberius Caesar (42 BC-37 AD), full names Tiberius Claudius Nero.

Emperor of Rome from 14-37. Stepson of the man now regarded as the first emperor, Augustus Caesar (63 BC-14 AD).

Torah.

The first five books of the Old Testament: Genesis, Exodus, Leviticus, Numbers and Deuteronomy, forming the basis of the Jewish religion.

Tribunes, military.

Usually young men of equestrian (i.e. knightly) rank, each commanding a cohort. In practice their role tended to be more administrative than military, the centurions, expecially the *primus pilus*, wielding more effective power.

Tribunicia potestas.

Tribune of the Plebs, a prestigious Roman office used by Augustus as a stepping-stone to absolute power.

Varus, P. Quinctilius (d. 9 AD).

Commander of the Roman forces defeated in the disaster of the Teutoburg Forest. He committed suicide as a result.

Virtus.

Courage. Literally 'manliness,' from *vir*, man. Later extended to include all admirable qualities, hence our word 'virtue.'

Year of the City DCCXLIX.

The Roman year 749, corresponding to our date 5 BC.

Yom Chamishi.

Fifth day of the Hebrew week, beginning at sunset on Wednesday.

Yom Revi'i.

Fourth day of the Hebrew week, beginning at sunset on Tuesday.

Zealots.

A group committed to obtaining Judaea's freedom from Rome by military action. Possibly linked to the Essenes, whose religious views they tended to share.

Zeus.

The chief Greek deity, identified by the Romans with their god Jupiter.

About the Author

ROGER BUTTERS is a native of Stafford, where he has lived all his life. He was educated at the local King Edward VI School, then a grammar school, apart from a brief spell at Denstone College, from which he ran away (twice). Following his father into the legal profession, he  qualified as a solicitor in 1962 and practised in Stafford for several years before retiring to give more time to writing and other interests.

In the 1970s he was a director of Stafford Rangers FC, and at various times has tried his hand at aviation, chess, owning racehorses, and Shotokan karate. He has obtained a couple of degrees at the Open University, and is a member of the University of the Third Age. His interests at present include the local theatre, gardening, and trying to improve his shaky grasp of French and German. One thing he has never tried is marriage.

His first published novel was *His Excellency* (Robert Hale, 1979) a novel of the Napoleonic War. Altogether he has published over a dozen novels, and two local histories of Stafford, jointly with the borough archives officer, Nick Thomas.

Further details are available at his website address:
www.rogerbutters.uk